THREE FRENCH HENS

ALOHA CHICKEN MYSTERIES: BOOK 7

Josi Avari

Quill
Canyon
Press

Want to know about new releases, free books, and fabulous prizes? Sign up for my newsletter!
josiavari.com
and connect with me on facebook

Also by Josi Avari

The Aloha Chicken Mysteries

Nest Egg (Book 1)

Hen Party (Book 2)

Hard Boiled (Book 3)

Hen Pecked (Book 4)

Home to Roost (Book 5)

Sunny Side Up (Book 6)

Three French Hens (Book 7)

Empty Nest (Book 8)

Bad Egg (Book 9)

Chick Flick (Book 10)

Chicken Out (Book 11)

Egg Nog (Book 12)

Love Birds (Book 13)

Spring Chicken (Book 14)

Over Easy (Book 15)

Walking on Eggshells (Book 16)

Fly the Coop (Book 17)

Love Nest (Book 18)

AND INTRODUCING TWO NEW COZY MYSTERY SERIES!

The Word Witch Mysteries

Spell it Out (Book 1)

The Desperate Strangers Travel Club Mysteries

Stranger on the Seine (Book 1)

* * *

This is a work of fiction. Similarities to real people, places, or events are entirely coincidental.

Three French Hens

Cover art and illustrations by Richard Lance Russell

See more at richardrussellart.com

Chapter One

When she thought about it later, Saffron would be most surprised that she hadn't recognized the sound of eggs breaking. It wasn't the steady, measured crack-and-plop she was used to. Instead, it was a rapid-fire popping, splashing sound that made her duck for cover.

Too late. A flying brown oval hit her, collapsing against her cheek and sending an arc of gold sailing through her field of vision.

Involuntarily, she reached up to wipe the slimy egg off her cheek. The popping continued and as she looked around desperately she saw its source.

Dylan Sawyer, middle-aged rancher, was standing by Saffron's egg cart at the head of the Tuesday Morning Egg Line, snatching eggs from cartons and pelting his brother Wyatt's pickup with them. Saffron realized she hadn't been the target, rather, she had simply been the victim of a stray egg.

Wyatt, inside, scrambled to roll up the passenger's side window from his seat behind the steering wheel. His hair was plastered with yolk, and shards of shell clung to his face.

The egg line stretched down Saffron's long driveway—a snaking train of cars whose drivers had come to pick up a dozen or two dozen eggs from Saffron's Hau'oli ka Moa—the Happy Chicken—egg farm as they did every Tuesday morning. The locals got a discount by driving out and picking their eggs up each week, and Saffron kept the line moving so they could get on their way to work. The Christmas garland she'd hung just last night, with its red tinsel and silver bells, stretched down alongside them, reminding her that she had less than two weeks before her big Christmas Eve party. And now this mess —one more thing she would have to attend to before she could finish preparations.

The egg line had been going so well, too. She had just handed Dylan and Wyatt Sawyer their egg orders and had moved to the next car while they were supposed to pull away, but Dylan had apparently decided to use his eggs on his brother instead of saving them for the skillet.

"Mr. Sawyer!" Saffron ran forward and grasped the carton of eggs in Dylan's hands, "Stop that!"

Dylan surrendered the carton and snatched another one from Saffron's egg cart. He seemed almost oblivious to

Saffron's presence as he lifted the eggs three at a time and sent them sailing toward the blue Ford where his brother sat. Wyatt was howling from inside the cab of his truck, cursing Dylan with a variety and intensity of words Saffron had never heard the quiet man use before. He gave up on rolling up the window and bailed out the driver's side door, taking cover behind the hood of his pickup.

There was no way Saffron could have seen what he would do next. She was as surprised as Dylan when Wyatt popped up from behind the hood and let fly a handful of eggs toward them. When the eggs hit and their fragile shells shattered, when the shards of shell clung to her skin and burst out into the morning air around her, when the cold and slimy innards of the eggs plastered themselves across Saffron's forehead, chest, and shoulder, she wished she knew a few more words to say.

Eggs were raining like bombshells around her and arcing up from Dylan's egg-cart armory to explode with dull thuds on the roof, windshield, and hood of his brother's pickup.

"I'm getting that calf back!" Dylan shouted, lobbing a handful of eggs.

"I'd like to see you try. That's my calf, and it's staying in my barn. You try to get your money-grubbin' hands on it, and you'll be sorry!"

"*You'll* be sorry you stole it!"

"Can't steal what's already yours!"

"That's Betsy's calf and you know it!"

"You leave Betsy out of this!"

"Betsy's in it! She knows you snuck over and took that calf out of the barn. She knows you're a lyin', cheatin', no-good—"

It was then that Officer Bradley, the town of Maika'i's only police officer, and a loyal Hau'oli ka Moa customer, stepped in.

Saffron didn't even see him coming until he put his uniformed body between her and a falling egg. She heard it splash on him and saw the spray of yolk and clear albumen that covered the badge on his chest.

Fury made his already powerful voice deafening, "That's enough!" he grabbed Dylan by the left arm, his knuckles white.

Dylan's right hand froze in midair, cocked above his shoulder with one dark brown egg and one moss green one clutched in it.

Wyatt took the opportunity to send one more sailing at his brother's head before crouching back behind the pickup.

Bradley spun Dylan toward him. His voice was low and menacing when he said, "you have twenty seconds to tell me what's going on here." With his free hand, he made a sweeping gesture at the carnage around them.

"It's not me you ought to be man-handling, Bradley," Dylan shouted, "Wyatt's the one that stole a prize calf from my barn last night!"

"Can't steal what you rightfully own," Wyatt shouted back, his voice muffled by the fact that he was still crouched behind the truck.

"Get out here, Wyatt," Bradley commanded, "and see what you two idiots have done."

Saffron blinked as she pulled her gaze from the brothers and looked around. Nearly her whole week's egg crop was smashed and smeared on the blue truck, the ground, and the two brothers. It dripped off the running boards of the pickup and streamed down the headlights, pooling in the sand of the driveway.

"What kind of calf is this that would make you two act this way?" Bradley asked, wiping his free hand across his badge, then on Dylan's shirt, "A golden one?"

"Almost. She's a purebred Charolais," Dylan said, pride and reverence glowing in his voice, "outta my best heifer."

"From my best bull," Wyatt interjected.

"And what's this about somebody stealing?" Bradley asked,

his voice as calm as if he was talking to two kids who'd been caught with their hands in the cookie jar.

"He took that calf from my barn last night," Dylan said, his hand tensing around the eggs again. "Don't deny it!" he shouted at his brother, "I saw her when I drove by your place this morning."

"Not gonna deny it, you bet I took her, and her mama. After I found out you were double-crossing me with that French fella. You're not sellin' that calf—she's going back into my herd like we agreed."

"Didn't agree on anything," Dylan said, "that's my cow and my calf and I'll sell her if I want to!"

"Okay, okay," Bradley said, "what's Betsy think about all this?" For the first time since the egg hit her, Saffron thought of Dylan's wife, the diminutive, dark-haired Betsy who ran the Sawyer ranches with a keen eye and an iron fist. Saffron looked up toward Dylan's red pickup, parked at the front of the line, blocking in his brother's truck and the rest of the customers. There was Betsy's outline, her trademark black braid sitting precisely down the middle of her back. She was not watching, seemed more interested in the swaying palms straight out the front of her windshield than she was in her husband's egg attack.

"You leave her out of it," Dylan said.

"I don't think we will," Bradley said, "Betsy!" he called, walking forward three steps to slap a hand on the fender of the red pickup, "You'd better come on out here, too!"

The slight shoulders inclined toward the door just before it opened. Betsy's red boots dropped out onto the sand. They were embellished all over with metal studs, and Saffron wondered if they hurt her feet. If they did, she didn't show it. She approached with a completely controlled expression.

Saffron took in her olive complexion, her hair, black as a

spider's back, her wide belt-buckle, her pearl-buttoned shirt. She could have been on the cover of *Rancher's Magazine*.

"Yes, officer?" she asked sweetly.

"Your husband here's been chucking eggs at his brother. Miss Skye's eggs, I might add."

Betsy looked around, but showed no visible reaction to the carnage.

"They say this is about a calf," Bradley said, "you know anything about that?"

Betsy turned her steely eyes on Bradley, "sure do," she said, "Wyatt stole our calf last night, just before we brought a client over to make a sale."

"And does Wyatt own any stock in this stock?" Bradley seemed pleased with his play on words.

"He *thinks* he does," Betsy said icily.

"That's not what I asked," Bradley said, a warning in his voice.

"Of course not. If you want to know the truth, he doesn't even have any right to the cows he's got on his place over there. They all ought to be ours—they're from Dylan's herd."

"Now, wait just a minute! Dylan and I *both* built that herd. I just took a few of them instead of my fair share cuz I was tryin' to avoid a feud after ya'll got married!" Wyatt cried, taking two steps toward Betsy. Dylan tried to wrench free of Bradley's grasp to get between his brother and his wife.

"Uh-uh," Bradley interjected, "you're staying here, Dylan. Wyatt, keep one hand on your truck. We're not having any fist-fights here this morning."

The Hawaiian sun was up now, and a few of the egg line cars were making three-point turns in the driveway, turning around and heading back toward the main road. Saffron didn't blame them, they had to get to work. That's why the egg line worked so well—when it was running right it was quick and easy for the commuter crowd.

Bradley noticed them, too, "You're gonna pay for all these eggs," he told Dylan, "and any that Saffron doesn't get to sell because you ran off her customers."

Dylan looked at Saffron for the first time and mumbled an apology. Wyatt echoed it from his place by the front of his blue truck.

"And, you're gonna lend her a cow for the live nativity at the Christmas Eve party," Bradley winked at Saffron. He must have seen her fliers around town, must have known how hard she'd been looking for animals to participate. She needed sheep, a cow, and if there was a miracle, she might even get a donkey. She had the hens of course, but a live nativity with only chickens just didn't seem right. Bradley went on, "Now, I don't know what we'll do about this calf-stealing situation, but I do know that if the two of you pull any more business like this, you're both coming to my jail until I figure out what's what. You got that?"

The men nodded, hanging their heads.

"That goes for you, too, Betsy," Bradley warned.

The woman raised her chin defiantly, but gave a curt nod of agreement.

Bradley, satisfied that the immediate threat was over, barked, "Now pay this girl and get these filthy trucks out of here."

* * *

HALF AN HOUR LATER, Saffron had finished with her few remaining customers and was standing by herself looking at the dark spots in the sand where the eggs still sat congealing. She fetched a rake and shovel and started tidying up.

She had to shoo her roaming hen and rooster, Tikka and Curry, away from the tantalizing eggs scattered in the driveway. Though chickens loved eggs, letting them eat raw ones was a terrible idea. Sometimes they got a taste for them and would break the eggs in the nests to eat them. She'd never had that problem in her flock, and she wasn't going to start now.

Instead, she scattered a few handfuls of scratch grains: wheat, cracked corn, and millet, to keep Tikka and Curry busy while she cleaned up.

"Can't have it looking like this for the party," she said out loud.

"The party is going to be sensational," a voice said, surprising her. Saffron turned to see her father, who had recently come back into her life, walking up the driveway alongside the long Christmas garland. Beside him was her adopted Tutu, or grandfather, Mano. Both were carrying beautifully wrapped Christmas presents.

She smiled in spite of the morning's antics.

Her father, Slate Skye, gave her a quick hug, and Mano greeted her with the honi, a traditional island greeting where they touched their foreheads together and breathed in deeply.

"What are you two doing out?" Both men lived in Maika'i, and it was an effort for them to come all the way out to the egg farm—especially since they insisted on walking. Saffron's father had found himself an apartment on the beach, not too far from Mano's house, and the two walked nearly everywhere.

"Playing Santa!" Mano said, holding his gifts aloft, "We went shopping."

"We also stopped by Juno's bakery," Slate said, tapping a pale purple box atop the others, "and we brought malasadas!"

That was exactly what Saffron needed after her exciting morning. The rich, sweet Hawaiian donuts had a way of soothing the soul.

"Did you get the special Christmas flavor of the day?" Saffron asked. Since Halloween, Juno's had been advertising a "Twelve Days of Christmas" promotion that was supposed to start today: December 12th, and run until Christmas Eve.

"Sure did. Eggnog custard!" Slate said.

"So 'ono," Mano said, using a word that always went with delicious food.

"I had to carry them so Mano wouldn't eat them all before we got here," Slate said.

"Better check his fingers for sugar," Mano retorted. Malasadas were rolled in sugar, which usually came off on your fingers when you ate them.

The two had been friends in their youth, and Saffron enjoyed seeing them spending time together now.

"I'll put these in the house," her father volunteered, and Mano reached for Saffron's rake.

"You've got more important things to be doing," he said, "let me help you." He raked a moment, then said, "how'd you make this mess, anyway?"

Saffron sighed and told him about the excitement that morning in the egg line.

Mano giggled, "I would have liked to see that."

Saffron loved how he always saw the humor in things. He had the best outlook she'd ever encountered.

"They picked a busy day to go nuts," she sighed.

"That's right," Mano said, "hatch day, huh?"

Saffron nodded, "It should happen any time."

"Can we go see her?" Mano had been keeping an eye on Saffron's broody hen, Cupcake, who was sitting on a clutch of eggs given to her by the wildlife department. The eggs were from a pair of Nene—wild geese which were Hawaii's state bird and whose species' survival was precarious. The wildlife department was trying to rebuild the population of the beautiful striped birds, and they had asked Saffron to see if Cupcake, who had been pining to hatch eggs, would take care of the Nene eggs.

And she had. Cupcake was an excellent mother. She stayed with the eggs every minute, turning them, cooing to them, and fluffing her ample feathers over them to create a dome of warmth where the little Nene goslings could grow.

The eggs were enormous. From what Vance Carlyle of the wildlife department told Saffron, they were even larger than most goose eggs, though the Nene was a smaller species than other geese. If Cupcake hadn't been so vigilant, one might have gotten chilled or left out, but she was meticulous at turning them and rotating them in the soft, feather-lined nest she'd made so that each one stayed the perfect temperature for incubation.

Saffron and Mano entered the egg house and walked down to the farthest pen on the right. This was Cupcake's "Broody Palace," as Saffron referred to it. Vance and the wildlife people had come in and fixed it up with pristine sand on the floor, cameras for viewing activity in the nest, thermometers to measure the temperature and humidity in every corner, and even little automatic sprayers that could come on if the humidity fell too far or the temperature climbed too high to be optimal for the Nene eggs.

Saffron had added something, too—a vintage wood couch with midcentury modern curves that was much more comfortable than it looked. It had been in one of the cottages she rented out, but she'd needed a comfy place to settle while she was observing Cupcake. She'd spent several hours snuggled in on the couch, feeling a soft breeze through the wire-covered windows and listening to the happy sounds of Cupcake's contented guardianship of the eggs.

Today, Cupcake clucked a greeting, and Saffron scooped some of the chicken's favorite scratch grains from her apron pocket and poured them from her palm into a little sandy depression directly in front of the mother hen.

Cupcake would not leave the nest except a few moments a day to eat and drink, so she appreciated having the treat delivered to her. She purred and trilled as she picked out the best bits first. Her favorite was the cracked corn.

Cupcake was leaning forward, snatching a bright yellow sliver of corn, when Saffron saw it. The smooth gray eggs looked like big pebbles peeking out through Cupcake's remarkable plumage. She was a special breed called a Blue-Laced Red Wyandotte, and her feathers were a beautiful auburn edged with gray. Underneath Cupcake's fluffy skirt, on the wide end of the Nene egg, was a distinctive triangular hole.

"Pip!" Saffron pointed, too excited to think of any other words, "That egg has pipped!"

Mano leaned closer and grinned broadly. It was the first sign that hatching had begun. The gosling inside had broken through the shell.

"What's the order again?" Mano asked, his voice bright with excitement.

"Pip, zip, pop!" Saffron replied, "They'll break through the egg—that's the pip, then they'll rotate inside, cracking a circle all around the circumference of the wide end of the egg— that's where the air sac is so they can breathe while they're working. Then, when they've zipped, they can stretch out and pop that end of the egg off and hatch!"

"Pip, zip, pop," Mano said.

Saffron heard something and leaned in closer. A wheezy chirping was coming from inside the egg, "Do you hear that?" she asked. Mano nodded.

Cupcake trilled back, sounding like the world's most encouraging parent. She raised up and stepped back slightly, to the edge of the nest, keeping close enough for the soft feathers of her chest to lend their warmth to the eggs, but pulling back enough to give the eggs some space. For a second, Saffron saw a little beak hovering just behind the triangular hole in the egg. She could see it rise and fall slightly as the gosling breathed.

Saffron's heart jumped when she saw an even larger hole in

the second egg and a hole with a jagged line running from it in the third egg.

"It's happening!" she couldn't keep the excitement out of her voice, "We'd better settle in. This is hard work for them. It could take a while."

And it did. Saffron, Mano, and Saffron's father, Slate, sat on the couch and kept an eye on the eggs all morning.

They watched as each egg developed a crack, then a gap in the shell as the crack ran all the way around the wide end. Little wings and spiky wet goose down peeked out of the widening gaps in the shells.

All the while, Cupcake was calling to her babies, encouraging them, pecking off a stray shard of shell, peering closely with one eye at their progress.

And all the while, Mano and Slate were making trips to the kitchen, bringing back the egg nog malasadas.

The sugary Hawaiian donuts they'd brought from town were the perfect snack for the sweet and wonder-filled experience of watching the goslings fight their way into the world.

Saffron couldn't contain a gasp of delight as the first gosling gave an enormous push and threw back the confining shell, stretching his long neck and letting loose a squeaky honk.

He was wet—a panting little creature plastered with black and silver streaks that were his baby feathers. Saffron knew from her research and from the papers the wildlife division had given her that he would fluff up eventually as he dried off.

Cupcake didn't seem to mind his bedraggled appearance. She was, it was easy to see, the proudest mother that ever hatched an egg. She nudged him with her beak, cooing to him, and opened a protective wing over him as he lay awkwardly splayed, half-in-half-out of his egg. He chirped back, lifting his enormous beak for her to peck a stray bit of shell from.

There was a sweetness about their interaction and a wonder about the whole process. Though the day had been trying so far, the new life that had just come into the world brought with it a bright new perspective. It was, according to tradition, the first of the twelve days of Christmas, and though there were no partridges to be found, one sweet gosling had graced Hau'oli ka Moa Egg Farm.

Chapter Two

In all, Cupcake had three babies to look after by the next morning. Three awkward little silver goslings, with too-big feet and bright eyes. Saffron checked on them just before Nik, her boyfriend, pulled into the yard to pick her up.

She'd been looking forward to this day for weeks, since Vance Carlyle had given her two tickets to the world's most elite poultry show, being held in Honolulu this year.

The World Poultry Premier Classic drew exhibitors from all over the world, who brought their chickens, pigeons, ducks, geese, quail, and other poultry to be judged by the CUBA—Companion and Utility Birds Association—judges. Saffron couldn't wait to see all the breeds of chickens she'd seen in the show's flier. Many she'd never even heard of.

Nik was more interested in spending some time in Honolulu than he was in the chickens, but he was cheerful and pleasant as always as they drove through the city streets in his station wagon, snacking on malasadas they'd picked up on the way out of Maika'i at Juno's Bakery. It was day two of the Christmas Malasada Countdown, and the flavor of the day was Gingerbread.

She never would have believed that the sharp tang of ginger and the sweet ooze of powdered sugar glaze would taste so good as a donut, but that was the magic of malasadas—they were versatile and always surprising.

Honolulu was in full Christmas mode. There were strings of lights on the palm trees, plastic Santas in short-sleeved Aloha suits, and everywhere, the poinsettia bushes were blooming. Some of them were as tall as trees.

All the trees were putting on a show. Nearly every palm had its trunk wrapped with strings of lights. The monkeypods' spreading branches shone, as well. A forty-foot fir tree caught Saffron's attention as they drove. It was decked with lovely glittering ornaments, with a star on the top. A beautiful seashell mosaic at its base spelled out, *Mele Kalikimaka.* Saffron was glad she'd worn her Christmas slippahs—flip-flops that were woven with shiny red and green ribbon and decorated with tiny seashells arranged in the shape of Christmas stars.

The show was no different. The parking lot was lined with candy canes.

As they searched through the aisles, Saffron's eyes narrowed when she saw a big red pickup truck parked in one of the stalls. If she had any doubt that it belonged to Dylan Sawyer, the doubt was erased by the three shattered eggs dried across the tailgate.

She hoped she wouldn't run into Dylan and Betsy. She didn't have anything nice to say.

The poultry show was being held in a wide park by the beach, under long canopies that shielded the birds and participants from the warm morning sun. There were garlands of poinsettias strung along the aisles along with several Christmas trees fully decked with tinsel and reflective balls. But the real ornaments of the show were the birds. Tables under the canopies held square cages filled with every size, shape, and color of bird imaginable. Saffron had seen photos of many of the birds in the show booklet that had come with her tickets. The photos themselves were exquisite. Rather than just using stock images of different breeds, the association had hired a portrait photographer to capture the true personality of various birds in the show.

Saffron had been pouring over the photos ever since she got the booklet. The portraits were funny, serene, sometimes poignant. Saffron and Mano were cooking up a new marketing campaign for Hau'oli ka Moa Egg Farm, and she wondered if there was any hope of getting the photographer who had captured the show birds to shoot some photos of her hens. His professional name was unusual, though. When she'd called the association to see who had done their photography, they said the photographer went by the professional name Blue. They didn't give out contact information, so she was hoping to run into him here.

The trouble was that Blue was reclusive. She'd found no photos of the man himself.

"Keep an eye out for someone with a camera," she told Nik.

"Found one," Nik pointed to the woman next to them. "Found another one," he pointed to the man on the other side of the aisle. Nearly everyone was photographing the birds.

Saffron gave him a wry look, "Very funny," she said, "I don't mean people with their smartphones. A professional photographer, with a fancy camera."

He grinned playfully. Saffron liked his sense of fun. It made every outing more enjoyable.

"Can you believe all these birds?" she asked. The canopies, tables, and cages went on and on.

"That's a lot of chickens," he agreed, "how many do you think there are?"

Saffron had looked for that answer in the booklet, but it didn't say. Maybe because when it was printed they weren't sure exactly how many would be coming. But someone must know. Scanning the aisle, Saffron recognized a poultry show official wearing a gold name tag.

"Excuse me," she asked the rather stern-looking woman.

The woman turned toward Saffron. She had a distinctly kite-shaped face, with narrow temples and a small chin, widened by broad cheekbones between. She was dressed smartly in an expensive navy skirt and jacket set that shone under the canopy-filtered rays of the Hawaiian sun. The woman's hair was pulled back into a tight bun, covered almost completely by a black beret. Saffron didn't often see people dressed so formally. Most islanders, even when they were dressed up, went for comfort and flowing fabrics. Her outfit, along with the clipboard she carried, gave the woman an intimidating air.

"Yes?" she asked impatiently.

"Um, how many birds are in the show?" Saffron stumbled.

"Three thousand six hundred and twenty-four," the woman rattled off. Saffron was taken aback. She'd expected only a general estimate. She thanked the woman and started off down the first row with Nik.

At the head of the row was a table filled with awards. They were bright and beautiful, flowing and shining and catching the light. Ribbons, medals, and plaques stood ready for the judges to hand them out to the best birds. The awards started small and got bigger. The smallest were brass "Participant" medals, and the awards grew in proportion to the prestige of the award. There were nineteen "Best in Class" trophies—gold pedestals with little statues of different types of poultry atop them. In the center of the table, standing two feet high, was a shining silver cup.

Saffron leaned in close to it. It was exquisite—reflecting the colors of the awards around it in its mirror surface. On it was a detailed engraving of a hen and a rooster and the words

"World Poultry Premier Classic Show Champion." There was no doubt that this was the top prize available. Saffron looked out over the thousands of birds and wondered which one would take that silver cup home.

Saffron tore herself away from the awards table and moved along the row. She peered into a cage where a jolly round red rooster looked back at her from above a fluffy white beard of feathers. "Nik," she called, "come check out the Santa chicken!"

Nik looked skeptical, "Is that beard fake?" he asked, "Who would do that to a chicken?"

Saffron shook her head, "Nope, it's a real trait that some chickens have. I have some bearded ones. They can also get those fluffy feathers on their cheeks, and then they're called muffs."

"It's a good look for him," Nik said, "I hope the beard looks as good on me."

Saffron squeezed his hand, "Thank you for being my Santa for the Christmas Eve party," she said. It was one more thing she didn't have to worry about.

"No problem. I like to spread Christmas cheer," he caught her eye and smiled down at her.

Saffron looked away just as she nearly ran into a couple moving at a fast clip down the row of cages. They didn't even say *excuse me*. Spinning back around, she eyed the departing couple. Those studded boots. That black braid. It was Dylan and Betsy Sawyer.

"That was close," Nik said.

"They didn't even act like they knew me," Saffron huffed.

"Do they?" Nik swiveled his head to watch them go.

"That's the Sawyers. The ones that destroyed my egg crop yesterday."

He squinted, "Hm. Maybe they were too embarrassed to speak to you, or they were just focused on something else."

Just then, a big black and red rooster next to them let out a deafening crow which set off several others in the cages around him, "Well, there are certainly plenty of distractions around here," Saffron acknowledged.

The next row held tiny, miniature chickens. Saffron knew they were bantam breeds—smaller than the standard fowl she kept at the egg farm. They were so small and delicate that Saffron was worried when she saw a young exhibitor reaching in and pulling one out. They looked so fragile. He reached in under the chicken's chest and grasped it, holding his two middle fingers under its breast bone and his index and pinky finger on either side of each leg.

When he lifted it out of the cage, he turned immediately to a man in a gold vest standing in the center of the aisle with a clipboard. A judge.

The exhibitor held the chicken in front of him, then smoothly and swiftly pivoted his hand and raised his arm so that both the hand and the chicken were on his shoulder.

This was a way of handling birds that Saffron had never seen before. The little chicken was right at eye-level for the judge. The exhibitor tapped the bird's beak to encourage it to look one direction, then the other side to get it to look the other direction.

The judge leaned in close, studying the chicken, then leaned back and jotted something on his clipboard. The exhibitor rotated the bird down again and spread one wing, then the other. He ruffled the feathers backward, then smoothed them into place again.

What most amazed Saffron about watching him show off the bird was how amazingly calm the little chicken was. It sat totally at ease in his hand, blinking lazily as if this pivoting and swirling were the most routine thing in the world.

Saffron supposed it was. If the bird traveled the world to shows like this one, it was probably very used to being handled this way. Saffron's hens, besides being much bigger and heavier than this bird, were also much more spirited. They'd never stand for being shown off like that. If she tried, there'd be a lot less judging and a lot more flapping and squawking and protesting going on.

Not that the other showbirds were quiet by any means. The whole park was filled with the noise of them clucking, bawking, trilling, and cooing. Saffron had spent enough time in her egg house being scolded and confided in by her own birds that the racket didn't bother her in the slightest.

Nik, on the other hand, was looking more bored with each passing second. As the exhibitor put the little bird back in the cage and the judge moved off down the aisle, Saffron saw Nik sneaking a look at his watch. They'd only been here half an hour, and he was already chafing to leave.

She laid a hand on his arm. "You don't have to stay, you know," she said, "I'll be fine. I want to see every chicken here, so it could take a while. I know you love the city. If you have something else you'd rather do, please feel free to go. You can come pick me up later."

Nik brightened, "Are you sure?" he asked, already turning toward the nearest exit.

"Of course!" Saffron thought it might even be more interesting to look around without him. That way she could explore what she wanted to without worrying she was boring him.

Nik craved adventure. He surfed the biggest waves, cliff dove, and wanted to learn to pilot a helicopter. The serene world of chickens held little interest for him.

Saffron watched him go, then turned back to the room full of fascinating and unusual poultry.

* * *

Hours had passed and Saffron had barely noticed. She had walked nearly every aisle and near the end of the crested breed section—the section where chickens whose feathers on their heads grew straight out like wild hairdos instead of laying down flat—a flash of gorgeous color caught her eye.

It was a hen, being carried by a large man with jet-black hair. The hen was a beautiful peachy color, with a creamy undercarriage and a few warm apple-colored freckles across her wings. Saffron had to know what she was—she'd never seen such delicate coloration before, or such fluffy under-feathers.

She followed the man, trying to catch up and ask him what breed of chicken he was carrying. He turned down an aisle and Saffron followed him, dodging her way through people and birds.

A beautiful, lilting melody drifted down the aisle. Saffron registered that it was growing louder the farther she went down the aisle. It was light and bubbly and somehow fit right in with the clucks and trills of the hens around them.

When she caught up to him, Saffron found that the bird wasn't the only uniquely beautiful thing the man had in his life. He stopped beside a row of cages where a very lovely young woman stood singing.

She had long, straight hair the color of buttercups. Her mouth was turned up in a smile, and her face had a look of joy. It was her song that Saffron had heard. She was also noticeably pregnant, and very near her due date, Saffron guessed.

"Hugo!" the young woman cried, "they've all made it into the final round!"

The man Saffron had followed tucked the hen he was carrying under his arm and hugged the golden-haired girl, "I knew they would, Cherie!" He had a thick French accent.

"They are the prettiest hens here," she said. Then, noticing

Saffron lingering behind the man, the girl called out, "Do you have hens you're exhibiting?"

Saffron shook her head, "No, no. I've got an egg farm on the other side of the island. I'm just a spectator here."

"Oh, then you must come and meet my girls!" the girl stepped around the man and reached for Saffron's hand, pulling her forward. "I'm Sophie Leblanc."

As she spoke, Saffron detected a slight accent. Not as strong as the man's, but present nonetheless.

"I'm Saffron Skye."

"What a charming name."

"Thank you. You have a beautiful voice."

The girl blushed, "Oh, you heard my song?"

"Yes, but I didn't understand the words."

"It's a French song," Sophie said, "Il est bel et bon." She looked up at her husband. "It's a song where two women are talking about how handsome and good their husbands are, and one says, 'he does the chores and feeds the chickens,' and the song is all about how the two of them sound like hens cackling about their husbands," the girl giggled. "I thought it was appropriate for the day."

Saffron found herself smiling. "It did fit well." One of the remarkable hens, as if to punctuate the point, cackled heartily.

The girl laughed. "This is Antoinette," she placed Saffron's hand on the chicken the man was carrying, "and Hugo, my husband."

Saffron tried to think of a proper greeting, but she was so surprised at the feel of the chicken that she was momentarily without words.

It was, without a doubt, the softest chicken she'd ever felt. Antoinette's feathers were so soft that Saffron almost couldn't feel them under her fingers, so silky she almost didn't believe they were there at all.

"She's so—"

"Soft!" Sophie cried, "I know. She is the perfect Faverolles!"

Saffron tried to repeat the word. "Faverolles?"

Sophie giggled at the pronunciation. "Very close. It's her breed."

Saffron had not heard of that breed. She studied the chicken and wished Nik were here—it had the fluffiest beard and muffs she'd ever seen. "Her feathering is remarkable! Look at those muffs!"

"You know chickens, then?" Sophie asked.

"I have over a hundred hens myself," Saffron said proudly.

"One hundred! So many!" Sophie looked delighted.

"My egg farm is in a little town called Maika'i. Like I said, it's on the other side of the island."

"Maika'i?"

"It means great, or awesome."

"Is it?" Sophie asked, a little wistfully.

Saffron couldn't stop herself from smiling as she thought of her little town, its people, and her farm, "Yes. It is awesome." She patted the chicken again, gleaning a scowl from Hugo. "But none of my hens are this color, or are quite this soft. Would you tell me more about this breed?" she asked.

"Faverolles get their name from a village in France," Sophie said, "Near Hugo's village, where we live."

"Are you from there, as well?" Saffron asked, stroking the chicken.

"No, no, I'm an American. I grew up in the Midwest, but my mother was French. That, combined with living in France for three years, has given me a little accent. I'm flattered you thought I was from there."

Hugo seemed to be growing impatient. Sophie hurried on, "The Faverolles are sweet and friendly," she said, "they're dual purpose, so they are good for eggs or meat. But mostly, they're wonderful companion chickens—they're so gentle and funny."

There was a plaintive look in Sophie's eyes that Saffron recognized. The girl was lonely. These hens were her friends.

"What color are their eggs?" Saffron's special color perception had sparked a quest to assemble the most colorful egg basket possible. Back at the egg farm she had hens that laid mint-green eggs, hens that laid sky-blue eggs, hens that laid cocoa-colored eggs, and many more. But she was still on the look out for some tints. "I've been looking for some pink egg-layers," she finished.

Sophie's face brightened and she turned to the table. Reaching under, she extracted a beautiful rose-petal-pink egg.

"Oh!" Saffron couldn't help herself. She had perfect color memory—an extensive catalog of every shade of every color that she'd ever seen—and she'd never encountered this exact pink before, "That is exquisite!"

"Here," Sophie held it out, "You take it."

Saffron reached for the egg with reverence. It delighted her.

But Hugo's hand was faster. Like a viper, he struck out and knocked Sophie's hand sideways. The egg flew in a short arc and shattered at Saffron's feet, oozing golden yolk into the rich green grass of the park.

"Hugo!" Sophie scolded.

His upper lip drawn back, he sneered at his wife, "Are you crazy?" he barked, "She is probably a spy from the competition. You would hand over our eggs so that she can hatch one of our champions and beat us at next year's show?"

Saffron, taken aback, tried to reassure him, "oh, no, no, I don't breed chickens, I'm just a spectator."

"Ha!" his tone was harsh, "You know eggs. I saw your eyes —you know that our colorations are special. It takes a practiced eye to differentiate between remarkable birds and eggs and common farmyard specimens. You have a trained eye."

He had her there, "It's not because I'm a competitor—I

just have a good eye for color. And you're right. I've never seen such beautiful color in birds."

"Sure," his voice was acid, "An eye for color."

Sophie tried to pull the conversation back. It was obvious she was enjoying Saffron's company and didn't want her to go, "I'm glad you noticed the coloring. In the Faverolles breed, there are several different colorations," Sophie went on, "Our girls have the salmon coloring. We've worked so hard to get them just right."

"And we have done it," Hugo said, his voice jutting into the flow of conversation like a stone tossed into a stream, "she just won the Best of Class Award."

Sophie's lilting tones washed back in, "which means that she and her two sisters," Sophie waved a hand at two more exquisite birds in the cages, "Babette and Claudette, are all in the running for Show Champion! They each won their class!"

Saffron didn't know everything about the show, but she knew what Show Champion meant—a huge cash prize, breeding contracts, and general poultry-world fame and fortune.

"Congratulations," she said, "they are beautiful."

"They are exquisite," Hugo corrected her. She looked up into the big man's face. He had heavy brows and dark, brooding eyes. "Which you seem to recognize." Saffron stepped back slightly. His face looked sculpted, modeled into an expression of stern disapproval. She pulled her hand back and he shifted the hen and locked her in an empty cage next to the two others, equally beautiful.

"Oh, let's keep them out a moment," Sophie plead with her husband, "they've been in so long!"

"And they'll be in longer," he said gruffly, "they've got the rest of today as well as the ride home. And when they get there, we'll put them in the bamboo cages. They don't need to be getting exposed to the prying eyes of our competitors," he looked pointedly at Saffron.

"Aw, but I could carry them around, let them see the other birds. Give them a change of scenery for some variety."

Hugo shook his head. "Absolutely not. I don't want their feathers mussed for the Show Champion round later." Sophie looked disappointed. "Anyway," he said, laying a hand on her protruding belly, "you're already carrying enough." Between them passed a look of tenderness that made Hugo seem, for a moment, almost warm. Saffron sensed it was time to go.

"Well," she said, "good luck!"

"Merci!" Sophie called, "Au revoir!"

"Au revoir!" Saffron tried out the words on her tongue, and though they didn't come out just right, Sophie seemed to appreciate the effort and smiled broadly.

Hugo stood behind his wife, his eyes piercing. He fixed a scowl on Saffron and a cold chill ran down her spine as she hurried away from him down the aisle.

* * *

SAFFRON TRIED to shake the feeling of dread that Hugo had left with her by searching out the examples of breeds she had back on the farm. She made her way to the Wyandotte's section and walked along looking at the heavy-bottomed hens with their perfectly laced feathers, edged in contrasting colors. Cupcake was a blue-laced red Wyandotte, which meant that her feathers were a rich rust color in the center and their points were edged with steely gray lacing. It looked like armor.

Where Cupcake had an occasional feather that was fully red, though, these birds had nothing out of place. They were absolutely perfect. Saffron would have hated to try to judge between them. They all looked exquisite to her.

She thought about the salmon Faverolles, each so pristine.

It must be difficult to keep their feathers so clean and soft when they had traveled so far.

Saffron liked things in their places. She was, at heart, an organizer and had been, when she lived in Washington, DC, a little neurotic about having everything just right. It was a way of maintaining control in a life she had felt she had little control over.

She had gradually changed when she'd come to the islands. Both the breezy, sandy landscape and the care of over a hundred hens whose standard of tidiness was markedly lower than hers had changed her. Now, she left her shoes in the living room, wore flowing fabrics, and sometimes didn't make her bed.

But because she had been, at one time, so obsessed with perfection, she saw it rearing its head in some of the competitors.

They were polishing beaks, arranging feathers, and trimming toenails all down the aisle. They didn't look up as Saffron passed, just kept their eyes on the bird they were working on. Occasionally, she saw them glance to the side to compare their entry with the one next to it. Saffron's color vision helped her detect either the scarlet flush of triumph flooding their faces as they detected their bird was superior, or the blue-green wash of envy creeping up their cheeks if, instead, they felt theirs was inferior.

It looked miserable to Saffron, always wondering if the judge would like the bird in the next cage better than yours. She supposed that was what was wrong with Hugo—ambition that had turned to paranoia. He couldn't trust anyone, couldn't even allow his wife to have friends lest they turn out to be spies trying to steal his poultry secrets.

Saffron felt sorry for Sophie.

Chapter Three

Saffron took photos of the silkie chickens—little balls of fluff—to send to her friend the Empress back in Maika'i. The Empress had a pet chicken who rode on her lap as she moved about in her wheelchair. The chicken's name, of course, was Princess. These silkies were perfectly groomed and tidy, but none of them as beautiful or with as much entitled sass as Princess had.

"Excuse me," a man's voice, laced with indignance, caught Saffron's attention as she leaned over to snap a photo of a steely silky with a particularly wild topknot, "you're in my shot."

She turned to find herself face-to-face with a shining round camera lens. She stepped back, mumbling an apology.

The photographer didn't acknowledge it. Saffron felt a little prickle of annoyance. She waited for the shutter click, then stepped deliberately back in front of the lens to get her own shot.

"Are you finished?" the man asked impatiently.

"Just about," Saffron tilted her camera.

The man was suddenly at her elbow, "Not that way. Take it from the top like that and all you'll get is a blob in the center of your frame." Without asking permission, he took her smartphone from her hand. "You have to think about angle. With chickens," he crouched in front of the cage, "there are three angles from which you can shoot to really capture their shape. Use the breastbone to figure out the composition. You can position your camera slightly above the breastbone to capture more plumage, slightly below the breastbone to focus more on the carriage of the head, or behind the breastbone to focus more on remarkable tail feathers or wings."

As he spoke, he moved her camera around and when he handed it back to her, there were three perfect shots of the silky. She recognized the style immediately.

"Wow," her earlier annoyance had evaporated, "Can I ask, are you Blue? Did you do the chicken portraits in the show booklet?"

He eyed her, "Why do you ask?"

Saffron jumped in, "I admire them. I own an egg farm on the other side of the island, and I wanted to see if I could hire you to shoot some photos of my birds and eggs—for marketing."

He considered, "Hawaiian egg farm," he spoke almost to himself, "could work for the *Modern Homesteading* spread." The photographer looked her in the eye, "Maybe. But I'd have to change my tickets. I'm supposed to leave tomorrow morning. Is there anyplace to stay over there?"

Saffron tried not to seem over-eager, "I have three cottages at the farm," she said, "and they're vacant the next two weeks."

She was glad that since she hadn't wanted to deal with renters while she was trying to pull together the big Christmas Eve party, she hadn't made the cottages available.

Blue nodded, "Fine. I'll be over tomorrow afternoon. I don't know how long I'll stay. I have projects I may need to shoot for."

He looked her in the eye, "My services are very expensive."

Saffron blinked, trying to think of something to say in response.

"Of course, I suppose your cottages are also quite expensive. So, I propose, we swap. I stay in your cottage, you get photos of your hens."

Saffron couldn't help but grin, "That sounds perfect."

"Perfection doesn't exist in the real world," Blue said, "Only a photograph can be perfect."

They exchanged information and he went off down the aisle hunting for his next subject. Saffron skipped a little as she passed the rest of the silkies.

* * *

As THE DAY WORE ON, Saffron found herself watching the people as much as the chickens. These, too, were a rare breed. While she loved her chickens and was inordinately proud of everything they did, from their eggs to their different calls and clucks, the exhibitors were far more obsessed with their birds. For many of them, the breed of chicken they showed, as well as the individual birds, were their lives—their identities. There were Plymouth Rock people, Sussex people, and Orpington people. Each had a distinct opinion about why their breed, and their bird in particular, was vastly superior to all three thousand six hundred and twenty-three others in the show. They would stop Saffron and give her their opinions or show off their prizes and their poultry.

Some of them even resembled their birds. One, in particular, caught Saffron's attention from across the room.

He was a tall man, gangly, with thin wrists sticking out of the sleeves of a black suit jacket. He had a long, beak-like nose and small lips, pursed in concentration as he shaped the toenails of what seemed to be a large rooster he was holding like a baby. Saffron couldn't see its head, but its feathers were fascinating: mottled black and white. The man's most striking feature matched that coloring. Atop his head was a spray of spiky silver and black hair, sticking out in every direction.

The man looked up, catching sight of Saffron staring at him, and before she could avert her eyes politely, his face split in a grin. He waved her over with the hand in which he held the nail trimmers.

Saffron was caught now. She couldn't simply ignore him, not when she'd been staring at him. She worked her way to the aisle where he was and approached him.

"You have an appreciation for the Mottled Houdan," he said, smiling.

"Do I?" Saffron had no idea what that was.

"Obviously," he said, "I saw you eyeing Lyle here," the man shifted, boosting the big rooster up and righting him.

Saffron bit her lip to keep from laughing as she came face-to-face with Lyle. This was the most comical chicken she'd ever seen: black and white spotted, its head was covered by an enormous crest of black and white feathers, a nearly perfect ball that looked like a spiky version of a clown's wig. She couldn't stop herself—she reached out to touch it.

"Oh, no!" The man pulled the bird back at the last second, "I know that puff is tempting, but you can't touch it. It's perfect. A broken feather right now, before I take him for final judging, would be a crisis of catastrophic proportions!"

Saffron understood, "Oh, I'm sorry!"

"You can pat my hair if you want," it was at that moment that Saffron realized how far the remarkable resemblance between the man and his bird went. His sleek black suit caught the light in a unique way. Just as the bird had irregular splotches of white, the black suit shone with subtle silver threads in an uneven pattern that gave it suit a slightly mottled texture, as well. He wore a silver tie and a glittering chain around his neck with a silver medallion on the end of it. The medallion had wording—too small to read unless she got uncomfortably close—and an embossed chicken in the center. His crown of hair that matched Lyle's was the icing on the cake. She pressed her lips together, fighting a rising giggle. The man tipped his head obligingly in her direction, "I'm Gavin Godfrey," Saffron gave his spiky hair a cursory pat. It was surprisingly springy.

"Nice to meet you," she said as he righted himself and Lyle the Mottled Houdan came back into view.

"He is a remarkable breed," she said.

"Mottled Houdans are the *most* remarkable breed," his tone was not arrogant, it was factual. "Dual purpose, you know— good for eggs and meat. They were developed for the market. They bear confinement well, and they are sensational-looking."

Saffron wouldn't argue that. Lyle was bobbing his fluffy head around, peering at her from under the tips of his feathers. Not only was his crest profoundly striking, but he had a comb like she'd never seen before. It almost seemed wrong: two lobes, like the wings of a butterfly, rose above his eyes like exaggerated eyebrows.

"Is that," she tried to think of a delicate way to ask, "usual? His comb?"

Gavin's face grew stormy, "not usual at all," he said huffily, "very unusual. But absolutely perfect according to The Standard."

He said the last two words as if they had great weight and meaning.

"The standard?" Saffron asked.

Gavin's eyes grew even wider, "Of Perfection?" he asked. When Saffron gave him a little shake of her head to show she still had no idea what he was talking about, Gavin heaved a great sigh.

"The American Standard of Perfection is the bible for poultry exhibitors," he said firmly, "A book that lists what a chicken should look like in every aspect. It is the absolute authority on every characteristic of each breed of chicken. It is what we aspire to, what we endeavor for our birds to reach." He didn't say *what we worship*, but it was implied in his tone.

"Oh," Saffron said, trying to convey that she understood when she didn't.

"Lyle *is* perfection," Gavin said proudly. "He conforms to every point of The Standard. He's going to be the Show Champion," the man's beady black eyes shone with the hunger of ambition.

"Oh?" It was the second time that day Saffron had heard such a claim. Saffron tried to judge in her mind how Lyle would stack up next to the Faverolles she'd seen earlier.

Gavin seemed astounded at the question in her voice, "But of course he is! Look around at all these…" he waved a hand, an expression of near-disgust on his face, "*yard birds*," he said the words as if they tasted terrible in his mouth. "None of them has the conformation, the carriage, the plumage, of Lyle. Not to mention his excellent showmanship."

Just then, though, Lyle was trying to scratch his beak with his foot, which was not a particularly impressive pose.

Gavin tapped the bird on his back, between his wings, gently, and Lyle snapped to attention. Saffron had never seen such a well-trained chicken before. It was as if the rooster knew exactly what he was supposed to do. He straightened, stretched his neck, and tucked his beak. He rearranged his wings and fluffed up his glossy feathers. He really was a showman.

Gavin looked on, bursting with pride, and slipped the rooster a shelled sunflower seed. Lyle gobbled it up and then resumed his pose.

"How did you teach him that?" Saffron asked, thinking of the flighty, willful hens she had at home. She couldn't imagine any of them standing so still, much less posing on her command.

"Lyle has been in training for eighteen months. Two sessions per day of three hours each, since he hatched."

"That sounds grueling."

"Oh, it is," Gavin assured her, "but it's the price of *perfection*."

That word again. Perfection. It seemed everyone in the show was obsessed with it. Even their bible was called *The Standard of Perfection*. It seemed an exhausting quest. Saffron had once been obsessed with it, too, but had found much more joy in the surprises and revelations that came with imperfection.

"Of course, there are other, more subtle ways in which Lyle is superior," Gavin said. He launched into a discussion about the lay of the hackle feathers on Lyle's neck. Saffron tried to listen, but was distracted by the sudden calm in the aisle around her. The buzz of exhibitors and attendees that had been swarming the area was flowing out of the aisle, all in the same direction. She glanced across the cages and saw that the same thing was happening in every aisle.

"Sorry," she interrupted, "what's happening? Where are they all going?"

Gavin glanced around, "Well, to the show ring, of course. The Show Champion will be announced soon——" he checked his watch, an enormous steel affair that made his wrist disproportionately bulky under his shirtsleeve. He smiled widely. "I hope you'll be there to see Lyle become the most revered chicken in the world."

The phrase made a smile begin to push up behind Saffron's best efforts at an earnest face, "I will."

"You'd better get over there if you want a decent seat," he said, "It will fill up fast, and there's only so many seats where you can see the ring well. I hope you'll be able to spot me."

Saffron glanced again at his crown of spiky hair. "I don't think that will be a problem," she said. He gave her a puzzled look, and she was afraid he'd guess what she meant and be offended, so she asked the first question she could think of.

"Will you be going right over?"

"No, first I'll be checking in with the judges to certify that Lyle is the bird that won his class earlier. Every Best in Class chicken must be verified. They'll check his entry sheet and details, then I'll move onto the photography tent, where they'll chronicle his superiority, then we'll proceed to the ring for the judges' final decision."

"Good luck," Saffron managed, wondering briefly if wishing both Sophie and Gavin good luck meant that she canceled out the good luck altogether.

"I appreciate the sentiment," he said, "but we won't need it. Lyle will win. Losing is not a possibility."

Saffron gave a little wave as she moved down the aisle. She glanced back once at the two remarkable hairstyles as she was caught up in a crush of people at the end of the aisle, all headed in the same direction.

After a few steps, they came to a halt. The information that was passed back along the line said that the gates to the show ring were closed until the competitors went through the eligibility check and the photography and put their birds in the cages in the show ring. Spectators would have to wait in line until then.

The minutes stretched on, ticked by, crawled. Saffron observed the people around her and found a huge array of them. Some were obvious fans of certain breeds or breeders. Others looked like they were tourists who had stumbled into the poultry show by accident. Still others were clearly real farmers. All were surprisingly patient, as if they'd paid for the ticket solely to wait in this line. There was a lot of chatter about who would win the Show Champion, and Saffron heard the words Houdan and Faverolles.

She even saw Gavin and Lyle hurrying by past the crowd, shined up and ready for final judging. She figured Hugo and the hens were somewhere up there, too, along with the best birds from some of the other classes. She heard people talking about them, and there were several she recognized. A Langashan was apparently competing, and a Dominique. It would be interesting to find out who won.

Finally, after what must have been an hour, it was announced that the ring was open and people could begin finding their seats. The line flowed along, shuffling and bumping like logs on a spring stream. The vast aisles were empty of people, all the chickens settled into their cages. This aisle was wider, but with all the people it felt very crowded. Large canvas tents stood off to one side, looking like oases of tranquility. On them were signs that said "Judging" and "Photography" and "Admissions." Saffron could see, far down the big park, in the direction they were going, a show ring with bleachers surrounding it. It was going to take a while to get there. She wished she hadn't spent quite so much time talking to Gavin. She doubted she'd find a very good seat now.

Saffron's phone buzzed and she moved to the edge of the stream of people and answered. She could barely hear Nik asking if she was ready yet. He'd be back in twenty minutes or so.

Saffron darted out of the line of people and ducked behind the canvas admissions tent where it was quieter. "Sure," she said, "but I want to see who wins the Show Champion title and the silver cup. Come into the show ring and find me. If it's not over by the time you get here, we'll watch the end before we go."

Nik agreed and Saffron hung up. She couldn't face going back into the crush of people. As she looked around, she saw that she could cut through the white tents and go directly to the ring. There were no signs saying she should keep out, so she charged ahead.

If she hadn't noticed a particularly beautiful peach-colored feather on the grass, she might have hurried right past the judges' tent. But she did notice it, and she stopped to pluck it from the ground as a little souvenir of her day at the poultry show. She heard the angry voices before she could start walking again.

"Get it through your head, Hugo!" a woman's stern voice was saying, "You won't win. Your birds are not going home with this cup!"

There was a hollow chime, like a bell being hit with a mop.

"You'd better reconsider that decision," Hugo's voice was unmistakable, icy and menacing, "or this will be the last show you judge."

"If you win, it will be the last show I judge. I'm telling you, he knows, and he won't hesitate to reveal it if I choose your bird. You've made him furious. I've never seen him so irate.

He'll tell them about us and then I'll be stripped of my status in the organization."

"I'll make sure you are if you *don't* choose my hen," Hugo growled. "I've got other information they'd be particularly interested in. Like the way you're completely disregarding The Standard in order to further your own economic interests."

"I know The Standard inside and out. I could no more disregard it than I could disregard my heartbeat."

"Coeur? You have no coeur."

"You always were a spoiled child, just like your father. You've never learned that you can't always have what you want."

"I can have what is rightfully mine, though. No matter what I have to do to get it."

"Be reasonable!" the woman's voice was high with fear or rage, Saffron couldn't tell which, "There will be other competitions!"

"None in which I will have the opportunity to sell—" Hugo stopped himself, "Never mind."

The woman's voice became even more shrill, "*sell?* You'd sell your heritage? Your birthright?"

"It's not something I expect you to understand," he said.

There was the sound of spitting. Saffron knew she had heard too much. She edged away from the tent.

"Is someone there?" called the woman's voice. Then, in hushed tones, she growled, "Get out of here before someone sees you. Go through the photography tent."

Saffron froze just as Hugo pushed his way through the canvas flap and raced for the tent across the path Saffron was standing on. She pressed back into the shadows, not breathing, and hoped he had not looked her way. He was carrying one of the three hens, though Saffron couldn't determine which one from here.

She glanced at the feather in her hand. Its color was a perfect match to the chicken he was carrying.

He ducked through the opposing tent flap into the photography tent.

Saffron eased out of the shadows, but dove back in as the judge hurried out carrying the silver cup. It was the stern-looking woman she'd spoken to before, the one who knew exactly how many chickens were at the show. The judge glanced around and slipped behind the photography tent.

Saffron kept an eye on the flap of the tent in case Hugo came back out. She was surprised to see the flap kick out suddenly right behind him, as if he'd stepped back into it, startled.

Saffron heard noises. Not loud, but distinctive. They were the sounds of a struggle. Blows, grunts, and shuffling feet. The hen squawked, a cry of alarm.

Low, angry voices slipped out of the tent flap followed by what sounded like a punch. Saffron couldn't understand the words, but it was clear someone was having a disagreement. The racket grew: a table sliding, the clanging of falling equipment, cries of outrage and surprise.

Saffron heard running feet, more voices, and a grunt.

Just as Saffron made her mind up to go into the tent and see what was happening, the sound of a ringing bell filled the air. All other sounds stopped abruptly and Hugo Leblanc fell backward through the flap, the chicken gone and his hand to his head.

He landed heavily on his back. As his hand fell free of his head and flopped onto the grass, Saffron could see it gleaming with blood.

Had the chicken attacked? Had he run into something? Saffron ran forward. Hugo was horribly still. His feet were still in the tent. The tent flap brushed his shins. Sticking out next to him, half-covered by the tent flap, was the big silver cup, splashed with red. Saffron found her voice.

"Help!" She screamed with all the strength her lungs and rushing adrenaline could muster, "Help!"

The noise from the rushing crowd on the other side of the tents must have drowned her out, because nobody came.

Saffron was alone with what was, very obviously, a dead man.

Chapter Four

The Honolulu Police were very thorough. Saffron told her story three different times to three different policemen. She answered a lot of questions: Why she was there between the tents, what she had seen and heard, why she had blood on her hands.

She'd tried to help Hugo. Had tried to stanch the flow of blood from his head, had done CPR until the paramedics pulled her away, arms trembling, and said there was nothing more she could do.

In the end, none of it helped. He had been dead before he hit the ground, and nothing Saffron did could change that. As she sat watching the police officers swarm the scene, she wished she hadn't wasted time trying to save him. Instead, she should have taken the time to look for clues about what had happened to Hugo Leblanc.

His face hadn't relaxed into peaceful repose. Instead, the very expression he'd drilled Saffron with as she said goodbye to Sophie earlier was etched onto his features: brows lowered, mouth bunched tight and pulled downward in an angry scowl.

The police weren't inclined to answer Saffron's questions with the same willingness she'd answered theirs. They wouldn't confirm, for example, that the stately silver cup engraved with a hen and rooster was the weapon that had cracked Hugo's skull. But Saffron knew it was. She had seen its crushed side, the hen and rooster splashed with red.

They wouldn't tell her any details, in fact, but she gathered some anyway. She listened as the officers cleared the tent, declaring no sign of anyone inside. She overheard as a sergeant with curly black hair made a report to the chief that another competitor was seen in the area moments after Saffron began screaming for help. She saw the light flash off an officer's badge as he knelt and gathered scattered feathers from inside the flap of the photography tent. Those feathers were not just peachy. They were black and white—mottled, Saffron would have called them, and she was sure they came from Lyle.

As she sat drinking a small can of apple juice one of the paramedics had brought her, she studied the crime scene. The police had fixed back the tent flap, letting light into the interior of the photography tent.

The tent had been crowded even before the four police officers began combing it for evidence. Saffron could see tables—some of them upended or flipped completely over— and photography lights and a big backdrop for shooting chickens with their owners. On the floor near the door was a lightbox. It was made from light material on a wire frame, and would have been surrounded, she thought, by the lights that were scattered around the tent now. She assumed Blue had used it for his exquisite chicken portraits, but it was bent and mangled now. It was obvious there had been a real struggle inside.

Saffron heard a familiar voice, and from where she sat on the back of the ambulance, she could just see around its side to a table where the chief of police sat. When Saffron looked, she saw the judge—the woman she'd heard talking to Hugo—on the other side of the table.

The woman was distraught, "Yes, I was meeting with him. I was meeting with all the exhibitors before the final judging for best in show. So were all the judges."

"And you argued with him?"

"You must be firm when dealing with exhibitors. Everyone wants an unfair advantage. I am committed to the equity my position requires."

"That doesn't answer my question."

"Yes, I argued with him. Only because he expected an unfair advantage."

"And why was that? Why did he think he deserved that advantage?"

Saffron glanced over and saw the woman's thin mouth pressed closed. The judge folded her arms, creating a wall between her and her interrogators. Saffron knew the answer to the question. What had the woman said to Hugo just before he died? *If they find out about us.* Hugo had obviously thought he deserved an advantage because of some connection he had with the judge.

Saffron eyed the woman. She was no expert in extramarital affairs, but the stone-faced, gaunt woman just didn't seem like she'd be one to carry on with a man easily half her age. It could be a romantic entanglement, but Saffron didn't find that likely. So if it wasn't that, what *was* the connection that the judge was so desperate to hide?

There was no time to ponder that, though. A ruckus around the side of the photography tent drew her attention.

A large policeman, his broad shoulders straining against his navy uniform, was wrestling someone out of the third tent— the admissions tent. As he turned, Saffron immediately recognized the shock of black and white hair on the struggling man. It was Gavin.

"Let me go! I have no idea what you're talking about!" Gavin cried, "I have only a few minutes to get into the ring!"

Saffron looked around for Lyle, but there was no sign of the rooster.

"I doubt any of us are going to the show ring now, Mr. Godfrey," said the judge.

He looked over at her in alarm, "What do you mean?"

"A man is dead, sir," the officer answered for her and pointed toward the still form of Hugo Leblanc.

Saffron wished later she hadn't seen it. She wished she had glanced away, or that the officer had moved in front of Gavin, but she'd had a perfect view of Gavin's reaction to seeing Hugo on the ground, and the expression on his face was one she'd never forget. She would have expected horror, revulsion, maybe even regret. What she saw was a jubilant look of triumph. Gavin stopped just short of smiling, but his eyes shone and his chin lifted, as if he'd been waiting for just that news.

"You'll need to come with me, Mr. Godfrey," the officer was saying.

Gavin's expression faded, "Wait, why?"

"We'll need to question you," the officer said.

"Me?" the tips of Gavin's spiky hair danced as he shook his head vehemently, "oh, no, you can't honestly believe I have anything to do with this? Can you?"

Without responding, the officer guided him toward the knot of policemen who'd been interviewing the judge.

But Gavin balked, "That's ridiculous!" he fumed, "I'm not going anywhere with anyone to be interrogated. I have important matters to attend to."

"You'll need to account for your whereabouts for the last two hours," one of the policemen said, stepping up to look Gavin in the eye.

"That's easy," Gavin said, "I've been prepping my rooster

—" he broke off, looking wildly around, "I need to get to him. He's in a display cage in the show ring. Anyone could be there."

"We have officers minding the show ring," the policeman said, "the faster you answer our questions, the faster you can get to your rooster."

"You don't understand," Gavin grasped the policeman's sleeve, "he's very fragile. He gets upset easily if I'm not around."

"A man's lying dead on the ground and you want us to worry about your chicken getting upset?"

"Imbeciles! If Lyle gets upset, he could go into a molt. Do you have any idea what a champion rooster looks like in molt? Do you?" he was shouting in the policeman's face now, and Saffron was impressed at how unfazed the officer was, "A rooster in molt looks like a walking rotisserie chicken that's staggered through a pillow and glue factory!"

Saffron didn't point out that there were few, if any, factories that actually made both pillows and glue, and neither did the police.

"I don't care if he ends up looking like a mud fence," the big officer said, "you're not seeing him again until you answer a few questions."

"Fine!" roared Gavin, "Fine. I'll answer your questions if it will get me back to him faster."

Saffron saw him sneak one last look at Hugo's still form.

Another officer approached Saffron. She wondered if he knew she could hear the conversations.

"We'll need to get you on your way," he said, "the chief says you can go."

Go now? When they were about to question someone whose rooster was going up against the victim's hen in the show ring? That was unacceptable. Saffron had to stall.

She tried to think of some plausible reason to stay. She'd

recently become much more adept at fibbing. But nothing came to mind. In fact, as she rose to her feet, only one possible option presented itself.

Saffron swooned.

The officer caught her and helped her back to bumper of the ambulance where she'd been sitting. She tried to look weak.

"I'll get you some more apple juice," he said, "probably just a little bit of shock. It sometimes happens when people see their first dead body."

Saffron didn't correct his misconception. This was not the first body she'd seen. Not by a long shot.

She was glad when the officer walked away, though, and she could close her eyes and concentrate on what Gavin was saying.

"No idea," his tone was terse.

"So you haven't seen Mr. Leblanc today at all?"

"Only when I was watching him accept the awards for his hens in the ring."

"We know you had been in the tent. We've matched feathers we found to your rooster."

"Of course I'd been there. We had to get our birds photographed before the Best in Show awards were given."

"What about just now? Why did you come back and walk directly into the photography tent, even though it was crawling with officers?"

"I didn't really notice them. I was in a hurry to get back to Lyle. I was just grabbing something I forgot when I was there earlier to get Lyle photographed."

"What had you forgotten?"

"My pen," Gavin reached in his jacket pocket and produced a pen, "this one." He held up the exact pen Saffron would have imagined he'd carry: black and white enamel, with a Houdan rooster etched on it.

"We'll have to take a look at that."

"Tell me why you ran when we called to you."

Gavin flushed red with embarrassment, "Well, when I looked up and saw all the police, I realized I was in the wrong place. I just got scared."

"And ran to the admissions tent?"

"I was just going to go back to the ring and wait for the judge. I wasn't running because I'm guilty."

"That's what they all say," another officer said under her breath.

The chief held up a hand, "Can anyone corroborate your story, Mr. Godfrey?"

"I don't know. Maybe Hugo's wife. I saw her on my way back to the tent and told her I was getting my pen."

The chief turned to one of his officers, "Where's the wife?"

"We don't know, Chief."

"What do you mean, you don't know? Has she been informed of her husband's death?"

"Not yet. We can't find her, and the chickens are gone, too."

"Which chickens?"

"Three French hens. They were supposed to be in the final round of judging, but nobody's seen them in the ring. They're a special breed. Faver—somethings. We found their feathers in the tent with the black ones, near where the victim was killed. The judges are pretty upset about it. They say the competition can't go on without them."

"The wife has disappeared with the champion chickens? Then don't you think we should probably consider her a suspect?" The chief said wryly.

Saffron's heart stopped. Sophie? A killer?

She thought of the girl's sweet face and involuntarily shook her head. But then other things came to mind—Sophie's loneliness, Hugo's harshness—and the idea didn't seem so far-fetched. People could only be caged for so long before they broke out.

* * *

"Seriously, Saffron," Nik said as they climbed into his station wagon an hour later, "I can't leave you alone for a minute without coming back to find you surrounded by law enforcement."

That was true.

"It was weird," Saffron said, staring out the window at the sprawling houses and spreading trees of Honolulu, "one minute he was walking around, the next he was dead."

"I'm going to be dead when your dad finds out I left you alone at that thing," Nik said. Lately he'd been fretting about things more than usual. The source of his anxiety always seemed to be Saffron's recently returned father, Slate. It was as if Nik felt like her dad was judging him all the time, which, to be fair, Slate might have been. He was extremely protective of his daughter.

"Oh, he doesn't need to know about any of this," Saffron said. Truth be told, she had no desire for a lecture about safety and staying away from strangers, either.

The road wound toward the mountains and Saffron felt the calm of the islands settling back into her soul. It was nearly impossible to be anxious for very long when the emerald and charcoal of the monkeypod trees reached out to envelop you and the lacy hapu'u ferns cast their dappled light across the highway.

Saffron rolled down the window. A storm was moving in, and the air was heavy with a warm damp that filled her lungs and soothed her throat. It tasted like flowers and smelled like the sea.

Saffron found herself peering into the windows of each car

that passed by, and it was only after about ten minutes that she realized what she was looking for behind their mirrored finish —Sophie.

It bothered her that Sophie had disappeared. Part of her was very afraid not that Sophie had hurt Hugo, but the other way around.

And the hens were gone, too. That made her suspect Gavin more than anyone else. He seemed more than capable of almost anything and very motivated to win the competition. She wished she'd had a chance to interrogate the judges, especially the woman Hugo had been talking to. Saffron had told the police what she'd overheard, and they'd asked the judge about it, but she'd neatly sidestepped every question and had carefully avoided giving solid answers. The police seemed satisfied with her account, but Saffron wasn't. The woman was clearly hiding something.

Going through the Pali Tunnels, where the highway cut through the mountains, Saffron felt the temperature drop. Cool air rushed past her cheeks and made her think of December mornings back in the nation's capital where she'd grown up.

Christmas in Hawaii was not what she'd experienced in Washington, DC, but it was beautifully festive, nonetheless. There, a bitter chill would have set in by now, and every inside space would be glowing, inviting you inside out of the cold.

Here, it was the opposite. As they left the tunnels and made their way into the next town, every outside space sported lights, music, and Christmas figures: Santa, reindeer, Mary, Joseph, and the Baby Jesus, inviting you outside to walk in the sweet island air and think about that special night so long ago.

She liked to think that Mary would have found a warmer welcome here in Hawaii than she found in Bethlehem. No stable birth for the Savior here. Saffron had found the people here to be open and sharing. The people she'd come to love here would have given their own beds to the little family, she was sure.

She thought about Sophie, her baby nearly ready to be born, and hoped that whatever happened with the investigation into Hugo's death, Sophie would be well-cared for and treated with kindness.

". . . I hope that's okay," Nik was saying. Saffron realized he'd been talking to her for several minutes, but she hadn't heard him.

"I'm sorry, Nik," she said as they drove out of town and along the winding road next to the shoreline, "I wasn't paying attention."

It was then that she noticed his red cheeks, his grip on the steering wheel. What he'd been saying had been hard for him to say, and she'd missed it. She tried to explain, "I was distracted—I was just thinking of Sophie and hoping that the police would be gentle with her."

"It's okay," Nik said, "I shouldn't even be considering it, really."

"Considering what?" Saffron asked. She turned in her seat, fixing her eyes on his profile so he would know she was really listening this time.

"Well, I was just saying, you know those friends I met up with? Bart and Carlos?"

"Uh-huh?"

"They're going to surf the Soup Bowl for Christmas. It's supposed to be killer this year."

"The Soup Bowl?"

"Sure. It's in Barbados, like one of the world's three most epic waves, and it's perfect around Christmas."

Alarm bells were ringing in Saffron's mind, "Christmas? But I thought we were going to spend Christmas together?"

Nik did something Saffron had rarely seen him do. He grimaced.

"Did you just grimace?"

"No," his tone was unconvincing.

"You did. I saw it. It's the look you gave Bernadette at the cafe when she brought you that mac salad with the beans in it."

Nik's tone was firm this time, "Beans don't go in mac salad. That was ridiculous."

"She was just trying out something new. The woman has cooked the same menu for decades. She needs to change it up once in a while."

"Then she can experiment with something else," Nik said stubbornly, "Change up the pancakes or the milkshakes, but not the mac salad. I mean, maybe you can even get away with some grated carrots in there, some green onions. I once had some with diced pineapple that wasn't too bad, but adding beans is going too far."

"We're getting off the subject here," Saffron said, "What is it about spending Christmas with me that gives you the beans-in-mac-salad grimace?"

Nik reached for her hand, "Oh, it's not spending it with you," his voice was earnest, "I'd love that. In fact, I still want that. I want you to come to Barbados with me."

Saffron swallowed. "Nik, there's no way I can do that. I have this whole Christmas Eve party—the whole town's coming to the Egg Farm."

"Exactly. You won't even miss me."

That stung, "Miss you?" it was sinking in now, "You're really thinking of not coming? Of course I'll miss you. You're the only one I even want there."

"Because you need a Santa?"

"Not just that. You make everything more fun, Nik. You're the life of the party. You're the one I can count on to get me through if Tamara Duke comes complaining about the food or the music. Or if the sheep don't show up for the live nativity. I need you."

"I know, Saffron. Thanks. I love being with you, too."

Saffron waited. When he didn't go on, she prodded, "But?"

Nik let go of her hand and gripped the steering wheel again. The bulge of the muscle in his jaw and temple made Saffron's mouth go dry. He was never this tense.

"Everything's just a little too . . ." Nik searched for words, "I mean, it's just so *serious*. So formal. So heavy."

"What's so heavy?" Saffron managed to keep her voice from cracking, but just barely.

"I don't know. Christmas. I just don't know if I'm ready to spend it with your—" Nik stopped himself.

"Nik, what is it?"

"It's your dad, okay? I just don't know if I'm ready to do the whole 'Christmas with the family' thing."

Saffron blinked, "My dad?"

Nik tried to backtrack, "I mean, he's great and all, but he's kind of intense, and he wants to know where we're going and what my intentions are, and I don't even know where *I'm* going, much less where *we're* going."

"He asked you where we're going?"

Nik looked chagrined, "It's understandable. He's trying to protect you. I get that. But I'm just not ready for a, you know, big commitment."

"I'm not ready for a big commitment either, Nik," she said, "if you're getting that, it's just because my dad's still really protective of me. He's been gone so long, and his whole life was devoted to keeping me safe. He's bound to be a little watchful." She gripped the door handle, "and really, I kind of like that he's looking out for me. It's not something I had growing up."

"I know. I just, maybe, don't want to spend Christmas with him."

Saffron's stomach was churning. Nik didn't want to spend Christmas with her father, but having Slate there on Christmas morning was something she'd dreamed about her whole life. She'd bought her father an array of presents: new slippahs, two aloha shirts, a-fruit-of-the-month subscription from the local grocery store, the Paradise Market. She'd gotten him two books and a new harmonica. She wanted to see him open them.

She tried to explain all that, but what came out was, "but he's coming out from town to stay over at the egg farm. I can't just tell him not to come."

"No, I know," Nik shot her a pained look, "I don't want you to do that. I just probably won't be there."

Saffron blinked back hot tears. She had gifts for Nik, too: a surfer's backpack for his wetsuit, a surfboard rack, and a retro-styled waterproof watch. Now he was going to Barbados?

She wanted to say more, to tell him she'd thought about where they were going, too, and she didn't know, either. But all she said was, "I guess I'll just," she took a trembling breath, "miss you."

"I know. I'll miss you, too. But I'll be back in a couple weeks, and we can do Christmas then, when it's not so . . . loaded."

The terrible thing was that he was completely right. The defining characteristic of their relationship was that they had light and uncomplicated fun together, and the traditional Christmas-with-the-family that she'd planned—that she'd wished for all her life—was more serious and strained. It wasn't in the scope of their relationship. As an event planner, Saffron realized that she should have been more aware of her guest list when she was planning Christmas.

Nik glanced over anxiously, his usually relaxed face drawn into an expression of worry, "Say something, Saffron."

She forced a smile, "It's okay, you go to the Soup Bowl," she sighed. "I guess I'll need to find another Santa."

"Hawaiian Santa's a good gig," Nik chuckled, relief making his laugh louder than usual, "You get to come in on the canoe like a king, all the keiki just jumping up and down waiting for you to get to shore, Mano playing the uke to bring you in. It's fun—you'll have guys lining up."

"I hope so," Saffron said, shifting her gaze back out the window to the lowering sky.

Chapter Five

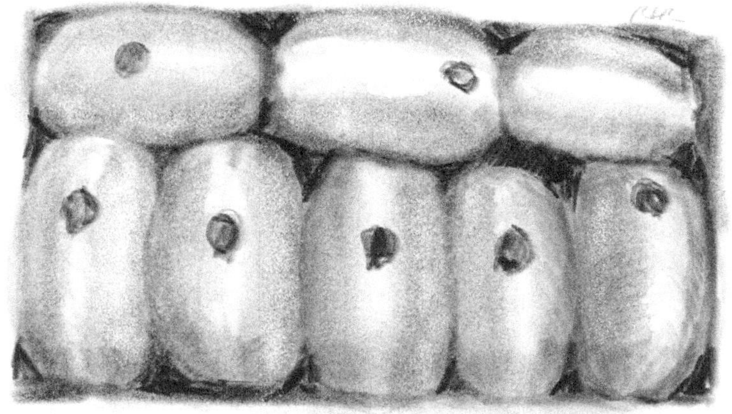

The next day, December 14th, at Juno's Bakery, Saffron found another treat she had not expected. Peppermint custard malasadas. Sweet and a little spicy, rolled in crushed candy canes and granulated sugar, the rich donuts tasted exactly like Christmas felt.

She'd come alone, since Nik was getting ready for his trip

to Barbados and Mano was working like crazy on some Christmas tikis one of the locals had ordered for gifts.

Saffron's father had gone down to Honolulu for the day. But Saffron wasn't going to miss Juno's daily malasada special. She had a personal goal to try every Christmas flavor.

It was strange to be alone out in town. She nearly always had Mano or Nik or her father with her, sometimes two out of the three, and sometimes all of them.

She took another bite of the warm donut. It was sweet and rich, with a delicate, pillowy shell. Inside, the smooth custard added texture and a punch of peppermint flavor.

"You like it?" a voice made Saffron turn. It was Theodore, Juno's nephew. He and Saffron had run into each other more than once since she'd moved here, and she'd grown to genuinely like the big kid with the bright smile.

"It's amazing!" Saffron grinned back, "How did you think to make peppermint?"

"It was actually Kinsey's idea."

"Ahhh," Saffron smiled, thinking of the sweet girl Theo had been dating. She was a new girl, Kinsey, whose family had moved here from somewhere on the mainland. Theo had fallen fast for her and the two were more or less inseparable now. Saffron suspected an engagement announcement any time.

"I think the whole promotion is ingenious," Saffron said, "With all the people who come to the islands to spend Christmas, it's perfect marketing. I think Juno was brilliant to think of it. And it's not just clever, it's also delicious! Who knew that Christmas malasadas would be so good?"

"And so popular!" Theodore waved a hand at the packed bakery.

"I know! I stood in line for an hour this morning for these," Saffron patted the box that held eleven more malasadas, some of which she planned to drop by Mano's carving stand later.

Theodore shook his head, "None of that for my favorite customer. You coming back tomorrow?"

"Of course! I'm not missing a single one of the surprise Christmas flavors!"

"Then you come in the back door and I'll get you a box ready."

"Really?"

"Sure. Gotta take care of our 'ohana."

Family. The word was as warm as the malasada in Saffron's hand, and just as sweet. Coming to the islands had given her family like she'd never known before—a whole town of people ready to help when she was in trouble and embrace her when she was alone. She thought, suddenly, of Sophie, who seemed alone even when she was with her actual family.

"Thanks, Theo."

He scooted a chair in next to a little table, gave the tabletop a swipe, then said, "Gotta get in the back and help keep this line moving. See you tomorrow."

"You bet," Saffron watched him go, glad that he'd found happiness. As he walked away, she thought of something.

"Theo?" he turned back to her, "Could I hire you to be Santa at the Christmas Eve Party?" she asked, hoping that this would solve the gap in her staffing. She'd been racking her brain to think of who she could ask. Mano was providing the music for the party, so he'd be busy all evening, and she needed her father's help with the food and wrangling the animals for the live nativity.

He considered, "I'd like to. What time would you need me?"

"Probably around seven?" Saffron had the outrigger canoe slated to leave the Laki Luau at quarter after seven so it would arrive at the egg farm beach at 7:30.

Theo gave an apologetic scowl, "Oh, man, I'm sorry, I have to work here until eight, then I told Kinsey I'd have dinner with her family. We planned on coming out to the party about 10ish, in time for the carols and the live nativity."

Saffron tried not to look too disappointed, "Okay. No worries. At least you'll be out there."

"Wouldn't miss it," Theo grinned.

* * *

"It's not toys!" Pastor Vaughn seemed on his last nerve when Saffron stopped by the church to check in with him about the carols. He was standing in front of a dozen restless children—the nativity's angel choir. "Try again!" he gave a signal to Estelle, the very old and very talented woman who accompanied the choir on the piano.

Saffron heard it. Clearly, the children were singing, "Toys to the world, the Lord is come." She suppressed a smile. The kids looked slightly baffled when Pastor Vaughn cut the music off again.

"Joy! Joy! Joy!" he cried, sounding less than joyful.

The kids, thinking he wanted them to say it too, chanted, "Joy, joy, joy!"

"No, it's *joy* to the world! Joy to the world, the Lord is come. The angels didn't want toys."

A little boy fixed his chestnut-brown eyes on the pastor. His voice was dismissive when he spoke, "Everybody wants toys."

The Pastor shrugged and sighed, "That's probably true, Liko." He looked at the squirming rows of children, "Let's take a little break. You guys can go into the rec room and run off some energy while I talk to Sister Saffron here."

Sister Saffron seemed a little formal, Saffron thought, but she didn't say anything. She wasn't a member of Pastor Vaughn's congregation, but like all the churches in town, he made her welcome when she dropped by.

"Just checking in on the carols and the nativity," she said,

"You're still planning on being there, right?" When Nik had backed out, Saffron had gotten nervous about the whole party. She'd sat down and made a list of everyone and every detail involved in this party for the whole town. She planned to spend today checking her list twice to make sure there were no more surprises.

"That's right. If we can get these kids to stop singing 'angels bending near the near the Earth to touch their hearts of gold,'" he looked at Saffron with pleading eyes, "You hear what's wrong there, right?"

"It should be *harps* of gold?" Saffron ventured.

"Yes! See, it's not that hard. Our littlest parishioners have apparently been singing it wrong their whole lives," he shook his head. "Hearts of gold," he muttered.

"Honestly," Saffron tried to soothe him, "I think *toys to the world* and *hearts of gold* are pretty cute. They're going to make the perfect angel choir." She dropped her gaze to the floor to keep a giggle from rising up. The kids were charming.

She was looking down at her feet when she noticed something—a piece of paper stuck to the bottom of her Christmas slippah.

As Pastor Vaughn rattled on about timing and enunciation, Saffron crouched down and pulled the paper free. It had obviously been torn from another, larger page.

She squinted at it. Handwritten, it was immediately obvious that it was in another language. *Trois poules françaises*, Saffron read. She didn't know what the words meant, but she'd worn these shoes to the poultry show yesterday. Maybe she'd picked this bit of paper up there.

The ink was unique: neither blue nor black, somewhere in the middle: a deep indigo with a slight silver glimmer on top. No disposable pen wrote this. It was the kind of ink you found in a fine, custom ink pen. She stuck the scrap in her pocket as Pastor Vaughn cleared his throat.

"We'll be ready," he said, "don't you worry. I'll work with them on the lyric situation. The mothers' group has almost finished the kids' robes, and the Tucker kids are ready to play their parts."

Ah, the Tuckers. Saffron's friends who ran the Tropical Adventures travel agency out of the old post office on Maika'i's Main Street. They had several kids—six? seven?—and the oldest two were just ten and eleven, but they were articulate and friendly kids who would do an excellent job at playing the principal roles in the live nativity.

"Do you have all the animals?" Pastor Vaughn asked. The community live nativity was apparently a huge and important tradition to the whole town. The responsibility of putting it on was passed year-to-year from one church to the next, with the city taking a turn as well. The city was in charge this year, and they had simply hired Saffron to run the whole thing. She felt a kinship with the spiritual leaders in town though, because each of them knew the challenge of organizing it.

"Still working on that."

"Well," he said, seemingly glad that she was running into a few bumps as well, "at least you'll have plenty of chickens. It may not be exactly what people envision, but as long as you have the spirit of the event, it will be fine."

That was true. "The same goes for you," she said, "Toys to the world."

* * *

WHEN SAFFRON PULLED up at the egg farm, she was surprised to see an unfamiliar figure on her lanai. Drawing closer, she gasped. It was Blue, the photographer from the poultry show. Amidst the drama of Hugo's death, she'd forgotten all about having him come and photograph her hens.

"I've been waiting for an hour," he said as she climbed out of her car and bounded up the stairs.

"I'm so sorry. I didn't know when you'd arrive."

"I told you I was coming today."

Had he? Saffron couldn't remember. Everything before she'd seen Hugo Leblanc killed seemed a little fuzzy.

Blue didn't wait for an answer, "Where am I staying, and where are the hens?" he asked.

Saffron was at a loss for words. She waved a hand for him to follow her along the wrap-around lanai and led him to the three little cottages behind the main house—what Saffron called the bungalow.

The cottages were painted bright colors—Pacific Teal, Banana Yellow, and Coral Pink. She let Blue pick the one he liked best. He went for the Pacific Teal Cottage, the one closest to the beach. She thought he'd like to get settled in, but he threw down his suitcases, grabbed his camera bag and said a single word to Saffron: "Hens?"

"This way," Saffron led him down the path to the egg house. She'd already been out early this morning to gather eggs and check on her hens, but they were just as glad to see her as if she'd been gone a week. The excited bawks and squawks, combined with the awkward, lumbering run that the hens broke into when they saw her, prompted Saffron to toss a few handfuls of scratch grains into each pen. While she was occupied with that, Blue went up and down the center aisle, peering in at the birds and occasionally raising his camera to his eye, aiming it at particular hens, and peering through it thoughtfully.

He was intent on his work. He didn't talk or look at anything besides the hens, not even at Saffron.

"What is this?" he asked, standing beside Cupcake's pen, "This doesn't look right."

Saffron chuckled, "That's my most unusual pen," she

admitted, "Cupcake there has been playing foster mom to these Nene."

"Nene?" Blue raised an eyebrow.

"Hawaiian geese," Saffron explained, "they're the state bird. Their numbers are declining, so the wildlife department is doing everything they can to hatch more healthy Nene, including giving some of the surplus eggs to Cupcake to hatch."

Blue crouched down and shot a couple of photos of the goslings though the wire of their run. "That's certainly fascinating," he said. He turned to her, his piercing blue eyes boring a hole into her own. "I will shoot your birds," he said, "but on one condition—you sign a photo release and consent to let me use some of the photos for a spread I'm supposed to be doing in a publication called *Modern Homesteading*."

Saffron considered, "That sounds fine," she said. She was flattered that her girls might be in a magazine, and she was excited to see what the master photographer could do with her already-beautiful birds.

Seemingly satisfied, Blue went back to work, bending and twisting, letting himself into pens, and aiming his lens at first one hen, then another.

The afternoon light streaming through the west windows was gold tinted with green by the wall of vegetation that climbed outside the egg house. Blue was capturing one of Saffron's prettiest hens, Tikka. Tikka had been the first hen Saffron had met here on the farm, when she was nesting in a pot on the stove in the abandoned bungalow Saffron now lived in. She was a beautiful gold and black chicken, with a low, folded rose comb and intelligent eyes. Saffron couldn't help herself.

"Gorgeous, isn't she?"

Blue glanced up. "Very nice," he conceded, "though

nothing compared to those peach-colored hens at the show yesterday."

Was he talking about Sophie's hens? "The Faverolles?" Saffron asked.

"That's right. Those may be the world's prettiest chickens."

Saffron felt defensive, but she couldn't argue that. "Sad that they're missing," she mused, "and that they didn't get to finish the competition. Did you get to photograph them?"

"No," Saffron was surprised at the bitterness in his voice. He went on, "I was supposed to, but that arrogant exhibitor wouldn't let me."

"Hugo?" Saffron asked.

The man looked startled at the name, "That's right. Said a photograph would provide his competition with too much information. He was convinced other breeders would study the photographs and figure out how to replicate his hens in their own stock." Blue shook his head, "I've seen people who were competitive, but that guy was over the top."

Was? The past tense? Blue must have heard about Hugo's murder. She tried a little fishing, "So you didn't get any pictures? Maybe you can contact him later and convince him now that the show's over?"

"He's dead," Blue said flatly. It made Saffron feel silly that she hadn't just come out and asked him, "and I won't get a chance to photograph them. The championship round was canceled because of the uproar, and those remarkable animals went missing," he lowered his voice, "along with the dead man's wife."

Saffron tried to seem surprised by this information. "Wow," she said, "that's terrible."

"But not surprising. Those birds were pure perfection." He said the last word slowly, like he was tasting it. "They would have made beautiful subjects for my portraits." he was gazing off into the streaming sunlight, deep in thought, "and they're worth unspeakable amounts, too. She was smart to take them and run. Maybe she sold them and took the money and ran away to paradise."

"She was already in paradise," Saffron said, nodding at the flowers outside the windows.

"Not as long as he was around," Blue said, "He was a brute."

Saffron wouldn't argue with that.

"But most of the competitors are terrible," Blue went on, "I don't like working with any of them, really."

"They're pretty intense, all right."

"Intense isn't the word I'd use. Maybe insane. Especially those top few—the champions. They're nearly impossible to deal with. They have all kinds of weird rules about their birds."

Saffron smiled, "I'll bet you've seen a lot of them."

"Sure. Just this week, I had to deal with a real doozy."

"Oh?"

"Another one of the champions yesterday. The Mottled Houdans guy—Gavin Godfrey. The name alone should have told me he'd be eccentric."

Saffron nodded, "I met him. He was a character."

"You should have seen him in the photo shoot, hassling that poor bird to stand this way and look that way. Just when the rooster would relax and I'd see a great shot taking shape, the guy would step in and tap its beak or poke its foot, and it would go back to looking like a statue. He took all the life out of every photo. I'm glad Hugo was killed, and the show was canceled so nobody ever had to see those photos. Probably would have ruined my reputation."

That seemed a little harsh, "Seems like a pretty high price to pay for your reputation," she said.

Blue looked up, "Oh, I'm just kidding, of course. It's very sad. I just pride myself on photographing the most beautiful animals in the most unique ways. There's a million pictures out there of show roosters standing at attention. Catch one flapping a wing, though, and you've got something special."

"I can't argue with your work. I love how you capture chickens."

"And you know I don't just shoot chickens, right? I do portraits of award-winning cattle, sheep, pigs, you name it."

"I didn't know. That seems like it would be challenging, too."

"Oh, it is. Cows are so big that you have to either do close-ups or shoot wide, but be very careful with your composition so you still have some drama. Pigs can be stubborn, although I find that a pocketful of marshmallows makes them very easy to work with."

"Do you have a favorite animal to photograph?"

His reply was quick, "Well, that's still chickens, by far. They have the most variation in shape and coloring and personality. They make the best portrait subjects."

Saffron was inclined to agree, especially when she saw Tikka peering curiously at Blue's lens. He snapped a photo.

Saffron eased into her next question, "So, you shot photos of random birds at the show and then also the champions?"

"That's right. The organization wanted both candids and portraits."

"You had your own tent for the portrait sessions, didn't you?"

Blue was distracted, pulling a box over from the egg gathering station to stand on while he got a shot of one of Saffron's Swedish Flower hens, Blossom. "Well, of course I did. If you're doing portraiture, you've got to have the right setup—the right backdrops, the right lighting—all of it has to be controlled."

"You said you saw Gavin before the Championship round. Did you see Hugo?"

Blue took a long time to answer. Saffron realized he was setting up his shot. Finally, after she heard the shutter click, he said, "Nope. I told you, he wouldn't let me photograph the hens. He wouldn't even come into my tent." He stepped off the crate and tipped the camera's screen toward her, revealing a gorgeous shot of Blossom scratching at a piece of corn in her pen.

Saffron was so impressed with the photo that she barely registered the nervous edge in Blue's voice. She was enchanted by the image of Blossom. "It's so playful, with so much movement and action. It catches her tricolored feathers so vividly! It's . . ." Saffron searched for good descriptive words, but only found one that would do: "perfect!"

Blue pulled back the camera and shook his head. "It's a nice shot," he said, "but it's far from perfect."

Saffron had forgotten Blue's obsession with perfection. She shrugged. "Well, good luck with the photos, I've got some Christmas presents to wrap, so I'll leave you to your work."

"Thank you," Blue retorted. Saffron tried not to notice the bitter tone in his voice and tried not to notice how happy he was to have her leaving. Blue, she decided, was not a people person.

Chapter Six

The next morning Saffron was on the road to Maika'i early. She had eggs to deliver to the Oceanside Cafe, the Paradise Market, and, most excitingly, Juno's Bakery.

What would the flavor be today? December 15th, the third day of Christmas. She was out of guesses. After peppermint and egg nog, what other flavors were there that went with Christmas?

It didn't take long to find out. Walking in the back door of the bakery with ten cartons of eggs, she was greeted with a heavenly smell.

"Freshly baked sugar cookies!" Saffron exclaimed as a grinning Theo met her with a pale purple box.

"That's right," he said, popping the box open.

Saffron set the eggs on the counter and reached for a malasada.

The granulated sugar coating on the outside had been supplemented with beautiful blue and white sprinkles. Biting into the donut, Saffron was caught up in the taste of warm vanilla. A sweet buttercream icing filled the malasada, sweet and buttery-rich.

She didn't say anything, just gave Theo a look of ecstatic approval. He laughed.

"Gotta get back to the crowds," he said, jerking his head toward the front counter which Saffron could see through the open kitchen door. It was teeming with people.

She waved a hand, shooing him along, and carried her sugar cookie malasadas out to the car, taking another bite as she went.

She told everyone she saw about today's flavor—her friends Tale and Baruti at the Paradise Market, Bernadette and Ed at the Oceanside Cafe, and Arnold and Viola Arrowood at Heluhelu Here, the bookstore on Maika'i's Main Street.

Saffron loved how the smallest things united this little town —new malasada flavors, or the live nativity. Back in Washington, DC, the only things she shared with her neighbors were complaints when the water in the apartment building was out. She'd had no idea what they did for fun, where they ate breakfast, even where they worked. Here, everyone was buzzing about Juno's new flavor, and by the end of the day, everyone would have tasted it. It made for close bonds and lots to share.

Most of her friends also knew that someone was staying in her cottage, though she hadn't been going to rent it this week. So she told the story of Blue the photographer at every place she stopped. That led into a discussion of the poultry show and the death of Hugo Leblanc, which most of Maika'i had seen mentioned on the news. They were fascinated to learn that Saffron had been there.

"Who do they think done it?" Baruti asked, leaning over the counter at the Paradise Market.

"When I was there, there were no real leads," Saffron said.

"I hear they think it was the wife," Tale raised her onyx eyebrows into perfect arches over her dancing brown eyes.

Saffron shrugged, "Well, that's one theory," she said.

"She take the chickens and run," Baruti interjected, "sounds like guilty to me."

"But I met her. She seemed so nice."

"You never know with people," Tale said, "You never know."

If Saffron had learned one thing, it was that, "You're right. I don't have any good reason to think it wasn't her, but I hope not."

They murmured sympathetically.

"Anyone else you think it could be?" Tale asked.

Saffron leaned over the counter, too. "Honestly," she said, her voice low, "I worry about the other champion. He seemed a little obsessed with winning."

"Makes sense," Tale nodded sagely, "he wouldn't want the awards to go on, especially if he thought he might lose."

"Well, I hope they catch whoever did it. I don't like the thought of a murderer running around on the island," Tale said.

"Let's not think of it then," Baruti reassured her, "Let's think of sugar cookie malasadas instead."

* * *

Sugar cookie malasadas were exactly what Saffron was thinking about later that afternoon when she wrestled the wheelbarrow out of the egg house, hauling a load of soiled sand from Cupcake and the goslings' pen. She was learning something about goslings—they were messy. And loud. When they were displeased, their wheezy squeaking cracked the air like an eggshell and made the hens in the other pens stop and look around for its source.

In fact, as Saffron left the egg house, she noticed nearly

every hen was outside in the outdoor runs. She wondered if that was due to their noisy neighbors inside.

Sweat ran down her temples. The sand was weighty, and the wheelbarrow's tire was slightly bent. But with a lot of effort, the wheelbarrow bumped and skidded along the path, down through the heavy jade shrubbery under the tall trees.

Despite her puffing and the burning in her arms and back, Saffron loved this part of the egg farm. The freshwater stream cut through here, running from the mountains behind the farm all the way down to the secret beach, where the chilly freshwater met the warm Pacific. Behind the stream, a little meadow, ringed with bushes, led the way to the slope of the first mountain behind the egg farm.

Called 'Ula'ula Mountain, it rose steep and grand against the blue sky. Saffron had never known why they called it 'Ula'ula. When Mano told her that, she'd been curious. The word meant "red" in Hawaiian, and the mountain, like all its sisters, was a thousand shades of green.

Except today. When Saffron finally dumped the wheelbarrow and straightened up to stretch the aching muscles of her back, she looked up to see a distinct patch of strawberry on the mountainside. It had never been there before, or at least she had never seen it. Saffron left the wheelbarrow and moved closer, stopping at the edge of the stream to squint up the mountain.

It was definite. Among the shamrock and seafoam greens, between the pine and the pickle greens, above the peacock-colored shadows, Saffron saw red. Like a single, huge blossom on the side of the mountain.

Saffron had always liked everything in its place. Back in DC, when she'd run her first business, *Every Detail Events*, she'd had an office where not a single paperclip was out of place. Everything had been labeled and divided into work zones: the flower area, the guest list area (where everything from addresses to stamps to food preferences were organized), the decor area.

Now, seeing the unusual splotch on the mountain, Saffron had to know why it was there. It seemed not to fit.

She splashed across the stream, feeling it tugging at her ankles, begging her to follow it down to the ocean and play. She stopped in the middle of it and looked down its brush-choked banks toward the secret beach. If only there wasn't so much to do, she might take the stream's suggestion and let herself be pulled down to the beach for a quick swim and a nap in the sand.

The hibiscus reached out over the edge of the water, their blossoms shining like jewels. A flash of movement caught Saffron's eye—too big to be a bird, too slow to be a wild pig coming to drink at the stream.

It was a flash, a second's glance. Saffron walked a few steps closer down the sandy bottom of the stream, but whatever it was had gone into the deep shade of the bushes, leaving only a nodding tiger-colored hibiscus in its wake.

Saffron thought about following it and discovering what had been visiting her stream, but her to-do list was a mile long and that splotch on the mountainside was calling her, too. Reluctantly, she turned back toward the mountain and splashed the rest of the way across the stream.

The meadow was cooling in the late afternoon sunshine. Saffron felt a chill as she began to push through the brush on the mountainside.

She was glad she'd worn long-sleeved work clothes. It was a real trek up the steep slope. She hoped she was going in the right direction—she could no longer see the patch of crimson ahead of her.

When she pushed through a final tall bush, she gasped.

The mountain was awash with Pua Kalikimaka—translated as Christmas Flower, and known back on the mainland as poinsettias.

They were a far cry from the twelve-inch plants she'd come to know back home. The ones that people left on your doorstep or handed over with a plate of cookies. The ones that ended up in their desiccated pots, dropping leaves, around January 9th before you tossed them into the dumpster.

These were different. They were lush, rich, vibrant. Their glossy green leaves made their brilliant red ones pop. The colors seared Saffron's eyes—cranberry and cherry, pale pink and cream. They reached up the slope as far as she could see. They were all sizes: tiny, egg-sized ones all the way up to towering tree-sized ones. They took Saffron's breath away. This is why they called it Red Mountain.

She was enthralled with the colors, the shapes of the leaves and branches. She knew, somehow, she was going to have to incorporate these beautiful leaves into the Christmas Eve party.

* * *

She told Nik all about the poinsettia grove when he came to say goodbye a little later. Over sugar cookie malasadas, they wished each other Merry Christmas, but Saffron felt melancholy in the moment.

"I know I'm letting you down," Nik said, ducking his head.

Saffron waved a hand, "Of course not," she replied, forcing lightness into her voice, "I'm glad you're going to get some monster waves!" And she was. Though she was sad he wouldn't be there, she was glad he was going to have an adventure.

Nik was made for adventure. He wasn't the kind of person who craved a cozy home Christmas. He wasn't, Saffron knew, the kind who settled in for carols and cookies. Maybe it was because he'd been abandoned when he was young, or maybe it was because losing his grandfather had cut the only real family ties he had besides those to his sister, who was off at college, but whatever it was, Nik didn't need people as much as Saffron did. He needed the wind and the waves, the rush of adrenaline, and the thrill of seeing something new. It was something Saffron had known about him, deep down, ever since she'd met him. She'd been drawn to him partly because of it. He seemed, somehow, outside of the realm most people dwelt in, where as they matured, they grew increasingly close to other people. Even now, when their conversation had turned serious, his gaze lingered just above her head, out the front room window behind her, on the ocean.

She tried to give him his presents, but he was driving down to the airport to meet his buddies, so he didn't want to leave them in the car in long-term parking. He promised to come by when he came back, which would be maybe a couple of weeks, but could be longer if the waves were truly epic.

They kissed goodbye. It was sweet, but brief, and she could tell that Nik's mind was far away at the Soup Bowl. Saffron waved as the station wagon wound its way down the long, sandy driveway.

Saffron had another malasada after Nik left.

She went down to the egg house and sat on the wood couch. Cupcake and the goslings were napping, the big blue-and-red hen fluffed up and the little silvery goslings nestled under her feathers, peeking out as if looking through curtains. Their eyes were closed in that dozy way that birds slept—not fully sealed shut, rather softly closed, with an occasional flutter.

Cupcake opened one eye to watch Saffron on the couch before drifting back to sleep herself. She was a picture of contentment.

Saffron didn't feel content. She felt restless and a little empty. She was excited to spend the first Christmas in a long time with her father, but she still hadn't fully accepted the idea that fun-loving Nik wouldn't be there.

"You've got plenty of love and support in your life," Saffron chided herself. "You don't need Nik, necessarily." But her heart wasn't in it. Why was it that you could have so much and still feel like something was missing?

"You understand, don't you, girl?" she asked Cupcake. Cupcake had wanted to be a mother so badly that Saffron had been forced to carry the hen around in a backpack to keep her from starving to death on an empty nest. It wasn't until Vance Carlyle had brought the eggs that Cupcake had felt complete and content.

Cupcake squawked in her sleep, as if having a bad dream, and the little goslings jumped, then settled back in again. Did chickens dream? Saffron wondered. If so, it wouldn't be visions of sugarplums that danced in their heads. Saffron imagined it would be visions of scorpions, or maybe visions of centipedes, or maybe visions of dustbaths.

The unusual calm from the brooding palace had tempted the other hens back into the egg house to eat and visit their nest boxes. Saffron heard them clucking to each other, squabbling, and chirping. Chickens had so many different sounds they could make. She had tried explaining this to people in town, but the only one who really understood it was The Empress, who carried her little silkie hen, Princess, with her everywhere.

The egg house was warm as the evening came on and the birds settled onto their roosts. Saffron stretched out on the couch and dozed a little herself as she was listening to them chuckle and settle. This was one of her favorite places to be.

It was the sharp click of a camera shutter that jerked Saffron out of a light slumber. She sat up to see Blue on his belly in the sand, snapping a photo of Cupcake's unusual little family. Saffron was glad she'd changed the sand, and that

Cupcake and the goslings were still sticking to their nest pretty closely. Otherwise, the floor in here would be filthy.

Blue gave her a little wave as she sat up.

"Sorry to wake you. I just like this early evening light."

"I like it too—how it brings out the blues and silvers in their plumage."

Blue lowered his camera and looked over at her, his eyebrows raised. "That's very perceptive of you. Most people don't know the first thing about light."

"It's not light I'm best with," Saffron responded, "It's color." She was growing ever more comfortable with her unique ability to see more colors than most people. Especially here on the island where there were so many colors to see, it was a benefit. But she still worried about how people would respond, if they would tease her like they'd done when she was young, so she didn't go into her color perception too deeply.

"Same thing," Blue said, squinting at her through the fading light.

"What?"

"The energy and frequency of the light waves are what we perceive as color," he said, "Without light, there's no color, and color is how we see light."

Saffron smiled. Explained like that, it made her color perception as natural as the sunrise and sunset. She appreciated that.

Blue pushed himself to his feet with some difficulty. For the first time, Saffron noticed that he had a bit of a limp.

"Are you okay?"

"Huh?" he looked down at his leg, "Oh, sure. Just twisted my knee a little," he left the brooding pen and went to shoot another hen who was cuddled up on her perch for the night, "on a rock." He added the last part like an afterthought.

Saffron thought of the big black lava point that jutted from behind the cottages out into the ocean. "Be careful if you climb the lava point," she said, "it gets really slippery with the spray from the sea."

Blue waved a hand dismissively, "I won't be climbing," he said, "I'm not much into the outdoors. Maybe the beach, but not anything much more exciting than that."

Saffron understood. She wasn't much for adrenaline, either.

Clarification came to her as the thought did. She didn't like adrenaline. Nik lived for it. It was what made them a good match—he tested her limits, and she helped him stay grounded. But it was also what would always draw them apart—this Christmas was, she could see, the first of many days they'd spend in very different places.

As the evening drew to a close, the thought made her a little sad.

Chapter Seven

There was no time for sadness the next day, when Slate and Mano came walking up the driveway. Saffron squinted out the front window. They had a box of Juno's malasadas, which she had expected. What she had not expected them to show up with was the grimy donkey walking between them.

Saffron ran out of the front door and down the driveway to meet them, trying to count the days until Christmas Eve in her head and think what she'd do with a borrowed donkey for that many days.

"Where did you get this?" she asked, her eyes feeling like they would pop out of her head.

"We bought him!" Slate said excitedly.

"Wait," Saffron held up a hand, which the little donkey immediately nuzzled with his soft nose, "you *bought* him? You own this donkey?"

"No," Mano said, "*you* own this donkey. We bought him for you!"

Saffron was speechless, partly because she'd thought they were only borrowing animals for the nativity, not buying them, and partly because the two old men looked so pleased with themselves that she couldn't tell them she didn't want a donkey.

"We saw him on the swap site," Mano said, glowing.

"The swap site? On the internet?" Saffron had picked up a few things there, and had gotten rid of a few things there, too.

"Yeah," Slate said, "He was just a couple towns over, so we went to check him out this morning, and we figured he would help you out with the live nativity, then he could help you out around here."

"Help me out?" Saffron tried to keep the edge of panic out of her voice. What in the world was she going to do with a donkey?

"Yeah, we know you haul those eggs up to the house on that cart, and you haul the sand in and out with the wheelbarrow. You're wearing yourself out," Slate said.

"We'd come do it for you, but we're old," Mano said bluntly.

Saffron felt a slight pang of guilt—she'd recently been gone for a week and Mano and Nik had attended to the farm. She thought for the first time of all the hard work he had probably done.

"Isn't he a little small for a donkey?" Saffron said, eyeing the animal.

Mano put his hands over the donkey's big ears, "Hey, he can hear you, okay?"

Slate laughed and spoke up, "He's a little too small for a regular donkey, but he's a little too big for a miniature donkey," he said brightly, "That's why we got him so cheap!"

He was certainly an affectionate creature. He laid his head against Mano's shoulder and scraped one hoof contentedly.

"Guys," Saffron said, steeling herself, "Thank you, but where will I put a donkey?"

"In the old barn!" her father said. Before Mano, Uncle Beau, and their friend Bud had built the new, modern egg house, Saffron's grandparents had kept the hens in a barn a little farther up the stream. But Saffron had only been in it a couple of times. It was overgrown and dusty.

"I don't think he's going to like it there," Saffron said, "you're going to have to take him back where you got him from."

Mano and Slate exchanged a look, "listen, mo'opuna," Mano began, using the term for granddaughter to soften his next words, "he's gonna like the barn a lot better than the place we got him. We can't take him back there. Jasper hates it there."

"Jasper?"

"That's his name that we gave him walking over here," Slate said, "You know, like they say was one of the wise men's names? It's Christmasy."

Saffron took another look at the donkey. It was obvious that he had not been well-cared for, but he was sweet and seemingly gentle anyway. She could see how Jasper had charmed the two old men.

Because Slate had been absent all of Saffron's childhood, she had never carried home a puppy and looked up at him, asking if he would please just let her keep it. If she had, though, she imagined she'd have given him the same face that he and Mano were giving her now.

Her resolve was wearing thin, "Maybe," she began, trying not to notice how their eyes sparkled with hope and they leaned forward with anticipation. Even the donkey seemed to be hopeful, "Maybe he can stay through the nativity, then we can find him a nice, new home after that?"

They took it.

"Let's show him his new home!" Mano crowed, thrusting the box of malasadas into Saffron's hands as he and Slate turned off the driveway to cut across the farm to the old barn. They seemed younger, somehow, walking through the tall grass with the donkey between them, like boys again. It was a glimpse of their growing up days, and Saffron couldn't help but smile.

Saffron opened the malasada box with a sense of anticipation. The scent of hot cocoa rose to greet her. She thought there was no way those donuts could taste as wonderful as they smelled, but one bite told her that she was absolutely wrong. Sweet, light, crispy-on-the-outside with a molten center of pure creamy cocoa goodness.

She stood savoring it before she followed the old men to the barn. They were inside, standing in one of the four stalls that opened onto the small pasture outside. The walls of the barn were lined with old nest boxes, from which Slate's mother and father had gathered eggs.

It was peaceful inside, and the donkey looked very content as he stood nodding in the stall. Mano and Slate had gotten busy tidying up the rest of the place.

"It's not nearly as bad as we thought it might be," Slate said, "Hardly any cobwebs in the stalls at all."

"And the pasture outside is just what he needs."

"What he needs is a bath and a brushing," Saffron said. The little donkey's gray hair was matted and tangled, splotched with mud.

"He does!" Mano said, "I know what we're doing with our day."

"I'm sorry," Saffron said, "you two are on your own. I still have to find out if the sheep are coming, and I have to find myself a Santa."

"Nope," Mano spoke up, "I got that covered."

"But I need you to do music," Saffron said, her stomach tightening at the thought of the party without Mano's music.

"Oh, I will," Mano held up a reassuring hand, "I got another guy to do Santa."

"You do?" Saffron's heart skipped, "Someone local?"

"You bet. Born and raised here."

Saffron allowed herself a sigh of relief, "One less thing," she said, then, stepping into the stall beside Mano, gave him a big hug, "Thank you."

* * *

SAFFRON HAD JUST GOTTEN off the phone with the owners of the sheep farm. They promised they'd be here on Christmas Eve with some assortment of sheep for the nativity.

Looking out the window, she saw a plume of dust kicking up behind a big black rental car screaming toward the house. Saffron walked out onto the lanai to meet whoever was charging up her driveway.

The crown of spiky hair that emerged from the big car was a dead giveaway: Gavin Godfrey. He looked immaculate, as he had before, and he smiled up at Saffron where she was standing on the lanai.

"Hello, Miss Skye!" he grinned, and his Adam's apple

bobbed up and down as he spoke. He was dressed differently than he'd been at the show, today wearing a t-shirt, khaki cargo shorts, and slippahs. He still had the medallion around his neck, though, hung by its glittering chain. She made a note to ask him about it later, "It's nice to see you again!"

"Gavin!" Saffron tried to ignore the fact that he was a suspect in a murder investigation and greet him with aloha, as she would greet any visitor to her farm.

"You're probably wondering what I'm doing here," he acknowledged, "Well, I remembered you saying that you have a variety of hens here, and I'm working on a new breeding project. I wanted to come and take a look at your girls for my research. I am selectively breeding for certain traits, and it would be helpful to see how those traits are expressed in a mixed flock." His tone was businesslike, but before Saffron could respond he added, "also, Lyle wanted to see you."

He reached back into the car and when he pulled his arm out, the striking rooster was perched on it.

"He did?" Saffron smiled.

But Gavin was being serious, "He said it was important that we visit you."

"Said?"

Gavin slammed the car door and he and Lyle climbed the steps onto the lanai, "Oh, you know how it is, Miss Skye, they talk to us," he stroked the bird's back, "other people may not understand, but I'm certain you will—they talk, in their own way, just as clearly as any human."

"That's certainly true," Saffron said, still a little foggy on how or why Lyle had communicated that he wanted to visit her, "and I am completely delighted to show you around."

"I thought you would be. You seemed so friendly at the show. It was a ray of island sunshine when you came around. So many people there are so competitive."

Saffron thought it ironic that Gavin would judge others for

their competitiveness when he was so obsessed with winning himself.

"Did you drive up from Honolulu?" Saffron was slightly confused how he had found her farm. She didn't remember telling him the name of the town.

"Yes, and I've got a room at a hotel in town. Don't mention Lyle. They don't know he's rooming with me," Gavin widened his eyes and put a finger to his lips.

"Good thing there are so many feral roosters on the island," Saffron said, "or someone would probably notice his crowing." She gestured to him to follow her to the egg house, and together they made their way around the lanai.

"I know," Gavin said with delight, "this morning, three roosters crowed before he did. Brilliant place, Hawaii."

"It really is," Saffron said. Lyle had flapped up to Gavin's shoulder and was bobbing along up there, surveying everything.

About halfway across the back lanai, Saffron stopped. A sharp popping sound was coming from the back stairs.

"Oh!" she said, holding out a hand to stop Gavin in his tracks, "I forgot about Curry."

"Curry?"

"Curry's my rooster. He lives on the porch. Usually he goes down to the egg house to visit the hens, but he's here."

Curry had met Saffron in her kitchen the day she'd arrived, a scrawny young bird with no fear. But now he'd grown into a strapping rooster, broad and tall, with deep red wings and long pointed hackle feathers around his neck.

He flapped up onto the porch, giving his warning call. Saffron had heard it before, when she or the flock was in danger.

"Easy boy," she was suddenly worried for Lyle's safety, "We'd better get him back in the car," she said over her shoulder.

But Gavin wasn't worried in the least. "Oh, never fear," he said, "there won't be a fight."

"Oh yes there will be," Saffron said, "Curry's very protective. He's not going to like having another rooster here."

Gavin waved a hand, "Trust me, it's going to be fine." To Saffron's horror, he lifted Lyle down from his shoulder and set him on the lanai.

"No!" Saffron said. But it was too late. Lyle was already jaunting over to where Curry stood with his hackles raised.

It was like watching the captain of the chess team trot out onto a football field to face a linebacker. Lyle's shock of poofy feathers danced as he jogged right up to Curry.

Saffron stepped forward to scoop up the unsuspecting rooster before he got hurt, but Gavin took her arm and stopped her just as Lyle reached Curry.

To her surprise, Lyle didn't throw up his hackle feathers and lower his head into the traditional challenge position. Instead, he squatted down, the bows of his wings raised, his neck tucked in, in what Saffron recognized as a common chicken acknowledgement of dominance.

Curry looked confused. He was obviously ready for a fight, but this strange bird didn't want to fight.

"They'll get along fine," Gavin promised, "Lyle doesn't fight. He's never met a chicken he couldn't get along with."

"That's crazy," Saffron said, "I thought the pecking order was wired into their brains."

"Maybe it is for most," Gavin said, "but not Lyle. He's a friendly chicken. Maybe it has to do with the fact that I showed him at three days post hatch, and he has been exposed to lots of different birds ever since? Maybe he doesn't feel threatened by other roosters because he's in cages next to other roosters all the time?"

Saffron couldn't explain it, but it certainly worked. Curry

lowered his hackle feathers and his angry *tuk-tuk-tuk* call changed to a questioning clucking.

Lyle straightened and scratched at the boards of the lanai. Scratching was a powerful social behavior for chickens. Saffron had seen one hen scratch the ground and start off a chain reaction that eventually had every hen in the egg house scratching the floor.

Lyle's scratching had a similar effect. Curry picked up the cue and scratched the lanai, then flapped down to the sandy driveway to scratch some more, and Lyle followed him. They wandered down the path, bawking to each other like they were old friends.

"That was remarkable," Saffron said.

Gavin laughed, "Yes, Lyle's a remarkable chicken."

When they opened the door to the egg house, Blue was inside shooting photos in the morning light streaming through the windows.

The reaction that Saffron had expected from the roosters she got with the two men.

Blue straightened, pushing his shoulders back and sticking out his chin, "What are *you* doing here?" he asked.

Gavin, too, tensed and seemed to swell in an attempt to intimidate Blue, "I could ask you the same question."

Saffron tried to intervene, "Blue's here taking photos of my hens," then, turning to Blue, "and Gavin's come to gather information for his new breed of chicken."

"That figures," Blue spat the words, "that the time-honored breeds wouldn't be good enough for him—he has no appreciation for quality."

"What is that supposed to mean?" Gavin took a step closer to Blue, and Saffron saw scarlet rising in their cheeks and around their mouths—a sure sign of anger and aggression, "Just because your second-rate photos couldn't properly capture Lyle's style and elegance."

"Elegance?" Blue waved a hand toward the rooster, who was conversing with a fluffy buff-colored brahma hen through the wire door of a pen, "you can't use the word elegant about a bird with that ridiculous poof of feathers sticking out like a clown's wig."

Gavin took each word like a bullet. He stepped forward, jostling Saffron out of the way, and pushed his face close to Blue, "you wouldn't know elegance if it pecked you on the nose!"

"Ha! I've seen the world's most beautiful animals. I've created images of them that stop people in their tracks. I know elegance, and grace, and style, and art—and your *yard bird* doesn't have it."

Saffron had heard the way Gavin had used that phrase yesterday, had heard the disgust in his voice that accompanied it. To him, it was like a swear word.

There was no way to stop him from lunging forward and knocking Blue to the ground, no way to stop Blue from leaping to his feet and grabbing Gavin by the shoulders, wrenching him sideways in an attempt to knock him off his feet as well.

"Stop it!" Saffron cried, her voice high. Lyle and Curry flapped out of the way, then, with a derisive backward glance at the combatants, flapped out the open doors into the calm Hawaiian morning.

The two were well matched. Gavin resisted Blue, but doing so was an intense strain. He grunted and heaved with the exertion. Their shuffling feet kicked up the sand on the floor and sent it into the air in puffs and clouds.

Gavin tried to throw a punch, but Blue was so close that he couldn't properly draw back, and the blow was ineffective. Blue let go and tried to grab at Gavin's throat, but Gavin ducked back, leaving Blue with just a handful of his shirt collar instead. Blue yanked on the collar, pulling Gavin closer and simultaneously snapping the chain around his neck and sending the medallion flying.

The two crashed into the wire door of one of the pens, their shoulders popping the staples that held the wire to the frame.

"Hey!" Saffron was mad now, more than she was scared, "Knock it off!"

They didn't seem to notice her. She looked around and snatched the only thing she could think of: a handful of scratch grains from the bag in the work area. She threw the grains at them, spraying them with cracked corn, wheat, and barley.

Though it couldn't have hurt them, it did seem to catch their attention. They stepped away from each other, shaking their shoulders and straightening their clothes. When Gavin looked up, he seemed abashed.

"I'm sorry, Miss Skye," he said, "I just won't stand here and listen to him say bad things about Lyle."

Blue opened his mouth, his eyes narrowed, and Saffron was sure he was going to say something to further inflame Gavin, so she snatched another handful of grains and drew back her hand in preparation for another volley. "Uh-uh," she said, "if you can't say something nice, don't say anything at all."

Blue didn't, apparently, have anything nice to say. He looked down, not meeting Saffron's gaze.

The silence grew, bringing a dull tension that seemed like an echo of the fierce scuffle.

"He could have broken my camera!" Blue finally said, cradling the camera that hung around his neck.

"You broke his necklace," Saffron pointed out.

"What?" Gavin looked down, scrambling with his fingers on his chest where the medallion usually lay. He looked around desperately, then knelt down, sifting through the sand in search of it.

Saffron had seen it fly, but when she searched where she thought it had landed, she saw nothing.

Eventually, even sullen Blue started helping them look. They looked in the pens, in the egg cartons, in the nest boxes. No luck. The medallion was gone.

Gavin was panicky, "I have to find it. I have to!"

"Is it valuable?" Saffron asked.

"It's valuable to me," he retorted, "I've had it since my first high school poultry show. It's my lucky charm," he laughed bitterly, "I always called it my 'clucky charm.'"

Blue scuffed a toe in the sand, "I'm sorry," he said, "I didn't mean to break it."

"What do you have against Lyle, anyway?" Gavin asked, his voice more sad than angry.

"Nothing," Blue waved a hand, "and I have nothing against any of these beautiful hens. I just can't say they're perfect if they're not. And, clearly, they're not."

Saffron thought about shoving him herself, "Are you aware that saying things like that could make people want to punch you?" she asked bluntly, "I mean, it seems obvious to me, but—"

"It doesn't matter," Blue said pragmatically, "The pursuit of perfection has never won anyone friends. Me telling a lie that they are perfection when they are not wouldn't help you or me. It might make you feel good, but it wouldn't be the truth. But when I see chickens like those Salmon Faverolles, and everything about them is completely perfect, and I photograph them and show them to the world, then people will take notice. They'll know I only use the word perfect when something truly is perfect."

"Well, it seems like a lonely, and sometimes dangerous, path to walk," Saffron said, feeling again, a little sorry for Blue.

"Maybe," Blue said, "but it's an authentic one."

Chapter Eight

Gavin and Lyle stayed for dinner that night, and Saffron enjoyed their company. She was especially interested in the new breed of chicken he was trying to develop. From what she understood, it was a combination of several breeds. Of course, he wanted Lyle to be the father, and he hoped that Lyle's remarkable crest and comb would make an appearance in the offspring, as well as his extra toe.

"Extra toe?" Saffron asked.

"Yes. Five breeds of chicken have five toes rather than the usual four: Dorkings, Faverolles, Houdans, Silkies, and Sultans."

"Fascinating. I know some of my hens have that extra toe in the back, but I didn't know it was so unusual."

"Quite unusual," Gavin said, "And quite distinctive." He polished off his bowl of chicken long rice. "That's why they'll be a key feature of my new breed: *the Godfrey*."

"The Godfrey?" Saffron had heard a lot of chicken breed names, and all of them sounded better than that. Except maybe Dorkings.

"Godfreys will be the most sought-after breed of them all,

combining the fabulous crest of the houdan and its butterfly comb with beards and muffs and delicate coloring and feathered feet, a docile personality, great egg production—even Blue will have to admit that it is the perfect chicken!"

Saffron cleared her throat, "So, about Blue. Things got pretty heated down there at the egg house today. Do you two know each other?"

Gavin nodded, "Sure. You get to know everyone on the show circuit after a while. He's such a hypocrite. He thinks we're eccentric purists, but he's the one who's the real snob." Gavin helped himself to more fresh sliced mango, "He can't even admit the beauty in a gorgeous specimen like Lyle."

"I admit that he seems harsh, but don't you run into that a lot with judges and stuff?"

Here, Gavin actually rolled his eyes, "Don't even get me started. Judges are the lowest creatures on the planet, as far as I'm concerned."

"Speaking of harsh," Saffron commented, raising an eyebrow at him.

"I'm sorry, but it's true. It comes with the line of work they've chosen. Think about it. Their whole job in life is to find fault, to discover what is wrong with a bird and weigh that against the flaws of the other birds. It makes for a sour perspective, let me tell you. They just go around looking for fault in everything and in everyone."

Saffron could tell there was history there, something with a judge that went beyond the ring. She pressed for details, "I can see how that would affect some people."

"Some people?" Gavin exclaimed, "All of them, is more likely. Take the five judges at the competition the other day: four men and three women, all of whom used to show at one point, but have completely forgotten how it feels to be on the other side of the bird. Bitter, dried husks, every one of them."

"Who were the judges?" Saffron asked. She was most interested in the stern woman she'd heard arguing with Hugo, but it didn't hurt to know a thing or two about the others, either.

"There is one judge from each of the top poultry-or-egg-producing regions: Asia, the Americas, India, Europe, Africa, Russia, and Australia. Suzume Sato is the judge from Asia; Perlita Moreno from Brazil representing the Americas; Arjun Khatri, he represents India; from Europe, Margaux Boucher, Afia Igwe from Africa, Vladimir Korsov from Russia, and finally, Oscar Hudson from Australia."

"You know them all?" Saffron asked.

"Yes, I've crossed paths with all of them on the show circuit," Gavin said, "and some of them are better than others, but none of them would be my first choice to spend an evening with." he snorted. "Although I have," he leaned in confidentially, "spent some evenings with one of them."

Saffron raised her eyebrows in a question, "Perlita Moreno and I dated some time ago."

"It didn't end well, I take it?"

"Not well at all. I felt like I was on a points system every time we went out. 'Your hair's too big, your enunciation is sloppy, your suit's too sparkly.' He heaved a sigh. I guess I just wasn't up to her standard of perfection."

"Wow. Is it awkward to have her judging your bird now?"

"Oh, she can't. There are strict rules about that. Whenever she's a judge at a show I'm in, we have to declare our past relationship at the beginning and she steps out of judging my class on grounds of a conflict of interest. She still judges all the others, though."

"So," Saffron clarified, "if someone had a relationship with a judge, they'd have to declare it at the beginning? What if they didn't declare it?"

"Both the exhibitor and the judge have to declare it," Gavin said, "if they don't, then the exhibitor can be disqualified, and the judge can have their certification taken away—

they won't be able to judge for the Companion and Utility Birds Association again."

"High stakes," Saffron said.

"Yes, and occasionally exploited," Gavin smiled, "Last year an exhibitor claimed a relationship to a judge just because she didn't want him judging her. It was totally untrue, they later discovered."

Saffron was enthralled with the intrigue in the showbird world, "What happened? Did she win?"

"Her birds were not of the quality to win, but it certainly disrupted the show."

"So, doesn't having someone from each of the regions encourage them to give preference to birds from their own region?"

"That's why there are seven judges. Theoretically, the other six should balance out any preferential treatment."

Saffron was lifting a forkful of noodles to her mouth when she saw Curry and Lyle drifting by outside the window. Not walking. Not flapping. Standing perfectly still, but gliding by the window, nonetheless.

Gavin saw it, too. Both scooted out their chairs and ran to the door. As it opened, the soft, hollow clip-clop of hooves on the boards of the lanai greeted them. The little donkey was walking by outside, and the two roosters were happily settled on his back, taking a ride.

Gavin gasped in delight, "what a beautiful burro!"

"Thanks," Saffron managed as Gavin barreled out to stroke the donkey and fawn over him.

"You've made a new friend, Lyle!" Gavin said, scratching between the donkey's ears, "What is his name?"

"Jasper?" Saffron was bewildered. This was not the ratty, scroungy donkey she'd seen earlier. He'd been washed and brushed and was the fluffiest, sweetest-looking animal she'd ever seen. His big ears swiveled toward her and he turned his head to look at the roosters on his back with big, gentle eyes.

"Is that a question or is that his name?"

"No, that's . . ." Saffron hesitated, ". . . that's his name. He just came to live here today, so I didn't recognize him for a moment."

"He is just the sweetest thing," Gavin said.

"I suppose he is," Saffron shrugged. She still wasn't sure about having a donkey in her life, "But I'd better go figure out how he escaped the barn."

"That's okay," Gavin said, "We've got to be going back to our hotel, anyway."

Saffron was itching to ask him about Hugo, to see if he could give any extra information, but she was weary and she still needed to get Jasper back to his stall. Gavin collected Lyle and together they drove off in the big black car.

Saffron looked at Jasper. He wasn't wearing a collar or a halter or anything. How was she going to get him back to the barn?

She had some rope in the house. Maybe a loop of that around his neck? She turned and walked back to the door.

When she pulled it open, she jumped in surprise. Jasper was at her elbow. He had followed her across the lanai.

"Will you come with me?" Saffron asked, "Without a rope? Will you just follow me like a dog?"

It didn't seem likely, but it worked. She walked toward the stairs, and Jasper followed. She walked down the stairs, and Jasper clip-clopped down them, too.

He followed her all the way back to the barn, Curry riding on his back, without stepping a hoof out of line.

When she got there, it was easy to see how he'd gotten out —the barn door was propped open ever so slightly with a rock between it and the frame. Mano and Slate must have been keeping it from latching while they worked. Saffron walked into the barn, letting Jasper trail behind her.

The building was wired with electricity, but Saffron didn't know until she tried the light switch whether it worked or not. It did. A dusty warm yellow glow filled the high barn. Some of the light bulbs were out, but the ones that remained did a good job of brightening up the place.

Saffron led Jasper to his stall and checked the half-door. It, too, was blocked with a small rock. "Your silly old friends wanted you to be able to roam all over the barn, huh?" Saffron asked. She leaned down and picked up the rock, chucking it across the barn floor, which was soft with the protected dirt of several decades. As she was leaning down, she felt the uneven texture of the door and looked more closely at it. It was beautiful. The entire door was carved with interlacing patterns of leaves and flowers. She had never been close enough to the door to see that before.

"Come on, now, Jasper," Saffron waved a hand as she opened the stall door, "time for bed."

Jasper gave a little shake and Curry leaped off, flapping, then the donkey trotted happily into his stall, where he turned and looked at her so contentedly, so sweetly, as if he were the happiest donkey in the world to have his own stall filled with warm straw and grain and hay to eat.

Saffron leaned against the half door as she shut it. It was warm tonight, and the breeze through the big barn doors tasted as sweet as the hot chocolate malasadas she'd eaten earlier. She double-checked the door.

"It's nice and tight now," she said, "But you can get out into the pasture through your back door if you decide you want a little wander. Remember, though, there's a highway over there, and a mountain over there, and the ocean over there, so don't go out of your pen. It's dangerous."

She reached over and scratched him between the ears, then

under his chin. He really was quite sweet. Maybe she could learn to appreciate having a donkey around.

Saffron was looking at Jasper when she sensed someone else nearby. It wasn't a bad feeling—not a chill up her spine or a wash of dread. Rather, a warm presence that made her turn expectantly toward the door, looking for a friend.

But there was nobody there. Only the warm evening breeze blew in through the door to greet her. Saffron was sure someone had come in. She searched her brain to think why she was so sure. Was it something she had heard? Maybe the creak of the barn door or the scuff of a shoe on the dirt floor? Or something she had seen? A shadow playing across the wall or a flash of color at the edge of her vision?

She couldn't pinpoint it. Maybe Gavin had poked his head into the barn on the way out but had, for some reason, decided not to disturb her. She wished he had. It would have been less disturbing for him to speak than to leave her with this unsettled feeling that she had just missed someone.

The next day, she didn't slip in the back door of Juno's Bakery to pick up her malasadas. Instead, she sat out in the front with the Walking Wonders, a group of older ladies in town who had gained notoriety for walking as a group every morning despite their age. They were some of Saffron's first friends in Maika'i, and they adored Saffron as much as she did them.

Her friend Fumi ran Maika'i's little kitchen store, and today, true to form, she had brought Saffron a new egg gadget to try out. It was a long, flattish, plastic spoon.

"It's for peeling hardboiled eggs," Fumi was saying. Her brown eyes danced as she pretended to demonstrate. "It supposedly slips right in there and pops the shells off."

Saffron thanked her and promised to try it out and give a full review.

"You are our resident egg expert," said one of Saffron's favorite members of the club, Mrs. Betty Claus. She looked stunningly like the Mrs. Claus of Christmas fame, and she had promised to come in the canoe with Santa on Christmas Eve and hand out the cookies to the keiki—the children—as they waited to tell him what they wanted for Christmas, "And I hear you even know a thing or two about eggs as weapons after this week's egg line."

"You heard about that, huh?" Saffron asked, sighing.

"Mijita," said Consuela Limon, the owner of Tiki Thrift and Trade, the little second-hand store, "half the town had front row seats to that."

It was true. Saffron had seen several of the ladies in the line that day, "It was a mess."

"And we didn't get our eggs. Let me tell you, those two brothers have had an earful from more than one person in this town this week."

The thought made Saffron feel both a great pity for the two men and a little vindicated, too.

"They'll think twice before bringing their family feud to your farm again!" Tillie Allbey, a platinum blond, shook her head.

"I would never have known they were brothers," Saffron said, "the way they were fighting, you'd think they were worst enemies."

The Walking Wonders tossed a look around the table. It was a sad look, and an impatient one.

"They used to be just the opposite," said Lani, an honorary Wonder like Saffron, who didn't actually walk with the ladies, but who did enjoy meeting with them at the bakery every couple of weeks, "They were inseparable, running their daddy's farm together after he passed away."

"What happened?" Saffron asked. She knew family fractures, and that they could sometimes be hard to understand.

The Wonders spoke almost in unison, and they all said the same word: "Betsy."

"Oh," said Mrs. Claus, shaking her head, "That girl breezed into town like a hurricane. She just had to see the Sawyer's herd—that was the year that Dylan and Wyatt's cows won all the awards at the livestock expo, and she came all the way from France to see them."

"How did she end up staying?" Saffron asked.

"Well, Dylan fell for her hard," Tilley said, "I think everyone in town told him one way or another that it wasn't a good idea, but he didn't have eyes for anything else after she got here."

Lani leaned in, "If you want to know my opinion, she never did want Dylan. She just wanted that ranch."

Saffron shook her head, "But she wouldn't have married him just to get that, would she? I mean, that's like giving up your whole life for—for cows."

"*Prize* cows," Tilley said, "Remember that. They're a special French breed, those cows, and I think Betsy's always been one to play the long game."

"That's right. She sure did that with the brothers. After she and Dylan got married, that girl just could not stand that Dylan and Wyatt were so close," Lani shook her head.

"Or maybe she couldn't stand that Wyatt was half-owner of the ranch," Mrs. Claus clucked, and Saffron remembered Sophie's song about the hens. She heard the tones of her own flock in the murmurs and sighs around the table as Mrs. Claus went on, "She had to get between them, then had to make sure to put some wedge between them that they'd never get over."

"What was the wedge?" Saffron was wrapped up in the history now.

At this, the usually chatty Wonders clammed up. Saffron

could tell none of them wanted to be the one to say it out loud. That only made her more desperate to hear it. "What?" she pressed, "What did she do?"

Finally, Miss Vinny Dingley, the most sour of the Wonders, and the most blunt, looked Saffron in the eye, "Oh, for Pete's sake, somebody's gotta say it. She," even Miss Dingley's voice dropped to a whisper as she revealed the word, "*seduced* Wyatt."

The women all let out sighs of relief that it was said and disapproval that it had happened. The word made Saffron want to giggle. It was such an old word, such a tight one. But as its meaning sank in, she realized there was nothing to giggle about. If that was true, no wonder Dylan hated his brother—that would be a betrayal too deep to forgive for a very long time.

"Ruined them both," Tillie sniffed, "Of course, Wyatt was too ashamed to look Dylan in the eye after that, and Dylan was hurt again every time he saw his brother. So her plan worked."

"The awful part is," said Mrs. Claus, leaning in, "I'm not even sure anything actually happened between Wyatt and Betsy."

There were exclamations of disbelief all around the table, but Mrs. Claus was quick to defend her theory, "Think about it —all she really had to do was suggest to Dylan that it had happened. He'd go after Wyatt, and Wyatt would be so hurt that Dylan could even believe it that he'd get just as angry back."

The Walking Wonders mulled this over until Theo arrived with their two dozen malasadas. He patted Saffron on the shoulder before hurrying back to the swarm of waiting customers.

The donuts were hot and perfectly fresh. They were dusted with cocoa, and inside filled with what Saffron recognized immediately as a smooth, more liquid form of Christmas fudge.

"Oh," exclaimed Mrs. Claus, "It's just like my mother's fudge! Down to that little hint of vanilla hiding behind the rich cocoa flavor!"

"And the creaminess!" Jan Lin, owner of a cell-phone store here in town, closed her eyes and let out a long, "Mmmmmmm."

Saffron was so caught up in the first few bites of Christmas Fudge Malasada that she didn't notice who had come in. She didn't see him freeze by the door, didn't see his gaze fix on her, didn't see him immobilized by her presence. She didn't see how long he stood debating whether to come over, and she didn't see the moment he turned to go without approaching her. She also didn't see him slip out and walk down the street away from Juno's Bakery.

Chapter Nine

Everything was coming together.

Saffron had stopped by on the way into town and talked to Matthew Bell, of Bell Ranch. They raised black Hawaiian sheep, and Saffron needed some for her nativity. The animals were remarkable, with long, broad horns that grew in corkscrews out the sides of their heads. Matthew had a beautiful mini-flock that he said he'd be happy to loan her: a ram, a ewe, and two new lambs. His kids had brought them out, and she'd verified that they were tame enough for the nativity.

She had sheep. The Sawyers were supposed to provide a cow. She had a donkey. She walked to the front of Juno's Bakery after the Wonders had left to see if she could get a guaranteed crowd at the Christmas Eve party.

Juno stepped out from behind the counter and enveloped her in one of his trademark hugs. He was a big man, bigger than she would have expected a baker to be, but it had always been clear that malasadas were his passion.

"Thank you for the extra eggs. I've needed them this week even more than I thought I would," he sneaked a glance at the crowd in his shop and Saffron could see his pride. "Now, what can I do for my favorite egg farmer today?" Juno beamed, "Need another dozen? It's on the house. Theo!" he turned to catch his nephew's eye.

"No, no," Saffron held up a hand, "It's nothing like that. It's just . . ." she wasn't sure how to ask, so she just blurted it out, "I was just thinking how incredibly special it would be if I could convince you to have some malasadas available on Christmas Eve, at the town's Christmas Eve Party," she waited for Juno to flinch and launch into why that was impossible, but his round face split into a grin, "I think that's a wonderful idea!"

"You do?" Saffron blinked.

"I do! The live nativity with a fresh malasada in hand? What could be better?"

"You can use my kitchen to cook them," Saffron offered.

Juno waved a hand, "Oh, no need. That's what the food truck is for."

"Food truck?" Saffron said.

"Oh, yeah. We have a food truck now. Bought it from the Taco Brothers when they retired. Now we hit the North Shore on slow days and sell to the malihinis!"

Lucky tourists, Saffron thought.

"We were going to have all our Christmas Flavors available that day anyway," Juno said, "So people could come back and get their favorites."

"That's a great idea!" Saffron would love another egg nog malasada.

They settled the details and Saffron left Juno with chalk in hand, writing "All Christmas Flavors Available on Christmas Eve at Hau'oli Ka Moa Egg Farm!" on his chalkboard in front of the bakery.

She was walking on air when she left. The whoosh of the waves along Maika'i Beach greeted her like laughter, and she veered off and walked down to the sand.

Kicking off her slippahs, she made tracks in the wet sand near the surf. The sand was honey-colored here, with flecks of ebony lava rock tossed in. The electric blue water lapped around her ankles, pulling at her feet and toes, again inviting her off her intended path for a swim. She watched as the seafoam raced in jagged lines up and down the beach. She watched as the water carried it up the beach, then left it behind, bubbles popping, before picking it up again and moving it slightly. It was a never-ending, living artwork, its lines constantly shifting, every picture new, original, and temporary.

Saffron looked around. She was alone on the beach, but for a moment had thought she sensed someone else's presence. It was like the feeling she'd had last night. When she turned and looked, though, the beach was empty.

It didn't stay empty long, though. Just as Saffron finished writing her name in the sand with her toes, she looked up to see Officer Bradley, as well as a navy-clad Honolulu officer, making their way down the beach toward her.

Her welcoming smile faded when she saw the look on Officer Bradley's face. She rushed over the few yards of sand between them, terrified that something had happened to Mano or her father.

"Saffron," he began, "there's been a development in that Hugo Leblanc case."

"We are not arresting you at this time," cut in the Honolulu officer. She recognized him—the big man who had hauled Gavin out of the tent. His name tag read *Havili*.

"Wait, arrest *me*?" Saffron took a step back.

"We'll need you to come with us," said Officer Havili.

Bradley held up a hand, "We just need to talk to you, Saffron, about—"

"The chief said specifically not to reveal any details of the situation until he could interrogate her," Havili said. That same unflappable attitude he'd shown with Gavin was on display again.

"I don't see how it can hurt to—" Bradley began, but Havili cut him off.

"Listen, we only involved you as a courtesy," Havili said. His tone was completely void of emotion, "I can take her over there myself if you don't want to abide by the chief's requests."

Bradley shot Saffron an apologetic look, "No, no, I'll drive you over. C'mon Saffron, the sooner you talk to the chief, the sooner this all blows over and you can get back to planning the Christmas Eve party."

Havili flinched, "you should be aware that you may not be at liberty to attend any Christmas Eve party," he said.

Now Saffron was scared.

* * *

TO HER SURPRISE, they drove her home. Hau'oli ka Moa was teeming with Honolulu Police Cars.

Saffron felt queasy. This could not be good.

She followed the officers all the way to the egg house,

where, leaning on her egg counter, she saw the chief she'd seen questioning Gavin.

The air in the egg house was dusty with the chickens' morning scratching. Outside, the i'iwi birds were trilling their morning greetings to the hens who'd wandered into the outside runs in search of a morning centipede. It would have been a perfect Hawaiian morning if not for the law enforcement everywhere.

"I'm going to cut straight to the chase here, Miss Skye. Any idea what these birds—" he pointed to the first pen where several of Saffron's hens had been joined by three of the prettiest chickens she'd ever seen, "are doing on your farm?"

"The French Hens!" Saffron gasped. She couldn't take her eyes off them. Sophie's Faverolles, without question. They were huddled in one corner, obviously completely terrified. She looked at the chief. "I have no idea," she said.

"How long have they been here?"

"This is the first time I've seen them," she said, thinking back, "Of course, there are a lot of chickens in here, and I've been a little distracted with Blue staying here and Gavin visiting—"

Gavin.

The crazy competitor was trying to frame her. "He must have brought them up yesterday," Saffron blurted.

"You saw Mr. Godfrey yesterday?" the chief nodded, and an officer at his elbow jotted that down on a clipboard.

"Yes, he showed up here, asking about my hens. He asked me a lot of questions about egg production—said it was for a new line of chicken he's developing."

"Are you aware that Mr. Godfrey is one of our leading suspects in the murder of Hugo Leblanc?"

Saffron was aware of that, but she didn't know if they knew that she'd been watching from the sidelines the day they questioned him.

"No," she said, "but it makes sense that he would be. I mean, he has means, motive, and opportunity."

"And, strangely, so do you."

"Right," she said, thinking fast, "on two out of three. I had means and opportunity, but what possible motive could I have?"

The chief didn't say anything, just raised a steady hand and pointed at the chickens in the pen.

Saffron saw it now. It was a good set-up. If she had the hens, they had probable cause to suspect her, even if she denied it.

"Are you working with Mr. Godfrey? Did you kill Hugo Leblanc so you and Mr. Godfrey could steal the hens, hide them here, and sell them when the heat is off?"

"No," Saffron managed.

"Did you plan to breed the hens and sell their offspring?" the chief asked, "was Hugo Leblanc in your way?"

Saffron concentrated on the sounds of her hens. They always calmed her, and this time was no exception, "You have a lot of questions," she told the chief, "Now, I have one for you: how did you even know they were here?"

"We got a tip from someone else you're connected to in the show world," the man said.

Saffron tried to think who she could possibly be connected to in the show world, but couldn't come up with anyone.

"A man named Blue called to tell us you were hiding these hens here," said the Chief, "and it's a good thing he did, or we would never have found them."

Blue. Gavin must have put the birds in the pen sometime during the night, and Blue must have seen them when he came down to the egg house this morning.

Saffron had been here early, as she was every morning, gathering eggs and filling feeders, but she'd been so intent on getting to her malasada date with the Wonders that she hadn't noticed the new hens.

"We're moving you up the suspect list," the chief said, "more and more coincidences keep adding up. You were at the scene of the crime with the victim's blood on your hands. You have the victim's stolen chickens here at your farm."

"You're right," Saffron admitted, "it doesn't look good. If I were you, I'd suspect me."

"Is that an admission of guilt?" he asked.

"No, but it should be a red flag to you," Saffron said, "Look, Chief, I've been involved enough in these things to know that it's rarely a wildcard like me who is responsible. Look at the whole picture. I've never seen any of these people, or these hens, before in my life. I didn't even know Faverolles existed until I saw them at the show. I've never spoken to any of these people—I'll happily give you all my phone records for the past year if you don't believe me. See if you can make a single connection—besides chickens—between me and any of these people, and I'll go with you happily. But you can't, because I don't know them, and I'm not the killer."

"It wouldn't take much to convince a jury that you are. I have enough evidence to bring you in."

"But that's not the business you're in, is it, Chief? You don't get where you are by taking the easiest suspect. You want the truth as much as I do, and I think you know you're not looking at it here."

The chief considered a long moment, "Pretty confident," he said.

"I can afford to be," Saffron replied, "I didn't kill Hugo Leblanc."

There was a long moment of silence between them, filled only with the trills of the i'iwi birds outside and the murmuring hens inside. Finally, the Chief sighed, "I believe you," he said. "But I also hear you're a bit of an amateur sleuth, so if I don't take you in, I'm going to need your word that you'll pass along anything you find out," his steely eyes bored into her, "which shouldn't be a problem if you really do want to find the truth."

"You got it, Chief," she said.

"All right," he said, straightening, "let's get back down to the city, guys."

Saffron waved a hand at the hens, "Are you going to take them? Did you bring a crate or something?"

"That's the other thing I'm going to need you to do. See, our evidence room isn't really set up for chickens. I'm leaving them here. I still need someone to make a positive ID on them anyway—I'll probably send up one or two of those judges we've been working with back at the poultry show—so if you could just keep them here, that would be great."

"They're welcome to stay," Saffron said, "but what if someone comes to steal them again? This isn't exactly Fort Knox."

"I hope they do come after them again," the Chief said, "that way we can catch them in the act," he sauntered toward the door, "just keep an eye out for anything strange."

* * *

SAFFRON TOOK his command to heart—she couldn't stop looking for anything strange. If the hens were too quiet, or too loud, if the sun went behind a cloud, she jumped.

She was keeping an eye out when Blue's rental car pulled up in front of his cottage late that afternoon, and she met him on his lanai.

"You called the cops and told them I stole those hens? Why would you do that?"

Blue seemed unfazed, "Well, first of all, I wasn't expecting to have to justify it to you. Why didn't they arrest you?"

"Because I didn't steal them, and I didn't kill Hugo. Why would you tell them I did?"

"How did the hens get here then? I'd know them anywhere."

"I don't know how they got here, but I didn't bring them."

"Well, it was my civic duty to report it."

Saffron supposed that was true, but it didn't give her any warm feelings for Blue.

"How are my photos coming?" she asked.

"I'll be finished in a few days. I'm editing some on the computer this evening. I'll let you know how it goes."

Saffron still wanted to see how he'd captured them, "Fine," she said icily, "just try to do it without bringing the police down on my farm again."

Saffron went back to the house and sat on her bed. Gavin. His name had been seething through her mind all day. He was framing her, she was sure of it. And he had seemed so nice. She had almost forgotten his erratic behavior at the show, his strange reaction to seeing Hugo's body.

She knew one thing—Gavin wasn't going to get away with it. She didn't know how she'd prove that he killed Hugo and stolen those hens. He probably planned to come back for them.

When had he sneaked them into the egg house? It must have been last night, when Saffron was putting Jasper away. Maybe that's why she had felt a presence in the barn—maybe he had stopped in to be sure she was occupied.

If only she could rewind time and see the egg house last night.

It was then that she remembered, with a clarity akin to the sun streaming through the egg house windows, that she *could* rewind time. Cupcake's broody palace had cameras. She had access to them.

It took her only moments to call up the application on her phone, and only seconds to figure out how to play back the streaming video from the camera most likely to show, in its background, that first pen.

She rewound to ten o'clock—around the time that she'd put Jasper away.

But all was still in the egg house then, with the exception of an occasional foray by one of the wobbly little geese to the feeder or the pan of swimming water.

Saffron moved it forward an hour, two hours, three, until she saw the pale dawn beginning to light the edges of the frame.

And there it was, a shadowy, bulky figure at the periphery, opening the door and setting down one hen, turning, producing a second hen, then putting down a third before securing the pen door and moving out of the shot.

Saffron sighed. She had proof that someone had put the hens in, and she was sure it was Gavin, but there was not nearly enough detail in the video to prove it. She couldn't make out his distinctive hair, and the figure was blurry in the minuscule light. The camera was too far away to make a positive identification. She'd have to keep looking for clues that led to Gavin.

Saffron heard Curry give his goodnight crow outside. She went to the window, grabbing his favorite treat, pumpkin seeds, which she kept on her dresser for saying goodnight. She pulled up the window sash and Curry leaped up, clucking, telling her about his day.

Looking past him, Saffron's eyes fell on a mottled black feather laying, gently curved, on the lanai.

Of course. She'd seen the police picking up the feathers in the tent. If they could match them to Lyle, it would at least be one piece of evidence they could build a case on. She called the chief.

Chapter Ten

Saffron was slow to get started the next morning. She sat in her living room watching the ocean beyond the palm trees. She knew there were things to be done, she just couldn't seem to get interested in doing them. Her mind was working on the mystery of Hugo's death.

The chief hadn't been too interested in the feathers. He said they already knew Gavin had been in the tent. Saffron told him about the shadowy figure caught on the egg house camera, and he said he'd look into it, but she didn't get the impression that he was as intent on finding the killer as she was. She was just going to have to solve this herself.

She thought back to what she knew. Hugo had been talking to Margaux Boucher, the judge, in her tent just before he'd been killed. He'd left the judges' tent and gone to the photography tent. Someone, maybe even Margaux, had met him in there. They'd struggled, and someone had hit him with the silver champion's cup.

After that, what? Hugo had been carrying one of the hens, so somehow someone had snatched it from him or after he was killed and before the police arrived.

Saffron closed her eyes, trying to picture the scene. Had she seen or heard anyone?

But it was no use. She'd been so focused on helping Hugo, on saving his life, that she had no memory of anything except his still form, CPR, and blood.

When she opened her eyes, Saffron let herself watch the sea for a moment, as if the sight of it would wash from her memory the jarring image of Hugo on the grass.

It worked. The coming and going of the waves was just what Saffron needed to calm herself.

Until, with a jolt, she realized something was in the water.

Saffron stood and walked closer to her window. Was it a sea turtle? It was big enough to be one.

But no, sea turtles were masters of the water. They rode the curls like surfers, flipping a lazy fin out of the water in what Saffron always called the turtle wave.

Whatever this was, it was at the mercy of the driving tide. Saffron grabbed her slippahs and ran for the beach.

Whatever it was, it was gray against the peacock blue of the ocean: a little sliver of silver peeking through the waves.

About halfway between the house and the water, where the palm trees made a line that edged the driveway and began the beach, Saffron realized what she was looking at.

"Jasper!" she screamed, breaking into a hard run.

The donkey must have gotten out of the barn again and wandered into the water.

She screamed his name again as she kicked off her slippahs and splashed knee-deep into the surf.

Jasper was ten meters out, his ears laid back. A monstrous wave swelled behind him, lifted him, and drove him closer to shore before breaking over his bobbing head. He disappeared into the sea foam.

"Jasper!" Saffron called to him just as the wave retreated

and he reappeared, rotated back toward the open sea, "Come here, boy!"

Saffron splashed further into the water, feeling helpless. The waves rose around her hips and lifted her feet off the sandy floor of the ocean.

Saffron swam. Through the swells of the waves, through the occasional spraying crash of water on water, further and further as the waves carried Jasper out twice as far as he'd been when she first saw him.

She kept her eye on him and worked toward him with focus. Two yards, five yards, ten yards. Every time she thought she might catch up with him, he drifted further out on the endless procession of waves.

They were in real deep water now. Saffron couldn't find the bottom if she wanted to. She'd only ever swam out this far with Keahi, the first few months she'd been on the island.

There was a coral reef somewhere out here, she knew, that sheltered the beach from the biggest waves, but she had no idea how close it was. She knew it could be extremely dangerous to both her and Jasper if they got caught on the wrong side of the reef—she'd seen whole logs pounded to kindling by the breakers on the reef.

Her arms burned. The sea was energetic today, and she fought to keep her head up and her eye on Jasper.

She had almost reached him when she realized she'd gone out too far. Her lungs were on fire, her legs and stomach tightening in cramps. She realized how foolish she'd been as she turned to look back toward the shore and found that the egg farm was just a dot on the beach. Her whole world reduced to one speck.

Her head went under and she kicked furiously through the pain and clawed her way up through a wave until she felt her head break through. There was water in her mouth, her throat, her lungs, and she coughed convulsively to clear it.

Her long, flowing dress dragged at her like seaweed, so she slipped her shoulders out and kicked free of it, trying to stay oriented.

When she looked again, she couldn't see the egg farm, or the beach, or Jasper. She coughed up more water. All she saw was the smooth hill of a wave behind her and another in front of her.

The water here was midnight blue, with translucent crests where it rose and the sun shone through the waves.

She wished for Nik, for his surfboard to float up beside her, or for Keahi, whose strong arms could lift her out of the water into a canoe, or Mano and her father, who, she was sure, would think of something.

But she didn't have them. She flipped onto her back, trying to float as pain seared her limbs and her head went under again. The waves were too big. She'd have to try to swim.

But she didn't know which direction to swim. The waves were disorienting. And her legs were becoming more useless by the second. She was alone in the Pacific with only a struggling donkey.

Except he wasn't struggling. As she went under and came up again, Jasper paddled up next to her, breaking through the waves as he swam.

He didn't seem panicked. His eyes weren't rolling, he wasn't flailing. For the first time, Saffron considered the idea that Jasper had not fallen into the water accidentally, that perhaps he had come in on purpose.

He seemed to sense she was in trouble. He swam up beside her.

Instinctively, Saffron grabbed on, using her ebbing strength to throw her arms around Jasper's neck. There was only one way to stay out of the way of his churning hooves: she let him drift under her and take her on his back.

His fur was soft and soaking against her cheek as she held

on. She was so tired that she had almost no idea of where he was going.

But the little donkey seemed capable, assured. He seemed calm, and that calm passed to Saffron as she let him tow her.

There was a jolt when Jasper's hooves found the sloping sand of the shore.

Saffron found the strength to hold on as he trotted out onto the amber sand, where he flopped down and she slid off, coughing up water and drifting off into a deep sleep.

He was still beside her when she woke up, laying with his body toward the sun and casting a shadow on the half-naked, exhausted girl by his side.

He'd dried out by then, and his fluffy, soft fur felt exquisite as Saffron gave him a hug.

"You saved my life," she said. Jasper blinked his big, sweet, brown eyes at her, stood, and shook the sand from his coat. Saffron found her slippahs and, with an arm around her new friend, went back up to the house to find some new clothes.

* * *

LATER THAT MORNING, Saffron was sitting outside the egg house on one of the little wooden benches where she liked to watch the birds forage. Her muscles were tired, but there were few other signs of her morning's adventure. Jasper was nearby, grazing at his leisure. Her gaze was trained on the Faverolles, who had tentatively followed her flock outside this morning.

With their puffy cheeks and beards, the Faverolles were comical birds, and they were even more so in a new environment. Saffron's chickens had been mostly feral when she'd come to the chicken farm and started taking care of them. They were adept at scratching for bugs and foraging for the sweetest seeds that fell into their pens.

The Faverolles, though, had never free-ranged, and they

were both delighted and terrified by everything. A nodding blade of tall grass sent them scuttling back to the door of the coop, and a darting i'iwi bird made them squawk with fright.

The best part, though, was when they became enamored of a scrawny beetle crawling along. Their instincts told them what to do, and they each trained an eye on him, but after that they were unsure. Where Saffron's hens would have snatched him up and crunched him like popcorn without a second thought, the Faverolles followed him, watching as he scaled stones and marched over blades of grass. They waddled along after him, the three of them in a tight knot, bumping and jostling each other while making a chortle that started low on the scale and ended high: what Saffron had learned was a curious sound.

They tripped on each other, ran into the wire surrounding the pen, and plowed over the grass. When the beetle got to the edge of the pen and wandered out in search of other adventures, the three hens huddled and held a bemused conference full of confused chirping.

"They look deep in thought," a voice said behind Saffron's bench. She turned to see Mano standing there.

She greeted him and explained about the Faverolles chasing the beetle, "They're just so funny to watch," she said, "like babies who have just gotten their first toys. They have no idea what to do with them."

She thought about the beautiful birds' lives so far. They'd only known their show cages—tiny, bounded environments with very few surprises. The image of the cages made her think of Jasper, and how maybe he needed to be able to roam. Maybe it was in his nature to swim and graze when he felt like it. The thought of cages also brought Sophie immediately to mind.

"They will get more comfortable," Mano assured her, "it's

inside them, they have the instincts. It just may take a while for them to figure it out."

"Chickens use social learning," Saffron said, "it's one of the things that makes them intelligent. Once they see another chicken doing something, they try it, then figure out how to do it for themselves."

"You call that social learning," Mano said, "we call it shared knowledge. It's important in any society. Now that these birds are a part of your flock, they'll learn quickly."

"I don't even know how long they'll be here, honestly," Saffron said. Then, looking around, she asked, "Hey, where's my dad?" It was rare these days to see one of the men without the other. She wondered briefly if she should tell them about her morning's swimming adventure, but quickly decided she'd better keep it a secret between Jasper and her.

"Wrapping Christmas presents," Mano said, "but he knew you'd be waiting, so he sent me ahead with these." He held up the pale purple box that Saffron had been looking forward to all morning.

She jumped up, "What is it what is it what is it?" She reached for the box. "What's the flavor today?" Her strenuous morning swim had left her starving.

Mano smiled proudly and opened the box. Inside, the malasadas were lined up, their sugared outsides gleaming like a fresh snowfall. They were different than usual, though. Their smooth, golden edges were flecked with color: bright red and green.

"Oh, no," Saffron drew her hand back, "they didn't."

"They did!" Mano's eyes were sparkling.

"Fruitcake? Fruitcake malasadas? That is a truly terrible idea."

"You don't trust Juno? Has he ever let us down before?"

Saffron shook her head, but she couldn't make herself believe it, "Fruitcake is the worst Christmas food of all. It's so bad that there are jokes about it—a whole subgenre of fruit-cake jokes."

Mano was helping himself to one, oblivious to her argument.

"More for me," he said, taking a bite.

Saffron picked up one of the donuts. She tried to fight back the memory of her first taste of fruitcake. It had been when she was ten, at her neighbor's apartment. The nice old lady had handed her a slice, and she'd thought it would taste delicate, like a warm vanilla cake.

She remembered looking at the chunks of red and green in the cake. She already had some trouble eating certain foods because of their colors: under- or over-ripe bananas, for instance, were as different from ripe ones in color as apples were from oranges. So when the neighbor had handed her that slice of fruitcake with its unnaturally crimson bits and otherworldly green chunks, she had known better than to taste it.

But what could she say? Mrs. Longorian was peering at her so kindly. Saffron very rarely had anything homemade, either. So she'd smiled and taken a big bite. It was dry. The red and green bits were gummy, and they tasted like medicine. There were bitter nuts.

Saffron remembered consuming it bite by painful bite as Mrs. Longorian beamed. She remembered choking on the marbly remnants of what she could only assume used to be fruit.

She'd gone home and lain sick on her couch for the rest of the day until her mom had come home.

To be fair, though, these felt nothing like that slice of iron she'd eaten so long ago. The donut was light and springy in her hand, as always. The flecks of green and red were, on closer inspection, tiny curls of lime zest and delicate slivers of guava.

Saffron took an exploratory bite. The sweet tropical fruit flavors blended seamlessly with the rich donut. There were finely chopped macadamia nuts. The donut tasted lightly of banana. It was seasoned with a little cinnamon and a little sharp clove that warmed the tongue and emphasized the sweetness of the lemon and lilikoi, also called passion fruit, custard inside. It was pillowy and rich and sweet.

Mano was looking at Saffron, smiling that "I told you so" smile without actually saying "I told you so."

"These are sensational!" Saffron admitted. She closed her eyes, and she could taste the heritage of this confection. The spices brought to mind Mrs. Longorian's creation so long ago, but it had been repackaged into a light, sweet, tropical delicacy.

"Fruitcake is making a comeback," Saffron said, taking another one.

* * *

SAFFRON AND MANO spent the afternoon gathering poinsettias from Red Mountain to make Christmas leis for all the townspeople.

Mano was an expert carver, a wonderful ukulele player, and a really terrible lei maker.

"Well, these aren't right," he said, holding up a knot of flowers and leaves.

"No," Saffron said, taking it from him and looking for any hole big enough for someone to put their head through, "Not quite."

The Empress had taught Saffron to make leis. One rainy afternoon before a baby shower for Saffron's friends the Tuckers, she and the Empress had sat in the Empress' big house and woven thirty leis. Saffron was pretty good at it now, but she wasn't an expert in the way the Empress was, and she didn't know how to teach Mano what to do.

"Uh, here," she took the one he was working on, "I can

figure it out if I'm actually doing it. She unwound the string from the stems of the flowers and worked to re-wrap it.

"You're good at that," he said from over her shoulder.

"I'm learning," she said, "I'm slow. The Empress could have made three for every one I've made."

"We should get her over here," Mano chuckled.

"We can't. She's in Honolulu with Lyza and Davis for Christmas."

"Oh, she's going to love that."

"But it means we're stuck here with no lei expert."

"You're on your way to being one," he said, "Just need to make about . . ." he squinted at the rack holding about twenty leis, "a thousand more."

She laughed. Mano always made work seem like fun.

"Well, I've got all evening," she said.

He picked up a blossom and handed it to her, "well," he said, "you've also got a helper."

Chapter Eleven

Saffron's hands were sore the next morning from holding the stems and string tight, from wrapping and skewering and braiding the leis.

She got through the Tuesday Egg Line with a smile,

though, and a sense of relief that she didn't see the red pickup or the blue pickup of either Sawyer brother.

The drivers of each car in the long line down the driveway all had something to say about last week's egg fight, so the line was a little slower than most mornings.

Jan Lin, owner of the cell phone store and one of the Walking Wonders, was particularly chatty about it.

"Dylan and Betsy came into my store yesterday," the woman was thin, with a smile a little wider than her narrow jaw. She was a master of the arched eyebrow, and her straight black hair was cut in a sharp, chin-length bob. It swayed around her oak brown eyes as she talked, "I told them what I thought about their antics in your egg line last week. Dylan seemed embarrassed, but Betsy was completely shameless," Jan shook her head, "I don't know why I was surprised."

Saffron handed a carton of eggs through Jan's window, "Thanks for looking out for me. How are you doing, Jan?"

Jan's only son, Sheng, had recently gone off to college on the mainland, leaving his mother with an empty nest. It had been very lonely for her.

"The house is too quiet," Jan said, looking down quickly, busying herself with placing the eggs in the floorboard and paying Saffron.

"Well, come out to the egg house any time," Saffron said, "it's plenty loud in there."

Jan laughed, "I might just take you up on that!" she put her car into gear, "you watch out for flying eggs this week."

"Oh, I will," Saffron watched Jan's car pull away and took a moment to rub her sore hands. She barely made it through the rest of the egg line before the lei-making ache came back with a vengeance.

But it had been worth it. Her extra refrigerator was brimming with colorful flowers, ready for the party. She looked at them again on her way down to the egg house. Green and red, a riot of Christmas color, they were beautiful.

But there was something off. One stack of the lei had been moved, and as Saffron investigated, she found a couple of bright red leaves on the ground in front of the refrigerator.

She peered in behind the stack that had been moved. She never could have seen it if she hadn't bent down to do a close inspection. Way in the back, behind the stacks of leis, was a little bundle.

When she opened it, Saffron was surprised to find a glass tube containing tiny white pills. She had never seen them before.

Shaking a few into her hand, she saw a little symbol that looked like three wavy lines. Printed below them was a string of letters and a number: dqe9.

Saffron felt a little chill in her heart. The only person that had been here yesterday was Mano. It was possible that they belonged to him. Maybe he'd put them out there and forgotten to take them home. Was he ill?

She took a deep breath and tried to calm herself by focusing on the limbs of the hibiscus trees as they swayed in the sweet morning breeze. Her gaze fell on the cottages.

Mano wasn't the only one who had been here yesterday. Blue was still here, in the cottage. Maybe these were his.

But he had a refrigerator in his cottage. Why would he put them here?

Saffron slid the pills back into the vial and the vial back into the fabric it had been wrapped in. She put the whole bundle back into the refrigerator where she had found it.

The egg house was bright and breezy this morning as Saffron went about her chores trying to avoid thinking about the mysterious pills in the egg refrigerator.

She peered into the first pen where her hen Tikka was scratching and pecking at the feeder with several other hens.

"Morning, girl," Saffron said.

"Brrrrrrk," Tikka responded.

The three Faverolles had settled in nicely. Babette and Antoinette were scratching and exploring around the feeder while Claudette pecked a few feet away from them. She was particularly interested in a little pile of scratch grains near the door.

Saffron froze. There, in the center of the pile, on the floor of the Faverolles pen, was a tiny white dot. She leaned down, peering through the wire in the door, and confirmed what she thought: it was one of the pills she'd just seen in the refrigerator.

Saffron scrambled for the catch on the door and threw it open. She reached for the grains, but not fast enough. She had just time to see the imprint on the pill: dqe9, before Claudette snatched it up and gobbled it. The pill was gone.

Saffron tried to breathe. How had the pill gotten there? Would it hurt Claudette? She was supposed to be taking care of these birds. What if someone had just poisoned them?

She thought immediately of Gavin. What lengths would he go to in order to get rid of the competition? And what if, somehow, her own hens got one of the pills? What would it do to them?

Saffron thought back. There had been no description on the vial, nothing to tell her what the pills were. She needed an expert, someone who would know, or be able to find out, what a prescription medication was.

She could only think of one person who might know. Though she hadn't spoken to him in months, she dialed Keahi's number with shaking hands.

He was a doctor, after all. He might at least be able to tell her what the pill was.

Keahi's voice held surprise when he answered. Saffron

skipped the pleasantries and told him immediately why she was calling.

As always, Keahi took her seriously. His deep voice carried with it a sense of calm. She often thought that was probably one of his strengths as a physician—he could make things seem okay.

"I don't recognize it off the top of my head," he said, "but I have access to a database where I can look it up."

Saffron waited, listening to the clack of computer keys on the other end of the line. She didn't ask him how Boston was, but she pictured him in his apartment, a snowy, gray Massachusetts December day outside his windows.

Finally, he cleared his throat.

"Nothing to worry about, I don't think," he began. Saffron breathed a sigh of relief. "It's not a human pharmaceutical. It's made for poultry. Some kind of seizure medication."

"Chicken medicine?" Saffron repeated.

"That's right. Whoever left it for Claudette, they must have meant to leave it."

Saffron felt the knot in her chest loosen. It wouldn't hurt the hen, anyway.

But that still left the question of who had given it to her, and why, and it still left Saffron with an uneasy feeling that someone had been to the farm without her knowledge.

Keahi spoke again, "how are you, Saffron?"

Saffron considered the question, "I'm good," she finally said, "I have a new donkey."

"I know!" Keahi's voice held an edge of laughter, "Tutu told me."

Though Saffron had assumed Mano kept Keahi informed about her, hearing it for certain made Saffron's cheeks grow hot. What else had her adopted grandfather told Keahi?

"Merry Christmas, Saffron," Keahi said, his tone gentle.

"Mele Kalikimaka, Keahi," Saffron replied.

* * *

AFTER HANGING UP WITH KEAHI, Saffron gathered the eggs and fed the chickens. She was heading up the path with the heavy egg cart when a squeaky braying from the direction of the barn drew her attention.

Jasper was ready for his breakfast. Saffron put away the day's egg crop, then hurried back down the path toward the barn. If she didn't get down to the barn, he'd be wandering up to the house to get his scoop of oats.

The barn was warm and damp inside. Morning light made bright rectangles where the beams shone through the open stall doors and warmed the deeper shadows in the corners and in the straw by the old nest boxes.

Jasper was waiting by his feed trough. He gave Saffron an enthusiastic honk as she came in and set to work on his oats as soon as she poured them into the trough.

Saffron stood beside him, stroking the soft fluff of his short mane. He'd saved her life in the waves yesterday. No questions, no demands, just swam over and took her on his back and swam to shore. Saffron couldn't help but love him for that.

She scratched between his big ears. He huffed and grunted —happy sounds. All it took to please him was a scoop of oats and some attention.

One of his ears was trained forward, but the other, Saffron noticed, was swiveled backward, toward the old nest boxes. That seemed strange until, from the corner of her eye, Saffron saw movement there.

She spun, staring over the stall divider at the piles of straw in the dim corner of the barn.

Nothing. All was still. But she had seen something move. She left Jasper in his stall and walked carefully along the row of stalls toward the nest boxes on the far wall.

She felt tension in her shoulders, in her arms. Could it be a mongoose? Rats? A feral hen? Saffron had dealt with all of them before, but they still made her nervous because each different type of intruder posed significant risks to her flock.

Not this intruder, though. As Saffron rounded the corner, as her eyes adjusted to the dimmer light in this part of the barn, as she stepped around a pile of old tack to get a good view of the straw on the floor, she found something that took her breath away. In the center of the straw, sleeping, curled on an old blanket, was Sophie.

Saffron approached quietly. The girl had obviously been here for days—her hair was matted, her cheeks smudged with black island dirt.

She was curled protectively around her protruding belly, like a hen shielding an egg. Saffron felt sorry for her—the straw couldn't be terribly comfortable.

She crouched next to the sleeping woman and laid a gentle hand on her shoulder.

Sophie jumped and, eyes springing open, scrambled backward until she was against the wall, staring and trembling.

Saffron held up her hands, "It's okay, Sophie. It's okay. I'm not going to hurt you."

Sophie's words came hoarse and hushed, "Please, please don't tell anyone I'm here."

Saffron spoke to her in the same tone she used with the hens when they were panicking, "It's okay. I'm here to help. I'm not going to tell anyone."

"They'll find me," Sophie said, tears brimming in her eyes, "I came here because you said you had a chicken farm, and you were so kind to me. But I can't let them find me. They'll put me in jail. I don't want my baby to be born in jail."

Saffron's heart was pounding, "Jail?" She asked gently.

"For killing my husband," Sophie said. Her accent seemed stronger today. The last word came out without an *h*: 'usband.

Saffron tried to keep her voice steady, "Did you kill your husband, Sophie?"

"Yes. I killed him," tears sprang to Sophie's eyes and made tracks down the grime on her cheeks. "I was afraid, so I grabbed Claudette and shoved him away. Then, the next thing I knew, he was dead."

Saffron considered this, "Did you hit him?" she asked.

"No, no, but don't you see? I pushed him away, and he fell. He must have landed wrong—broken his neck or something. I don't know. I couldn't stay. I ran away."

"Did you see him?" Saffron didn't know how to put this delicately, "dead?"

Sophie shook her head, "I saw in the newspaper that he was found dead and that they are looking for me."

Saffron *had* seen him. She had seen his head, had seen the cup. He had not died from a simple fall.

"Sophie, where were you when you pushed him?"

"I was in the photographer's tent with Antoinette and Babette. I told the photographer he could shoot the girls because I wanted to have portraits of them. Hugo was furious when he came into the tent."

Saffron fixed her gaze on the crouching woman, "Sophie, I don't think you killed Hugo."

"What?"

"I was there. I—" Saffron didn't know how much she should say with Sophie's fragile emotional state, "I saw him. He was killed with the trophy—the silver cup."

Sophie's eyelids fluttered briefly, as if she were remembering something, "The cup?" she said slowly.

"Yes," Saffron said, "he was hit in the head."

Sophie's eyes sprang open, and she shifted, pressing her back against the wall of the stall and straining to rise. Saffron moved carefully to her side and took her elbow to help her.

"Then I know who must have done it," Sophie said, "I know who must have killed my husband."

Saffron's eyes asked the question: *who?*

"Margaux Boucher," Sophie's voice was stronger now that she was on her feet—confident, even.

"The judge?"

"More importantly, Hugo's aunt," Sophie ran a hand across her belly.

"Hugo's aunt?" Saffron saw now what connection the two had been talking about.

"His father's sister," Sophie said.

"Why would she kill Hugo?"

"Because he was a threat to her illustrious career," Sophie nearly spat the words. She swayed a little.

"What do you mean?" Saffron needed to know exactly what Sophie was implying.

"If the Companion and Utility Birds Association had discovered that Hugo and Margaux were related, she would have had her judging certification stripped from her."

"But someone said that judges and exhibitors could simply declare their relationship."

"It must be done at the beginning of the competition. Margaux and the other judges had already awarded our birds their Best in Class titles when we found out."

"When you found out what?"

"That Margaux was Hugo's aunt."

"You didn't know before the show?"

Sophie shook her head sadly, "Hugo's father was estranged from his family. It was the birds that did it."

"The birds?"

"Our Faverolles. His family was a leading developer of poultry, cattle, and swine in France for generations. Hugo's father was the family scapegoat—ostracized as a child, told he would never amount to anything. But he had an eye for which birds to combine to improve the stock. When he perfected this line of Faverolles, he kept them a secret from his cruel family, then moved away and started his own farm, entering his birds against his father's in a local show. When he won that show, his family cut him off forever. Hugo was raised never knowing his father's family at all, except as rivals," Sophie was winded from talking so much, and her words came in little pants at the end.

Her breathing made Saffron nervous. She didn't know when Sophie was due, but it seemed possible that it could be anytime.

"Will you come inside?" Saffron asked, patting Sophie's arm reassuringly, "It can't have been comfortable for you in here."

"But I can't," Sophie said, "I have to stay hidden until I know for sure that Margaux killed Hugo, until I can prove it."

"But Sophie, this barn is no place for you to rest!"

"I can't risk being seen by a visitor to your house, or a customer."

Saffron thought for a moment. She couldn't leave the girl here, but she could see she wasn't going to come to Saffron's house, either.

The answer made Saffron smile as it came to her. The cottages.

"Sophie, I have a cottage—three, actually, though one is occupied right now—but I have two that are empty. They're beautiful, and comfortable. Will you stay there?"

"No one will see me?" Sophie said warily.

"No, not if we put you in the Coral Cottage. It's not far from the egg house, and it has a big hibiscus in front of it that shields it from the other cottages." Sophie looked hopeful. Saffron tried to sell it harder, "It has a beautiful view of the mountain behind it, and a big tub, and a brand-new, soft mattress."

Sophie caved, "Okay," she said, "but you won't tell anyone I'm here?" she grasped Saffron's arm, "promise me?"

"I promise," Saffron said, guiding Sophie toward the door and apologizing to the Chief in her mind. She wouldn't pass this info along just yet.

The lemony sunshine outside blinded them for a moment as they shuffled along together, up the path, past the egg house, to the cottage. Saffron eased Sophie onto the couch in the little front room and went straight to the tidy little bathroom to draw her a bath.

Once the tub was filling, Saffron sat on the couch with Sophie.

"You really don't think I killed him?" Sophie asked, her eyes pleading with Saffron.

"No, I don't," Saffron said, "I'm absolutely sure that you shoving him did not kill him."

"And you'll help me prove it? So I can stay out of jail?" Sophie's eyes were full of tears again, and Saffron wanted to comfort her.

"All you need to worry about is resting and getting ready to bring that baby into the world," Saffron said, "I will do everything I can to figure out what happened to Hugo."

"And you'll help me take care of my girls?" Sophie asked.

For a moment, Saffron was confused. Sophie must have seen it in her expression, because she clarified.

"Antoinette, Babette, and Claudette are in your beautiful henhouse," she said. Saffron saw it now. Sophie had brought the chickens with her, not Gavin.

"I didn't know where else to take them, and I couldn't leave them at the mercy of the other exhibitors. Claudette has a medical condition—she has seizures and must have her medication each day."

That explained the poultry pills in Saffron's fridge.

"Don't worry. They're very happy. They'll be safe here,"

Saffron consciously made her tone gentle and reassuring, but the look on Sophie's face quickly changed from relieved to panicked. She scrambled backward on the couch just as Saffron realized that the woman was looking past her, out the wide front window of the cottage.

"It's her!" Sophie hissed.

Saffron turned and followed Sophie's gaze. Outside she saw a string of cars had pulled up. Out of the first one stepped the trim, suited form of Margaux Boucher.

Chapter Twelve

Saffron sprang into action. She stood and stepped to the front window where she closed the blinds before stepping out the door and locking and closing it behind her.

She skirted the cottage and slipped into the egg house without being seen by the growing crowd of people in her yard.

When she emerged through the front doors of the egg house, she tried to keep a smile on her face as she recognized not only Margaux but also another two judges as well as Officer Bradley and Lieutenant Havili from the Honolulu Police Department.

"Well, this is quite the crowd," Saffron said cheerily as she approached them.

"We've come to positively identify the hens for the police department," Margaux said crisply, "If you would be so kind as to show us where they are?"

"Sure," Saffron said, waving a hand toward the egg house, "C'mon." She waited until the group arrived at the egg house doors to introduce herself to the judges.

"I'm Saffron Skye," she said, holding out a hand to a slight man with a pencil mustache.

"Vladimir Korsov from Russia," he said, taking her hand.

Behind him, a lovely woman with eyes the color of driftwood held out her hand. "Perlita Moreno," she offered.

Margaux did not offer her hand. Instead, she sneered. It was an expression Saffron had seen on Hugo's face, and it reinforced her knowledge that Margaux was related to him. She wondered how Sophie and Hugo had found out about the connection.

Part of her felt like blurting that out, like stating it for the officers and other judges to hear, but she held onto the information, biding her time until it might be more useful.

The group had moved into the egg house, and the judges spent the next few minutes inspecting the three French hens. Each had a clipboard. Perlita's seemed to be the hens' records from the show, which the judges were using to positively identify them. Vladimir's clipboard seemed to have the information of the other class champions, and Saffron realized that the judges were also trying to reach a decision on which of the birds that should have been in the show ring would receive the show champion title. Margaux was writing on her clipboard, in neat rows of perfectly even handwriting. It was too small for Saffron to see what she was writing from where she stood.

The officers stood to the side, discussing in low tones the crazy calls they'd gone out on. This one, with all its chickens, seemed to be ranking pretty high.

The judges stepped away and faced the officers, "These are definitely the missing chickens," Margaux stated.

"Okay," Bradley said, "I'll let the chief know."

"Is it still the chief's intention to leave them," Margaux looked around the egg house, her nose wrinkling, "*here?*"

Bradley, a friend of Saffron's, seemed to notice the woman's lack of manners. He squared his shoulders. "Yep," he said, "lucky chickens. Saffron will be looking after them with her own flock."

"I will be happy to take them back to my farm in France," Margaux said, "where they can be housed as show birds ought to be."

Saffron bit her lip. Of course Margaux wanted them back at her own farm. She had been angling for them all along.

Havili shook his head, "with their owners dead and missing, nobody has legal rights to take them anywhere," he said, "Chief says they'll stay here, so they'll stay here."

Margaux made a small, annoyed sound, then strode over to face Saffron. She pulled the top page off her clipboard and held it out.

Saffron took it, but before she could ask, Margaux stated, "It's a strict regimen of care for these fine birds."

It was. Saffron read, in Margaux's neat handwriting, a list of foods and amounts, two paragraphs of grooming instructions, and an hour-by-hour schedule of handling, resting, and exercise for the three French hens.

"Okay," Saffron said, realizing that any argument would be quickly quashed.

"I'm afraid it will have to be," Margaux shook her head, "though this is not the kind of place at all for champion showbirds."

Saffron felt her heartbeat pick up, and a swell of defensiveness rise in her stomach. She wanted to tell Judge Margaux exactly what she thought of that statement, but all that came out was an incredulous, "Excuse me?"

"Oh, don't get me wrong," Margaux hushed her, "it's absolutely the nicest egg house I've ever seen. But these birds should be housed in 2 foot by 2 foot show crates, with wire bottoms to keep them from scratching—which dirties the toenails—and enclosed sides to keep them from mussing each other's feathers. It's obvious these have been," she wrinkled her nose again, *"foraging."*

Saffron was no lifelong chicken expert, but she'd lived with over a hundred hens for some time now, and she knew a thing or two about them.

"Chickens love foraging," she said, and this time, before Margaux could reply, she cut the judge off, "they're made for it. And they're flock animals. They shouldn't be separated; they need a natural pecking order and the company of other hens to thrive."

"You're telling me my business?" Margaux's voice was shrill.

"I'm telling you that if you want a perfect chicken, buy a ceramic one for your shelf. I have dozens of perfect chickens in my house—a collection of decor gathered over several generations, so I know about them. You should buy yourself some nice bookends or a watercolor print of a chicken, buy yourself some hen-and-rooster salt and pepper shakers, or a cookie jar shaped like a Rhode Island Red that crows when you open it. But don't try to make a real, living, breathing animal into a piece of art. Don't try to comb and tease and clip and shine a hen into a statue. They're *alive*, they're *aware*, and they're *individuals*. Some of them are quirky, like me, some of them are snobs, like you."

Margaux sucked in a sharp breath. Saffron knew she should stop talking, knew she should maybe even apologize, but she didn't. She just kept going.

"I think your poultry show was beautiful—I think it teaches people about chickens and maybe makes them appreciate these utility birds a little more. But I think you've got it all wrong," she waved a hand at the other judges, "you've *all* got it all wrong. I wouldn't waste your time finding flaws in every bird you see, holding them up to 'the standard of perfection.' I'd spend my time finding the beauty in each individual, in appreciating them on their own unique terms, for their own unique qualities. If one hen has a little black on her hackle feathers, that just makes it easier to call her by name when you bring her favorite treat. If another has a crooked toe, that just means you can recognize where she's been scratching. You're looking at them all wrong, see—their unique features aren't flaws, they are strengths."

"And if a life in a 2" x 2" cage seems like a good place for a chicken, where they can't slurp up a centipede or give themselves a nice dirt bath or squabble over a juicy beetle with their flock mates, then think of your life without ever walking on the beach, or swimming in the ocean, or eating a delicious meal with your friends. Picture your own life without chocolate cake or laughing until you get the hiccups, or hiking to the top of a mountain to see the sunrise."

The judges' mouths were hanging open. It was likely no one had ever talked to them like this before.

"I, for one, am glad the girls get to stay here a little longer. I'm going to enjoy watching them live their lives as chickens are meant to, even if it's just for a few days."

When the flow of her words dried up, nobody said anything. The judges, stunned, filed out of the egg house and wandered up the path toward the cars they'd arrived in.

Havili followed them, but Bradley came over to Saffron and patted her shoulder, "You told them, huh?"

Saffron's cheeks were burning with emotion, "Some people are so blind," she said.

Lightening the mood, Bradley asked, "Have you really laughed so hard you got the hiccups?"

"Of course I have," Saffron said, "haven't you?"

A smile crept across Bradley's face, and the light of reminiscence touched his eyes, "Not for a long time," he said.

* * *

It was late that evening when Saffron, lounging in her pajamas, was struck with a horrific thought—December nineteenth was nearly over and she hadn't gotten today's malasadas.

She was not going to miss out on one day of the holiday event of the year. She jumped in her car and drove straight to Juno's Bakery.

Though it was late, Maika'i was buzzing. Rental cars clogged Holoholo Street—mainlanders here for the holiday—and the shops along the side of the road all tossed cheery yellow light out onto the boardwalk. They were still open, and Saffron's arm got tired from waving at all the locals she saw going in and out of the shops, their arms laden with packages.

There was only one light on, in the back, when Saffron pulled up, and it went out as Theo let himself out the back door and headed for his car.

"I missed it, then?" Saffron called to him as she climbed out and gave him a wave.

Theo's smile lit up the parking lot, "Of course not!" he said, reaching into the back seat of his car and extracting a box.

As she approached he tried to hand it to her, "Last box of today's flavor," he said. "You take it."

Saffron waved him off, "no, no, I'm sure you were taking that home for yourself. You've had a busy day—a busy week. And I can't eat a whole box of malasadas before tomorrow morning, when I'll be back for tomorrow's flavor anyway."

Theo wouldn't hear of it. He popped the box open, "I'm not leaving with all of them. If you won't take the box, at least taste one—you have to try all the flavors."

Saffron relented and took the warm pastry from his hands. She could smell today's flavor as soon as she touched it. The warmth of cinnamon filled the night air and mixed with the sweetness of the plumeria blossoms that drooped over their heads.

It was like biting into a warm cinnamon roll, except the experience was enhanced by the richness of the malasada pastry and the lightest brush of fresh lemon zest in the cream-cheese filling.

It would have been a tragedy to miss this culinary creation. Theo laughed when she told him so.

"Wait till you try our next flavor," he said.

"I'll get here earlier tomorrow," Saffron promised.

* * *

Driving home, the taste of cinnamon still warming every breath, Saffron thought of Sophie.

She had checked on the pregnant woman after the judges had left and had taken her some extra clothes.

For once, Saffron had been glad she wasn't a small person. Her clothes had fit Sophie—belly and all—quite comfortably. Sophie had finished her bath and was looking much more at ease. Her only concern now was her hens. She was relieved to hear that they would be staying at the farm until further notice.

"It's strange," she'd said, "but they are very precious to me. They've been the best friends I've had in years, since, since I stopped singing with the girls."

"You were in a group?" Saffron asked.

"Yes, when I was first married, and we moved to the village. Two ladies and I," her eyes were wistful, "We sang at local luncheons and community events, nothing too grand."

"But you stopped?"

Sophie winced. A fearful look crossed her features, "Yes. We couldn't continue. Hugo wouldn't stand for it."

"It must have been so lonely for you," Saffron said.

"Very. The farm was isolated, and besides that, because of the feuds, Hugo was very paranoid. He thought everyone was a spy wanting to steal his father's line of Faverolles. I couldn't socialize, or even talk to people on the phone, because he was so convinced that they were out to get his secrets."

"I'm sorry," Saffron said.

"I never should have fallen for him," Sophie said, "my mother warned against it. She saw something in him she didn't like," Sophie sighed, "I wish I could talk to her now."

Saffron felt a pang of empathy. Her own mother had died, and she knew the feeling of being adrift, of having no one to share your burdens with that really cared. She'd felt that way until she came to Maika'i and found a whole new family waiting for her.

"How long has she been gone?" Saffron asked.

"Gone?" Sophie seemed puzzled, then shook her head, "Oh, no, my mother isn't dead."

"Oh," it was Saffron's turn to be confused, "I'm sorry, I just assumed when you said you wished you could talk to her…"

"It's another casualty of Hugo's ambition," Sophie said, "And of my own foolishness and pride. I haven't talked to her for years, not since Hugo and I married and left for France."

That was even sadder, Saffron thought, "Is she still in the… where did you say you were from? The west?"

"The *Mid*west," Sophie corrected her, "Yes, she's still there, I think. She is still teaching at FIHS."

"FIHS?" Saffron asked.

"The French Immersion High School I graduated from," Sophie said, "She was a teacher there, and we used to eat lunch together every day in the cafeteria."

A tear slipped out of the outside corner of Sophie's eye, and she turned her head away. Saffron recognized the gesture —Sophie was trying to hide her sadness.

"You can be sad about it," she said softly, "It's okay to cry."

That had opened the floodgates, and Sophie had cried. She had cried hard for almost half an hour. When the sobs died down to sniffles, though, Saffron could tell it had done her good.

Saffron had left her with a refrigerator full of food and a cheap cell phone she'd picked up at Jan Lin's cell phone store in case Sophie needed help, "You could call your mom on this, if you want," Saffron had suggested gently.

"She won't want to hear from me now," Sophie had said, "But thank you for the phone."

"Call me if you need anything," Saffron said, "unless you go into labor—then, call 911."

Saffron didn't know much about having babies, but she did know that Sophie's baby seemed likely to come any moment. She wished that human babies were as predictable as avian ones. Exactly thirty days and the goslings had begun their hatch. Twenty-one days for chicken eggs.

The evening was warm and sweet, a perfect Hawaiian night. Saffron pulled to the side of the road next to one of her favorite beaches: Moonmist Beach. It was a little half-moon stretch of sand where the waves met the shore in a soft spray that made the air glimmer at the edge of the water.

Especially on a night like this, when the moon shone down almost full, but not quite, it was ethereal. The sparkling sand, the glittering air, the soft hush of the waves reaching up the sand, then retreating, then reaching again.

The night air was light here, soft and sweet with the taste of jasmine and salt. Because of the sea spray, it was degrees cooler than it had been back in Maika'i. It was a peaceful place, free from the bustle that seemed to be engulfing the little town just now, as tourists arrived to spend their holidays on the island and locals scrambled around buying their last-minute gifts.

Here, in the cool air, in the quiet hush of the water, in the twinkling of the stars overhead, Saffron could feel Christmas.

It was only a little over five days away, which meant her

party was only four days away, but she didn't feel panicky. Almost everything was ready, and the night's calm had seeped into her soul.

She wished everyone could feel this calm. Sophie's life was in an uproar just now—her husband dead, her baby on the way, estranged from her mother—and peace seemed far away for the young woman.

But that was the promise of Christmas, wasn't it? Peace on Earth and peace in people's hearts. Saffron hoped that Christmas would work its magic on Sophie.

Chapter Thirteen

Saffron woke on December 20th to a pounding on her door.

She'd been in one of those deep, hard sleeps that took a moment to wake from, so when she staggered to the door and saw, on her lanai, a large white cow and calf, she wasn't quite sure she was awake.

"Hello?" she called. The cow blinked slowly, and the calf came tentatively forward to lick Saffron's hand with a rough tongue.

"Brought your cow," came a raspy voice from somewhere on the other side of the big creature.

"Dylan?"

"It's Wyatt," the other Sawyer brother stepped out from behind the cow and stood scratching the head of the little calf.

"Oh, hi Wyatt," Saffron remembered now that Bradley had ordered the Sawyers to provide her a cow for the nativity, "thanks," she managed.

"Where do you want 'em?" Wyatt asked.

"This way," she said, grabbing a pair of boots and trekking, in her pajamas, toward the barn.

As she opened the big doors, she was glad Sophie wasn't in here anymore. She also realized it must have been Sophie who was propping open the barn door—Jasper hadn't gotten out this morning.

Wyatt looked over the barn with a critical eye. "It'll do," he finally declared. He led the cow and her calf to a stall and unclipped the rope from her halter before closing the stall's half-door. "Although if Betsy were here, she'd throw a fit about putting champion cows in a barn like this."

"I'm sure she would," Saffron said, "But I'm planning on cleaning it up in the next couple days."

"The cows ain't gonna mind," he said, then, "Always too fancy, Betsy." There was less bitterness in his tone than Saffron would have expected.

The little calf frolicked in the straw and stuck her nose out the outside door into the fenced pasture to watch Jasper grazing.

"I've got feed and instructions for them in the truck," Wyatt said, "But the main thing is, don't let my brother get ahold of that calf."

Saffron felt her eyes widen, "Wait. Is this the calf you've been fighting about?"

Wyatt ducked his head, "Yup," he said, "Bradley wants it on neutral ground while he waits to hear back from the judge about whose it rightfully is. So he says it should come over here for the live nativity."

It made Saffron nervous to have the responsibility of a prize calf, even if it was only for a few days, but Wyatt's mind was made up. He was heading back to his truck and wouldn't hear of taking the cow and calf with him.

Wyatt hauled a few days' worth of hay and grain into the barn, then met Saffron on the porch with a sheaf of papers. A quick glance told her that these were instructions on what and when to feed her new residents.

"I'll be back to pick them up the day after Christmas," Wyatt said.

"Are you coming to the Christmas Eve party?" Saffron asked.

"Probably not. I'm sure Dylan and Betsy will be there, and I'm not particularly inclined to run into them."

Saffron sensed a current of sadness under the bitter tone in Wyatt's voice. She wondered if he missed his brother.

"You guys had some good times, huh?" she asked.

"Sure. Our childhood was great. I was always followin' him. One time, when I was about seven and he was about nine, we got treed by this whole passel of wild pigs," he pointed back toward town, "in a grove just over there. I was sure we were gonna die—those pigs were furious. They were tearing up the ground underneath us and the trunk of the tree with their tusks, just in a frenzy." Wyatt had a faraway look in his eyes, and Saffron tried to picture him as a little boy. His face was weathered, his steel-gray hair cut short and bristly on top—it was hard to imagine him young. "I was just bawling because I was so scared, and I could barely hang onto the branch. Dylan must have figured out I was going to fall, cause he started barking like crazy. He had this perfect impression he used to use to bring the cows in, sounded like a big old hound dog, and wouldn't you know, those pigs froze and cocked their heads and hightailed it outta there," Wyatt shook his head, and the ghost of a smile flitted across the corners of his mouth, "It sure was somethin'. And you know, he never teased me for cryin'. Just got me down and cleaned me up with his shirttail and put his arm around me and took me home." The sadness in his eyes was pronounced now, and a long silence followed his words.

Saffron finally spoke. "You know," she said slowly, "It is Christmas. It's a good time for reconciling."

Wyatt flinched like she'd slapped him out of his reverie, "You and that preacher," he said bitterly, "always wantin' everybody to get along. Well, the road runs both ways, you know. It's not my job to apologize. I ain't done anything," Wyatt snorted, "Won't be no reconcilin' until Dylan gets his act together and apologizes for all he's done." The answer came so quickly, and sounded so practiced, that it was obvious to Saffron that what Wyatt was telling her was what he had said to himself, in his mind, countless times.

She didn't know what to say. Wyatt didn't seem to expect her to say anything, though. He just waved a hand toward the barn and cautioned, "Remember, don't let Dylan take them."

Saffron called to him as he stepped off the porch, "Wait! What am I supposed to do if he comes for them?"

Wyatt turned around and looked at her contemplatively. "You got a shotgun?" he asked. It took Saffron a moment to realize he was completely serious.

"No, I don't have a shotgun," she said, trying to keep her voice at a normal pitch. Still, incredulity had seeped in.

"I can bring one by," Wyatt nodded.

Saffron held up her hands, "No, no, no need. If he comes by, I'll figure something out."

Wyatt shrugged, "Up to you," he said.

That was all he said. Without a 'goodbye' or a 'see you later,' he got in his truck and drove away.

Saffron sighed. *What a waste,* she thought as she walked inside with the papers he'd given her, *to have a sibling and not even speak to him.*

Saffron had, when she was eight, wanted a sibling more than anything in the world. She had begged her mother for a sister or brother, had prayed for one, had written to Santa Claus asking that he leave one under the tree. Even now, when she saw Nik and Naia together, or watched the Tucker children tumble over each other and share tastes of their malasadas from sticky fingers, or saw any of the dozens of siblings in town, she felt a dull pang that she would never really know that kind of relationship: someone who had known her all her life, who had watched her grow and seen her change, who carried in their heart a picture of her as a child, an echo of her adolescent voice, an understanding of the challenges she'd faced in her life. She imagined someone who would know that the scar on her right knee came from a bike accident when she was seven—not because she had told them, but because they'd been there to run get her mom. She imagined someone who had been there when she walked across the stage at her high-school graduation, when she tore open the acceptance letter from the university.

But she had never wished harder for a sibling than the night she held her mother's hand and said goodbye. That night she longed for someone to share that pain, to understand the loss she felt, to keep her from being all alone in the world.

The memory of it brought stinging tears to her eyes, and she wiped them away with a rough hand. Anger made her chest tight—here Wyatt and Dylan had perfectly good siblings and they were just throwing that away. She would never understand people.

On the kitchen table lay the instructions for the three French hens which Margaux had left for her. She picked them up and slid the cow's care sheets underneath. Might as well keep them all in the same place, she thought. She felt like a zookeeper: feeding schedules, special diets, various species. She'd only ever had to worry about her hens before.

As she laid the papers down, something caught her eye. The page on top, where Margaux had written what she should feed the Faverolles, how much, and how often, looked irregular somehow.

It was a subtle color shift in the ink—something someone else might never have noticed. Saffron peered more closely at them.

The pen strokes on certain parts of the page were slightly more navy than midnight blue. Why would that be?

Saffron held the papers up to the light from the kitchen window and turned them back and forth.

It was only at one particular angle that she could see it: ghosted writing on the paper underneath the instructions.

Saffron ran a finger over the marks. They were indentions, probably where someone had written on a page atop this one and the pen's tip had pressed through, leaving lines with no ink. When Margaux had written the instructions on it, the ink from her pen had crossed over the ghosted words, causing the shifts in the ink color that had caught Saffron's eye.

Saffron tried to make out the words, but the paper was too cluttered with Margaux's instructions.

Saffron sighed heavily. It probably didn't matter anyway.

But she couldn't give up. She went to the drawer and extracted a pencil. Carefully, she laid the paper on the table and pulled the broad side of the pencil lead gently across the surface of the paper. An 'o' appeared, and her heart beat faster.

More shading with the side of the lead and more letters

appeared. Soon Saffron could see words emerging. But not words she could read. They were in French.

That made sense. Margaux was French, after all. Maybe it was something mundane: a grocery list or an appointment reminder. But Saffron had a hunch that it was something more important. More than that, she had a hunch it was something she'd seen before.

She squinted at the words, shaded like a sketch in charcoal and graphite gray. Three words drew her attention like a beacon: *Trois poules françaises.*

Saffron bit her lip and raced down the hall to her bedroom. She dug out the board shorts she wore the day after she'd visited the poultry show. For once she was glad she'd put off doing the laundry. In the pocket of the shorts she found the scrap of paper she'd found stuck to her Christmas slippah.

Her heart skipped when she laid the scrap of paper atop the page. Doing so confirmed her suspicion: the written words on the scrap and the ghosted writing on the instruction page were identical.

Saffron squinted at the rest of the page, trying to make sense of it. She wished she could read French.

She looked up in frustration, out the back door of the bungalow. There, in the lemony light of mid-morning, she saw the little cottages.

Sophie. Sophie could help her.

Saffron hesitated at the top of the lanai steps. She wasn't sure it was fair to ask a widow to translate a piece of evidence related to her husband's murder. What if there was something horrible written on the page? Something about Hugo?

But Sophie needed this mystery solved as much as Saffron did. Maybe more. And they were on a timeline. That baby was going to come, and there would be no hiding Sophie away then. She needed to be able to live freely, move around, and find her own life after Hugo.

The sun was hot on Saffron's back as, several minutes later, she sat in the sunny little kitchen space of the cottage and watched Sophie's face.

Sophie was reading the paper. Saffron fidgeted, trying not to guess what Sophie was discovering.

Her face was inscrutable—the sheen of her pale eyebrows level and the muscles around her mouth neither tense nor relaxed. Saffron couldn't even tell anything from her usual barometer: the underlying colors that surged beneath the skin, revealing emotions before people even knew they were having them. Sophie's face showed only the warm pink glow that Saffron assumed was caused by her pregnancy.

Sophie laid the paper down on the table and looked up at Saffron.

"Well," she said, "that's interesting."

"What is it?" Saffron leaned across the table, unable to contain her curiosity.

"It was a contract," Sophie said, "For the sale of *trois poules françaises*," she raised her eyebrows expectantly, as if Saffron would respond with shock.

"Which means?" Saffron prompted.

"Three French hens," Sophie said, her voice trembling with anger, or maybe fear, "I told you she wanted our birds."

Saffron sat back, processing the information. The sun through the window was hot on the top of her head, "Margaux wanted to buy them, wrote up a contract . . ." she was trying to imagine what happened next.

Apparently, so was Sophie, "I knew it! She wanted our hens, wrote up a contract, and I'll bet that when she showed it to Hugo, he refused and tore it up. Then, she killed him because he wouldn't sell them to her."

Saffron didn't say that she'd heard them arguing. She tried to fit what she had heard with Sophie's scenario. It was possible. But who had Hugo made angry? And what had that person stood to gain by revealing that Hugo and Margaux were related?

"How did you find out?" Saffron asked, "that Margaux was Hugo's aunt?"

"A note," Sophie closed her eyes, "left on one of the hen's cages. Hugo thought it came from Gavin Godfrey. But we don't know for sure."

"I heard them arguing," Saffron told Sophie. "Just before —" she tried to be gentle, "just before Hugo died."

"You heard Margaux and Hugo?"

Saffron nodded.

"So it could have been her?"

Saffron nodded again, "she was afraid that if she picked any of your birds for show champion, then someone would find out they were related and she would lose her credentials."

"That is reasonable," Sophie said, "and it's a perfect motive for her to kill my husband."

"Is there anyone else you can think of? That might have wanted to hurt Hugo?"

Sophie leveled her gaze at Saffron, "You met my husband," she said evenly, "what do you think?"

Saffron remembered the glowering eyes, the cruel scowl. There was no doubt that Hugo Leblanc had made himself some enemies.

Saffron thought through her list: Judge Margaux, Gavin Godfrey, even Sophie herself used to be a suspect. All of them with means, motive, and opportunity.

But who else had Hugo infuriated, excoriated, humiliated? Who else had he intimidated that might want him dead?

Saffron thought about that question later, as she drove into town and stopped at Juno's.

The line seemed exceptionally long this time, and she was happy to slip into the back door where Theo met her with a grin.

"Hang on just a minute and I'll get you some," he said.

He was working the back, as usual, while his uncle, Juno, took orders at the front.

Theo was skilled at the art of making malasadas. He took the little balls of dough and dropped them in the oil, then, while they were frying, used a huge pastry bag full of bright orange custard to fill several dozen that were waiting on the counter.

He dropped them into a big flat pan of tangerine sugar, shook the pan to roll the donuts around, and scooped them out three at a time, filling a box in seconds.

Saffron was grinning as he handed it to her, "I recognize this flavor," she said, "It was a family tradition at my house— my mom always put something special in the toe of my stocking: a Christmas orange."

"That's right—we came up with it by thinking of that tradition!"

Saffron could see Theo was busy, so she said goodbye and carried her box of Malasadas across the street to the beach.

The shadows of the palm trees were the color of plums. Settling into the warm sand, Saffron pulled out a malasada and bit into it.

The custard inside was sweet and creamy, an orange-vanilla flavor. She was surprised to taste, with the dyed sugar on the outside, a hint of sour and salty tastes. They complemented the sweet filling perfectly, bringing up the bright tones of the orange and the soothing vanilla flavor. Saffron knew what she was tasting: li hing powder, a fascinating Hawaiian tradition that she'd been quite surprised by when she first came to the island.

Li hing was a powder, made from pickled plums, which Saffron had first tasted when it was sprinkled on fresh pineapple at one of the Empress' luncheons. It gave the pineapple a tang that Saffron recognized now. It was popular here, and she'd since tasted it on mangoes, papayas, shave ice, and a dozen other foods. On these malasadas, it made the sweet doughnut even sweeter by its sourness.

Saffron thought about that. It was a great metaphor for life. Without the sour tones, how would you know what was sweet? Without the bad, how would you know what was good?

She finished off the treat and laid back, stretching her body in the sand. The hens, the egg line, the Christmas Eve party, the constant stream of visitors this week—all had worn her out.

She let her stress sink into the soft beach beneath her. She felt the heat, stored up from the day's rays on the sand, radiating into her back and her legs through her sundress. She pulled her wide-brimmed hat over her eyes and stared at the little squares of light that peeked through its woven crown.

Beyond it, through the squares, Saffron saw an incomplete picture of palm trees and bushes. A bright red square caught her attention. It was half an 'i'iwi bird, what mainlanders called a scarlet honeycreeper. It was brilliant red, with black wings and a curved beak. Saffron could only see its head and one shoulder. The rest of the brilliant bird was lost to the weave of her hat. The whole scene was like that: half images, bits and pieces of the world around her, the rest obscured.

This case was the same, Saffron thought. Just when she figured out one piece—where the Faverolles were, where Sophie had gone—she realized another was missing. It was like a puzzle that came with too few pieces in the box. There was a picture, she was sure, but whether she could put it together or not was uncertain.

Hugo had been murdered, there was no doubt of that. Someone had hit him hard enough with the silver cup to kill him.

Hugo had enemies—enemies in the show ring, enemies among the judges, enemies in his own family.

He had been power-mad, blind to anything but his birds and their supposed superiority.

Lying there, feeling the warmth all around her, Saffron felt a little better about the whole hopeless situation. That was one of the best things about Hawaii: it was hard to worry too long about anything in the tropical sunshine.

Christmas was nearly here. Saffron thought again about the differences between Washington, DC Christmas and Maika'i Christmas. Ukulele carols instead of handbell ones. The scent of plumeria and jasmine instead of coal smoke. Soft breezes instead of bitter winds. Saffron stroked her hands across the sand and moved her legs, making a sand-angel.

There were beautiful things about both places, but for this moment, there was no place Saffron would rather be than right here.

She thought about Keahi. She'd never spent Christmas time in Boston, but it was farther north than DC, and must be even colder. She wondered if he was homesick.

She should, she knew, be thinking about Nik. He was her official boyfriend. But she knew Nik, and she knew he wasn't homesick. He was, most likely, dropping over the crest of a monster wave in Barbados right now, home and Christmas the farthest things from his mind.

But Keahi was connected with home. He was connected in a deep way with Maika'i, its shores and scents, its sunbeams and breezes. He loved the people of this little town, too, and she knew it must be hard for him to be so far away. He would be missing them.

Just for a moment there in the warm sand, Saffron let herself miss him, too.

Chapter Fourteen

"I won't sing that!" Little Harley Tucker was facing off with Pastor Vaughn when Saffron walked down the path to the barn.

The farm was a hive of activity this morning, with the whole children's choir doing a run-through of their program, Slate and Mano helping the Walking Wonders decorate, and the last of the animals arriving. Saffron had just put away two doves and a little family of sheep when she came upon the standoff. The little girl was dressed in denim overalls and a red shirt. Her hair was in pigtails and her hands were on her hips.

"What do you mean you won't sing it?" Pastor Vaughn asked. His hands were spread wide in a gesture of placation, but there was an edge of annoyance in his voice, "you're the soloist. Silent Night is the pinnacle of the program."

"I don't know what a pinnacle is," Harley said, sticking her chin out stubbornly, "but it's rude and I won't sing it."

"Rude?" Pastor Vaughn's breath ran out before the word did, "How is Silent Night rude?"

"My mother says we don't talk about the shapes of people's bodies. Every body is beautiful."

That seemed a solid philosophy. Saffron stopped to observe. Pastor Vaughn seemed both perplexed and astounded.

Harley must have taken his expression to mean that he needed more explanation. She gestured at Saffron, "you know, like how Miss Skye is bigger than most ladies, but we don't say that."

Pastor Vaughn shot Saffron an apologetic look, but Saffron just stifled a smile. She was glad she was comfortable with her own figure. It made the little girl's comment endearing rather than searing.

Harley went on, "I'm not saying rude things about Jesus' mother, either."

"Okay, can you tell me what in the world it is you don't want to sing?"

"No."

Pastor Vaughn let out a long sigh.

"I don't want to say it out loud."

Saffron stepped in. She knew the Tuckers well, and was sure Harley would feel comfortable with her, "Harley, would you whisper it to me? Just tell me in my ear what you're worried about singing?"

Harley narrowed her eyes, weighing in her mind the morality of whispering rude things rather than singing them. She apparently judged it less of a sin, because she waved Saffron over with a nod.

Saffron knelt in the sand beside the little girl and Harley bent down to whisper in her ear.

"Just because a lady had a baby," Harley whispered, "doesn't mean we should call her round."

"Round?" Saffron blinked.

"Yes, you know, the 'round yon virgin mother'. Can't I just say yon virgin mother?"

Saffron fought back a giggle. *All is calm, all is bright, round yon virgin.* So that's where the problem was.

Harley was still talking, "It's rude to call a lady round. My mom hates that."

Belle Tucker was expecting again, and she was definitely round just now. Saffron could see how she'd be sensitive to that term.

"And she hates other words, too," Harley wasn't whispering anymore. With every example, her voice got louder, "big, and enormous, and huge," the little girl's hands left her hips and traced ever-widening circles in the air around her with each word, "and gargantuan, and colossal and humongous. But people keep saying them anyway. I don't want to say that about Jesus' mom."

Pastor Vaughn was silently pleading with Saffron, who was concentrating all her energy on keeping her expression concerned and understanding and keeping herself from laughing out loud.

"Just a little mix-up, Pastor," Saffron said, trying to sound reassuring. She spoke to Harley loudly so that he could hear the explanation, "I think it's so great that you don't want to say bad things about people. I wish more people were like that, Harley. It would make the world a better place if we had more Harleys in it."

The little girl glowed under the praise.

"But you don't have to worry about this one," Saffron said, "It's not the mother who's round, it's the light."

Harley's expression was suspicious, "The . . . light?"

"Right. 'Round is an old-fashioned way of saying *a-round*: the light is a-round the virgin," Saffron sang a few bars, aware that her pitch was far from perfect, "All is calm, all is bright, AROUND yon virgin mother and child," she traced a circle in the air.

Harley was quiet for a few seconds. Her eyes were narrowed as she processed that possibility, "All is bright around the virgin?"

"Yep," Saffron said.

"What does yon mean?" Harley asked, covering all her bases.

"It means that one over there—like yonder. Around that virgin over there, who's a mother, and her child."

"Baby Jesus."

"Right," Saffron smiled, "You want to try singing it and see how it sounds when you think of the light around the mother and child?"

"Okay," Harley said. She started to sing, and Pastor Vaughn scrambled to catch up to her.

The child's voice was, in a word, angelic. It was pure and sweet, and only slightly too intense when she sang, boldly, "All is bright, around yon virgin mother and child."

Harley stopped, satisfied, and nodded, "Okay," she said, "around yon virgin is fine."

Pastor Vaughn looked so relieved Saffron thought he might fall over. She left them to continue their practice.

Saffron stopped at the snack table that the Walking Wonders had set up on the lanai and snagged a finger sandwich. She saw that Mano and her father had also left something on the table—light purple boxes of Juno's malasadas.

What would today's flavor be? How could they keep thinking of new Christmas flavors?

Cracking open a box, Saffron inhaled the sweet, heavy smell of the cookies her German neighbor used to bring down to her apartment in DC when she was a little girl: hazelnuts.

The filling today was rich and chocolatey, with the smokey flavor of the nuts and crunchy little crushed nuts on the outside.

"Good, huh?" Mano said, reaching past her for one.

She hugged him with her free arm, "Delicious, and even sweeter since they were hand-delivered from town."

Mano, characteristically, glanced away, deflecting the

credit. Saffron was about to tell him how wonderful he was when a shrill voice interrupted her.

"You just want everything your way!"

Saffron turned to see Mrs. Claus stalking up the stairs of the lanai, followed closely by a fuming Jan Lin.

Apparently the decorating crew was having some challenges, too.

Mrs. Claus spun around, standing in exactly the same position as Harley had been, hands on hips, with her chin stuck out stubbornly, "I just think it should be done properly, or not done at all."

"Well, you can be the one to tell Saffron then," Jan Lin faced off with Mrs. Claus.

Saffron's gaze was glued to them. Mrs. Claus seemed to be trying to make herself larger, puffing up, sticking her elbows out and her shoulders wide. Jan, on the other hand, drew inward, crossing her arms, planting her feet, like an immovable pillar.

"You really think that the garlands should spread out from the canoe's landing site? That they shouldn't be placed in straight lines that lead to the barn? You'll have people wandering off all over the farm. You have to *direct* them," Jan said firmly.

"People know they're going to the barn. They don't have to be herded like cattle."

"Let them roam where they want and you'll have chaos. I think we all remember how well that kind of approach worked with your children."

Saffron held her breath. What a cruel thing to say. Jan was referring to Mrs. Claus' shiftless son and daughter, who had not turned out well.

Mrs. Claus was visibly upset, but to her credit, she did not strike back. Her words were clipped and her voice brimming with tears when she finally spoke.

"Jan, we all know how Sheng's leaving has affected you. We've been through it. It's difficult when they leave the nest. But that's no reason to be . . ." Mrs. Claus took a shuddering breath, "mean."

Jan was ready for a fight, Saffron could tell. What she wasn't ready for was Mrs. Claus' firm but honest approach. She looked around at the Walking Wonders, who had gathered on the lanai around the two women.

"I'm fine," she said, "I'm not upset. I'm fine. I'm glad Sheng is off living his own life at college. Glad that he can go and be successful and," her voice cracked, and Saffron saw a crystal tear race down the woman's cheek, "happy."

Jan turned then and hurried away from the scene, along the side of the house, toward the back yard.

Everyone else stood still and silent for a long moment before they moved. When they did, it was the Wonders, rushing in around Betty Claus like a tidal wave of compassion, reassuring her that her children's mistakes were not her own, exclaiming about Jan's thoughtlessness, comforting and clucking like Saffron's hens.

Mrs. Claus' eyes were brimming with unfallen tears, "It's funny she would mention my children. I just heard from Joey this morning."

There was general interest among the Wonders, and an anxious concern that Saffron knew stemmed from the fact that whenever Joey called, the news was bad.

"Yes," Mrs. Claus continued, "He's not coming home for Christmas of course, that would be difficult since he's in jail again. But they let him call home for the holiday, and he said he's starting to take some college classes in prison."

"That's wonderful," Tilley Allbey squeezed Mrs. Claus' arm, "steps in the right direction, Betty!"

Mrs. Claus smiled gratefully, "Baby steps," she said wryly. She took a moment to calm herself, then waved the ladies away, "Oh, we just have to remember that this is a difficult time for her," she said, "We've all been there."

The Wonders murmured in response. They'd seen their children grow and fly away, too. Saffron was, as always, impressed by their understanding.

Mrs. Claus' reaction to the confrontation was such a contrast to Wyatt's approach yesterday. He was holding on to the offenses, Mrs. Claus was letting them go. It only took one look at her rosy cheeks and the twinkle creeping back into her eyes to see which approach brought more happiness.

Saffron felt an arm around her shoulders and turned to see her father, "Emotions can be high around the holidays," he said.

Saffron looked at him with new eyes. He'd been in the witness protection program for thirty years, ever since she was small. They'd missed so many Christmases.

"Were holidays hard for you?" she asked, laying a hand on his arm.

He smiled, but his eyes were sad, "Oh yeah," he said, "I'd wander through the department stores picking out presents for you and your mom. Of course I never actually bought them. I couldn't send them to you without putting you in danger, so I just dreamed about it."

"Did you have happy holidays?" she asked, "Or anyone to spend the holiday with?" She'd often pictured him with another family, cutting their turkey, unwrapping their presents, but when he'd come back and she'd found out why he was really away, she'd realized there was no other daughter, no other wife that he'd spent those years with.

"Sometimes," he said, "A neighbor would invite me to have dinner with their family, or a local church would have an open-invitation party where I'd spend an evening. I went to concerts, you know, that sort of thing."

It made Saffron's heart hurt to think of Slate alone somewhere on Christmas.

"Did you?" he asked, "have happy holidays?"

Saffron nodded, swallowing a lump in her throat, "Mom made them special," she said, suddenly very lonesome for her mother. "She had to work the other days, but Christmas Day we always got to spend together." she smiled, remembering, "she'd make turkey and dressing and mashed potatoes and yams—way too much for just the two of us—and even pie. We'd freeze what we didn't eat, and we had those leftovers all the way through January sometimes. And she loved to go look at the Christmas lights, you know, around town. So about a week before Christmas, we'd pack sandwiches and a thermos of hot cocoa and go ride the city busses through the neighborhoods to see their lights." Saffron felt a little laugh rise at the same time she felt hot tears spill down her cheeks, "We got so many funny looks, just riding around like tourists late into the evening. There was this one bus driver who really got it, though, named Al. And whenever we could, we got on his bus, and he took all kinds of detours to go down streets with more lights, just for us. When mom asked him if he'd get in trouble for it, he just laughed and said, 'it's Christmas. Everybody got to slow down a little and see the lights.'" Saffron wiped her fingertips across her cheeks, "I never forgot that. To me, that's what Christmas really is—that feeling I got when I realized that he was going out of his way to do something kind for us."

Slate's eyes were wet, too, "I'm glad someone was taking care of my girls," he said.

Mano cleared his throat, "That's the spirit of Kalikimaka. It's not so different from aloha, either."

Saffron blinked. That was true. The island philosophy of aloha was love, respect, kindness, peace, and harmony.

Mrs. Claus was rallying. She and the other Wonders had taken a break to have some lunch.

Saffron thought of Jan, "I'll be right back," she said, reaching for an extra malasada and heading in the direction Jan had gone.

She found Jan in the egg house, leaning against the counter in the work area at the front, tears running down her cheeks.

"Hey," Saffron gave the woman a hug. She was slight, and Saffron felt like she might break her, but Jan hugged her back, tight.

"I'm sorry about that scene," Jan said into Saffron's shoulder, "I don't even know why I cared so much. It doesn't matter where the garland goes. I've just been so—emotional lately." A little sob shook her, "I didn't expect to miss him so much. And I guess I was counting on him coming back for Christmas more than I thought I was."

"The first Christmas apart is the hardest," Saffron said, her own eyes stinging as she remembered the Christmas after her mom died.

Jan pulled back and looked her in the eye, "I'm sorry I haven't been more thoughtful," she said, "I feel like I'm looking at the world in a whole new way."

"That's the gift that pain give us," Saffron said, searching Jan's face, "perspective." She held out the malasada, and Jan took it gratefully, "and compassion."

A squeaky little honk caught their attention, and Jan walked down the aisle to where the awkward little goslings were paddling in their swimming pool.

"Oh!" She cried, "they are so charming!"

Saffron tipped her head. She supposed that was one word for the noisy little creatures.

Jan let herself into the pen and sat on the couch. The goslings piled out of the pool and waddled over to her. Saffron pretended not to see her tear little bits off her malasada and share them with the babies.

She left Jan cooing over the goslings. As she walked toward

the door of the egg house she said goodbye to her hens. One of them, Sunshine, didn't look up as Saffron passed. That was unusual. Saffron stopped to see what was holding Sunshine's attention.

Letting herself into the pen, Saffron saw that it was a small, silver circle. She shooed Sunshine aside and picked it up.

Gavin's medallion! He would be so pleased she'd found it.

She peered at the chicken stamped in the center of the medallion, then tipped the silver circle into a band of sunlight and squinted to read the wording.

Saffron sighed with annoyance. The wording was in a different language. She couldn't read it. Squinting again, she saw *Nous perdrons quand les poulets auront des dents!*

It was, she was reasonably sure, French. The word *poulets* was familiar.

Saffron tucked it into her pocket and resolved to ask Sophie what it said when she went to check on her later.

For now, she had set-up to finish. She couldn't pause to visit Sophie or to contact Gavin.

She thought about Gavin as she worked beside her father and Mano to hang lights and string garlands. He was so competitive, so driven to win. She wondered what lengths he would go to.

She also wondered what he was doing, out on the island today. Some of the Wonders said they'd seen him around town with his wild-haired chicken: on the beach, at the aquarium, wandering the boardwalk. But he hadn't been back out to the farm. Saffron didn't know if that was suspicious or not.

Chapter Fifteen

Saffron was out early the next morning to get the chores done. With the furor of activity at the farm yesterday—the decorating and the song practice—she had neglected her birds a bit, and they let her know it as soon as she flipped on the lights in the egg house.

"Brrrrrrrk!" Tikka scolded from the first pen. This set off a chorus of disapproving growls and low chortles from the rest of the flock.

"Okay, okay," Saffron said, "I know. You're not the center of the universe this week, and you don't like that."

"I have no idea what you mean," a voice from the back of the egg house made Saffron jump. Her hand flew to the door handle and she stumbled backward just as Blue stepped out of one of the pens.

"What in the world are you doing in here?" Saffron gasped.

Blue stepped past her and switched off the light with an annoyed grunt.

"Trying to get a perfect shot of a roosting hen," he growled, "Leave the light off."

Blue stalked back to the pen he'd come from without further acknowledging Saffron.

She froze, not knowing exactly what she should do. She could see why a roosting hen would be difficult to capture. The chickens went up on their roosts at dusk and were off them by first light, scratching and foraging.

And they usually woke and often flapped down off their perches at the slightest disruption. She knew if she turned the wheel on the automatic feeder and sent food rattling down the pipes to each pen, every hen would be awake and clamoring for breakfast.

Similarly, if she started gathering eggs, that would draw at least some of them up to the nest boxes to investigate. She abandoned the chores and crept carefully down the aisle to see who Blue was photographing in the soft blue light of the Hawaiian morning.

It was Cleo, a beautiful Buff Brahma hen, whose enormous form rested on the roost like a heavy blossom. Blue had set up the shot from a low angle: slightly below the breastbone. Saffron remembered that he'd told her that would emphasize the carriage of the head.

Cleo's head was lovely. Black, with a collar of pointed feathers that stuck down over her lovely yellow feathers, it was tucked down into her shoulders, resting in blissful slumber.

The wire-covered windows were sapphire squares—the night outside fading slowly to day. There was a layer of cool air that had settled in the egg house overnight and now settled across Saffron's shoulders as she crouched behind Blue in the pen.

Saffron stayed still while he snapped his photos. She watched Cleo, who was still except for her slow breathing and the flicking of her eyelids.

"They dream, you know?" Saffron said quietly, "Birds have

REM sleep, just like humans. Although it's a lot shorter than ours."

Blue murmured, acknowledging her comment, but not responding to it. After three more clicks of his shutter, he spoke. "What could a chicken possibly have to dream about?"

"I've wondered that, too," Saffron said, "Centipedes, I suppose, and beetles."

"Laying eggs?" Blue added, holding his camera away from him and peering at the screen on the back.

Saffron leaned in to see the photos he'd just taken, "I wonder if they dream of more," she said, "maybe they dream of flying."

Blue looked up and pulled the camera away where she couldn't see it, "That's ridiculous."

"Is it? Why wouldn't they dream of flying?"

"They have tiny brains. They've never experienced flying, so they couldn't imagine themselves doing it."

Saffron felt her cheeks get hot, "But they've seen other birds fly," she argued, "they know it exists."

"You think they'd remember something they'd seen?"

Saffron opened her mouth to answer. She knew her hens remembered things—and people—they'd seen. But as the thought came to her, she pressed her lips together, the thought of flight dreams fleeing in front of another thought: if hens remembered things they'd seen, then would the Faverolles remember Hugo's murder? Would they know who killed him? And if so, how could they tell her?

Saffron left Blue in Cleo's pen and walked along the indigo aisle. The Faverolles were awake, scratching happily at the sandy floor. They looked up as Saffron approached.

Saffron communicated with chickens every day. She listened to their urgent calls and squawks and knew they needed food or they were scared or they were being picked on.

She listened to their contented purrs and knew they were safe and happy. She listened to them bicker and listened to them cuddle. She talked to them—about their eggs and the day's events, about her own life and its complexity. But now, looking at these three French hens, she felt the communication barrier between species much more sharply than she'd ever felt it before. If only she could just ask them, *What did you see when you were in that tent? Who hit Hugo?*

She thought the questions at them, then crouched and whispered them.

The Faverolles responded with popping bawks that told Saffron nothing.

* * *

SOPHIE LOOKED surprised when Saffron stopped in at the cottage later that morning.

"I didn't know you were coming by," Sophie said.

"I wanted to drop off today's malasadas," Saffron held out a little box, "chocolate-covered-cherry. They're delicious!" They were. Sweet chocolate pastry with smooth cherry custard inside, rolled in cocoa powder and sugar, they tasted like they were straight out of a Christmas chocolate sampler.

Sophie took the box, but didn't open it. "I'll put it in the kitchen," she said, "and have some later. I just ate breakfast."

She seemed anxious as she rushed into the kitchen. "You go ahead and sit in the living room," she said, "I'll be right back."

That was strange. The kitchen was just behind the living room, and Sophie had never minded Saffron following her in there before.

Saffron sat on the couch, waiting for the girl to return.

When she did, Saffron could see she was visibly shaken.

"Are you all right, Sophie?" Saffron asked, "I mean, are you feeling okay?"

"I'm fine," Sophie said quickly, "Just a little tired."

Saffron watched the pink wash of Sophie's complexion give way to a pale blue fear.

"Sophie," she said slowly, "You know I'm here to help, right? I mean, if you need anything—"

"I know," Sophie's eyes were wide.

"Are you in labor?" Saffron asked, "Should I call someone?"

"No!" Sophie's voice cracked on the word, then she calmed herself, "I'm not—not in labor. I'm fine."

There was a coarse silence between them, filled only with Saffron's intuition screaming at her and Sophie's ragged breathing.

Maybe if Sophie could relax she'd open up about what was troubling her. Saffron made other conversation by pulling out the medallion from her pocket.

"I brought you more French to read," she said with forced brightness.

Sophie took the medallion. Her eyes sparked with recognition.

"You've seen this before?" Saffron said.

Sophie looked up, surprised, "You're very observant."

"It's one of my gifts," Saffron said.

"This is a medallion from my high school," Sophie said, "It's from the poultry showing team."

"You had a poultry showing team in your high school?" Saffron asked, trying not to sound as incredulous as she felt.

"We were in farm country," Sophie said, "in the Midwest. We also had a cattle showing team and a seed germination competition."

"It's Gavin Godfrey's," Saffron said, watching Sophie's face carefully. She saw no change in the woman's features, "Do you know him?"

"Only from the show circuit. If he went to my high school, he must have been older or younger than me, because I don't remember seeing him."

"You said it was a French Immersion School?"

"Right. Everything was in French—classes, the lunchroom menu, signs, the music at the prom, everything."

"What does that say? Something about chickens, I see."

Sophie looked at the medallion again, tipping it into the beams of light that shone in through the window, "Nous perdrons quand les poulets auront des dents!" she read, "It means 'we will lose when the chickens have teeth!'"

Saffron squinted. That was not exactly what she had expected.

Sophie must have recognized her puzzlement, "It's a French saying, when the chickens have teeth—it means never," she searched Saffron's face, and explained further, "Basically, it says, 'We'll never lose!'"

That made sense for a competition team. It was, in fact, more fitting than most motivational slogans.

"Gavin said he got it at his first poultry show," Saffron remembered.

"Yes, they would have given them out to all the team members," Sophie handed it back to Saffron.

It was warmer since Sophie had been holding it in the sun, and it felt heavy and ominous in Saffron's hand, "We'll never lose." she said thoughtfully, "If he's had this since high school, I imagine it's a philosophy that's informed his life since then."

"Mmmm," Sophie agreed, "I wonder how committed he is to that philosophy." She met Saffron's eyes, "Would he commit murder to make sure he never lost?"

Saffron didn't like the knot in her stomach. There was no doubt that Gavin was obsessed with the competition.

"What if he killed Hugo?" Sophie asked, "Could we prove that?"

"I'm trying," Saffron said. She had to get more information. "Sophie," she said carefully, "I don't want to upset you. I've been worried about asking you too many questions. But I need to know anything you know about the day Hugo was killed."

Sophie shifted, almost imperceptibly. Her knees drew away from Saffron, her chin tilted back toward her opposite shoulder. Saffron wondered if that was because she was upset by the memory or if that was because she was uncomfortable with the topic.

Saffron charged ahead anyway, "Tell me more about the time between our meeting and—" Sophie took in a shuddering breath and wrapped her arms around herself. Saffron proceeded carefully, "and the last time you saw Hugo."

Tears made Sophie's already luminous eyes shine brighter, "Oh, it's so horrible," she said, "I was so selfish. If I had known what it would cause, I would never have done it."

"Done what?"

"Gone against Hugo's wishes. He didn't want our hens photographed, remember? He was certain another competitor would steal his secrets. But I wanted portraits of them. I wanted to frame the portraits and hang them in our farmhouse. I knew the girls wouldn't be with us forever—chickens only live ten or twelve years usually, and the girls are at the height of their beauty right now. I just wanted to preserve that," Sophie was bouncing her knee in a rhythmic, nervous way.

"There's nothing wrong with wanting that," Saffron said.

"Except that my arranging it led Hugo to his death," Sophie's tone was bitter.

"Why do you think that? Tell me what happened."

Sophie sniffed and closed her eyes, "See, the girls were

supposed to go into the ring for Show Champion judging." she pressed her lips together a moment, remembering, then went on with a trembling voice, "Hugo took them all in their carrier to the tents, where they would go through the verification process and judging. They would also have had their photos taken there, but he forbade it. He had to take each hen through verification and then judging. He put each hen in the carrier outside the photography tent, then went back to take the next one through verification and judging."

"I had arranged with the photographer to hide in his tent so Hugo would think the tent was empty. When Hugo finished the circuit with Antoinette, he left her in the carrier, and I got her out and let Blue photograph her, putting her back in the carrier before Hugo made it back with Babette. I did the same with Babette, but he was too quick, and when he came back with Claudette, Babette wasn't where he expected her. He came into the tent and saw what I was doing."

"Wait," Saffron said, "Blue *did* photograph the hens?" He had told her he never got to shoot them.

Sophie shivered, remembering, "Two of them. But when Hugo came in with Claudette, everything happened so fast. He grabbed for Blue's camera, and Babette flew. I caught her and put her in the carrier with Antoinette while the two men were scuffling. Claudette was afraid. I could see her beginning to have a seizure, so I tried to get her from Hugo. He knocked Blue down, and tried to push me away, but Claudette scratched him and he let her go. She flapped to me, and he grabbed me. I turned and shoved him," her voice caught, "I pushed him hard and he fell down, and I grabbed the carrier and ran. I knew he would be hurt, and furious. I didn't know he would die."

The last word ended in a little weeping hiccup.

"When I found you in the barn, you said you knew who

killed him," Saffron was about to say Margaux Boucher's name when Sophie reached up and put a hand on her mouth.

The girl's teary eyes were wide, and she shook her head, "Don't say it," she begged.

Saffron was puzzled, "Why not?"

If Saffron hadn't spent her whole life studying the complex color patterns that swirled under the skin of the people she knew, she wouldn't have known that Sophie was afraid. But she had studied and she did know. The girl was terrified. Saffron reached up and took Sophie's hand from her mouth. She held it gently, trying to be reassuring.

"What's wrong, Sophie? You don't want me to say it?"

"No, no, please don't. I can't stand to hear that name."

Saffron nodded slowly, "Okay. I won't say it. But what makes you think it was—" she paused to think of alternative phrasing, "that person, rather than Blue?"

Sophie considered this, "I don't know. I hadn't thought of Blue. He seemed so ill-matched to Hugo. I know that when Hugo knocked him down, Blue cried out. His knee was hurt, he said. I don't know if he was strong enough to go after Hugo again. And," Sophie hesitated on the name, "that other person was so angry when she found out they were related. She was so vehement and she had so much to lose."

"Do you think she always knew they were related?"

Sophie's bouncing knee intensified. She stood suddenly and put a hand to her head, "I'm sorry, Miss Skye, but I can't talk about this just now. I'm not feeling well." Sophie turned away from Saffron and paced the length of the living room, stopping beside a big pineapple-shaped mirror.

It was so abrupt that Saffron was disoriented for a moment. Then she felt ashamed. Of course this was too close a subject for the girl. She was expecting, she'd been on the run, her husband was dead. Saffron couldn't just charge in here and make her relive the whole thing. She'd have to go more gently.

"That's okay," she said, "you should get some rest."

"Yes," Sophie said, looking in the mirror, "I will. I'll rest."

"Do you want me to get you some water?"

"No!" Sophie spun around, "I mean, I'll get it. I'm just going to lay down. Can you see yourself out?" Sophie moved toward the door that led to the kitchen behind the living room.

Baffled, Saffron stood, "Sure. Of course."

"I'm sorry," Sophie said, "I'll see you another time," the girl fled into the kitchen, leaving Saffron standing in the living room.

She stood a long moment, absorbing the shift in the conversation, then she walked slowly toward the door.

As she left, she found herself at an angle to the big pineapple-shaped mirror on the wall. From here, she could see into the kitchen.

She couldn't see Sophie, who had moved to the fridge, but Saffron did see something else. The table. And on it, breakfast plates set out with the remains of eggs benedict, banana pancakes and pineapple juice.

Saffron bit her lip. Not one place setting. Two. Sophie had had company.

A thin filament of tension encircled Saffron as she let herself out.

* * *

SAFFRON WATCHED the cottage for the rest of the day, but saw no one arrive and no one leave.

When Saffron tried to check in hours later, Sophie hadn't opened the door. She had simply called through it that she was still not feeling well and needed to rest.

Saffron was uneasy when she went to feed the chickens that evening. She gave Claudette her pill and watched the Faverolles settle themselves onto their roost.

They were in the tent that day. She wished she could ask them what they had seen.

The hens stayed on her mind the rest of the evening. When she ate an Ono burger at the Oceanside Cafe with her dad and Mano, she was wondering about them. When she finally crawled into bed that night, she dreamed about having a long conversation with them.

Chapter Sixteen

The Faverolles were out and about the next morning, December 23rd, as Saffron finished tidying the barn and getting things ready for the nativity.

Pastor Vaughn and the children's choir were there doing a final run-through.

The farm was sparkling. She had swept out all the cobwebs

she could reach in the barn and washed all the saddle blankets from the tack shelves. She'd even wiped down the old saddles and bridles with leather conditioner, not because she planned on using them, but because she wanted everything to look nice. Even though she didn't plan on anyone coming into the barn, one thing being an event planner had taught her was that you never could predict where guests at a party may wander, so every space should be company-ready.

Antoinette, Babette, and Claudette were out while they went through a practice run with all the other nativity animals. She'd chosen the Faverolles to be in the nativity because they were so calm and so friendly. They were used to crowds, and they were used to staying in one place—they didn't roam like her hens would if let out.

In fact, Claudette was especially easy to keep track of, due to her favorite new hobby: riding around on Jasper's back. She stayed completely still, only flapping once in a while to regain her balance if Jasper made a quick turn.

And he was making a few quick turns. Though he didn't have a part in the nativity until the end, when the two oldest Tuckers would slip into the barn and Andy would lead Jasper out to the nativity scene while Piper rode on the donkey's back, he was out this morning.

He liked being with the other animals. In addition, Jasper turned out to be an excellent helper. The sheep had arrived, and when Saffron went through a practice run with moving the them to their spot for the nativity, she found Jasper was particularly good at trotting around the sheep and keeping them bunched up and in place. He seemed to take cues from Saffron and work to get the sheep where she wanted them.

Claudette rode happily, occasionally bawking at the sheep to give her input on where they should be, curling her toes in Jasper's wooly back to keep her seat.

Mano was as proud of the little donkey as he was of his own children.

"Look at him. So smart and helpful!" he said.

Slate, too, seemed pleased, "I think we did pretty well picking that donkey."

Saffron had to admit they were right, "You did do well. He's turned out to be a lifesaver here on the farm." She scratched Jasper's head, but didn't elaborate on how he'd pulled her from the ocean.

"And you haul that heavy egg cart out to the driveway every Tuesday," Slate said, "I'll bet he can help with that task, too."

"Maybe," Saffron eyed him skeptically, "do you think he's that strong?"

Slate scratched Jasper's head, eliciting a honk of happiness from the donkey, "He's plenty strong."

Jasper pulled away and made another lap around the sheep, nudging them toward the little knee-high fence that Slate and Mano had constructed off to one side of the barn door to keep the animals contained. On the other side of the door they'd built risers for the choir to stand on. Saffron was grateful they were so handy.

Jasper let out a squeak Saffron hadn't heard before. Glancing over, she saw his back leg drawn up in a funny way. He was hobbling. Claudette scolded him and shifted to make up for his uneven gait.

Though she didn't know until that moment how attached she'd become to the donkey, Saffron felt the cold grip of fear. What had happened? The field in front of the barn was uneven and covered in long, untidy grass. Had he stepped in a hole? She tried not to think about what happened when horses broke their legs.

"What is it, bruddah?" Mano went over and leaned down,

looking closely at Jasper's back leg and hoof, "Uh-oh. That's no good."

Saffron raced over, followed closely by Slate, and the three of them checked Jasper over.

Saffron saw a loop of something orange around his hoof, drawn and knotted.

"Baling twine," Slate said, "oh, man, that stuff is everywhere."

That was true. Used to tie bales of hay and straw that her Uncle Beau had hauled in for a few head of livestock, baling twine was useful, but also seemed to crop up in strange places like this. There was a whole pile of it in the barn.

"Okay," Slate knelt down beside the hoof. Jasper reached back to watch what he was doing. "You better not bite me, now. I'm trying to help," from his pocket, Slate pulled a folding pocketknife. The handle was mother-of-pearl, and it was about as long as Saffron's little finger.

Slate popped the blade open and gently worked it under the twine.

Pulling up on the knife, Slate easily cut through the twine, which fell away from Jasper's hoof harmlessly.

Saffron was so relieved that as he stood up, she hugged him. "Oh, I'm so glad you got it off. Once, one of my chickens got some on her toe and I had to take her to the vet to get it removed. The twine was way too tough."

Slate hugged her back, "No problem. This thing's so sharp," he said, "it'll cut paper edgeways."

Saffron had seen him do that—hold a piece of paper up between two fingers and let the weight of the knife carry it downward, slicing cleanly through the paper.

"Don't you have a pocketknife?" Slate asked, squinting at Saffron.

Where would she have gotten a pocketknife?

"I don't think so," she said, "there might be one in Uncle Beau's old desk."

Slate snapped the blade closed, "Well, you have one now," he said decisively, holding the iridescent knife out to her on his flat palm.

"What? No," She shook her head, "You need it."

"I'll get me another one," he said placing it in her hand. "You can't run a farm without a pocket knife."

Saffron took it. Its weight in her hand, and then in her pocket, a reminder that she had a father, that he was right here, and that she could count on him.

Jasper did a little leap of joy and cantered off around the field and back, Claudette bouncing along for the ride.

Claudette's more grounded sisters, Antoinette and Babette, looked up from where they were pecking in the dirt in front of the little fence and clucked to each other. Saffron thought of the song Sophie had sung the first day they'd met. It did sound like hens cackling to each other.

The thought of Sophie made Saffron nervous. She still didn't know who'd eaten breakfast there yesterday, and Sophie's curtains had remained drawn all morning.

A flash of white caught her eye as Mano led the big cow and her calf out to their spot. She'd be staked beside the risers where the choir would sing, behind another knee-high fence that should keep the little calf where she was supposed to be.

Standing back, Saffron liked the looks of it: the cow and calf, the choir, the sheep and hens, and in the center of it all, the big weathered barn, watching over the nativity.

It was going to be beautiful.

If Pastor Vaughn could keep calm, it would be, "Florida?" he was saying, "Florida?"

Saffron listened. The children were singing,

"Angels we have heard on high
Sweetly singing o'er the plains,

And the mountains in reply

Echoing their joyous strains!

Glo-ooooo-ooooo-ooooor-ia."

But as Saffron tuned in and paid closer attention, she heard it. Someone was singing "Flooo-ooooo-ooooo-ooooor-ida."

"Gloria!" Paster Vaughn cried, "Who's singing Florida?"

The children picked up on it and more of them began singing Florida.

Mano and Slate were standing by the cow, watching and listening. As the children broke off their ragged chorus, they walked over to the Pastor.

"Did you hear 'Florida'?" He asked them.

Mano and Slate exchanged a glance, "Maybe once or twice," Mano said.

Pastor Vaughn rubbed his temples.

"They still sound just like angels, though," Slate said, "even if they sing the wrong words."

The kids had oozed off the risers and were crowded around the cow and calf, petting them and feeding them shocks of grass. The patient mama treated them as the children they were, with patience. Occasionally, she reached out with her long rough tongue and gave one of them a lick, causing giggles and delight.

Pastor Vaughn sighed, watching them. A smile broke through his weary features, "You know what?" he said, "you're right."

Parents were arriving to pick up their little ones.

"Are we done, Pastor?" Andy Tucker called, beginning to gather his many siblings.

"Yes," the Pastor replied, his voice lighter, "Everyone come in your costumes tomorrow."

"Any homework?" Called Liko Kapule.

"Just practice your glorias," the Pastor called.

"Practice our Floridas?" a little voice piped up.

The rest of the children shouted in unison, "Glorias!"

* * *

THERE WAS an air of solemnity as Saffron, Mano, and Slate sat around the kitchen table in the bungalow that night. The sun was slipping into bed, pulling the teal blankets made by the waves up over its face, and the evening breeze was flowing in through the screen door.

"This is it," Saffron said, her gaze fixed on the pale purple box in the center of the table.

"The last flavor," Slate said.

It was silly, Saffron knew, to feel sad that there would be no more surprise Christmas flavors. But she was sad.

"I've been looking forward to these every day," Mano said. He felt it, too.

"I know. Christmas is always full of anticipation," Saffron said, "It's always something you look forward to, but this has been especially exciting."

"I guess tomorrow we can still look forward to trying all our favorite Christmas flavors again," Slate said, trying to cheer them up, "Juno's bringing out the truck, and he'll have all 12 flavors, huh?"

That brightened their spirits.

"Okay, let's see what the final flavor is."

When they opened the box, they couldn't immediately tell. The malasadas inside looked ordinary.

They each took one, and without even counting down, bit into them at the same moment.

Saffron felt her eyes close involuntarily. The taste was exquisite. It was as fluffy as fresh-fallen snow, as bright and sweet as the Christmas star. Marshmallow. Impossibly light and rich and creamy. It was a glowing fire and a warm cup in your hand. It was culinary perfection.

Saffron murmured the only thing she could think to describe it, "So ono," she said.

AFTER MANO and Slate headed back to town for the night, Saffron took some of the malasadas to Blue. He was sitting cross-legged on the floor, working on a laptop computer. He called to her to come in, but snapped it closed as soon as she set foot inside. She hoped she could press him for some information. He'd lied to her, about not shooting the Faverolles at the show, and about how he had hurt his leg.

He waved her gift onto the end table by the couch.

"I don't have time to eat right now," he said, "I'm finishing up the editing on these photos for *Modern Homesteading*." He didn't sound like he was in a chatty mood.

Saffron squealed a little, "Can I see?"

"Absolutely not," Blue was curt, "You'll see it in the magazine. And I'll give you a download link for your photos when I've finished editing all of them."

"Okay," Saffron said, "Does this mean you're leaving?"

"I'll fly out on Christmas Day," Blue said, "That's when it was cheapest to change my tickets to. Apparently nobody wants to travel on that day."

Saffron could see why. A little thrill shot through her as she realized on that day she'd be with her dad. She wouldn't trade a minute of that for cheap airfare.

Blue was done with speaking. He waved her out impatiently, opening up his laptop as she left. Her questions would have to wait.

Saffron made her way from there to the coral cottage. There was a single light on in the living room window, but the curtains were still closed. She was beginning to worry about Sophie. Who had visited her? Was she in danger?

Voices from inside stopped Saffron in her tracks. One of the windows was open just a little, and on the cool air streaming out of it came two voices.

"I don't feel like it, okay?" Sophie's voice was high and emotional.

"I'm not giving you a choice," It was another woman's voice, older than Sophie, with a light French accent. Margaux.

Ten horrible images streaked through Saffron's mind: guns, poison, the bloody silver cup.

She pulled out her master key and slammed through the door into the cottage.

Sophie was standing against the wall. She turned shocked, terrified eyes to Saffron. In front of her was . . . not Margaux Boucher.

A small woman with rosy cheeks and a flowing silver bob stood holding out a steaming cup.

"Back away," Saffron said, pulling out her cell phone, "Sophie, are you okay?"

But it wasn't the woman Sophie seemed afraid of. It was Saffron herself.

"Who are you calling?"

"I'm calling the police. I knew someone was in here threatening you. I should have done it sooner."

"Threatening me?" Sophie said, "No, no, you've got it wrong. Saffron, hang up the phone, s'il vous plaît." Sophie rushed away from the woman and took Saffron's arm, "Saffron, this is my mother, Pauline."

Saffron hung up the phone.

"Your mother?"

The older woman smiled warmly. She certainly didn't seem threatening now.

"What's in the cup?" Saffron was still wary. Her heart was still hammering in her ears.

"Chamomile tea," Pauline said, "Why don't you sit down

and have a cup, too? I know how wonderful you've been to my girl here."

"How did you . . ." Saffron looked from one to the other, "Oh," the truth dawned on her, "the cell phone."

"I took your advice. I called her," Sophie's eyes were soft as she looked at her mother, "I didn't think she'd even want to talk to me, much less see me. But she was on the next plane here."

Saffron's shoulders relaxed with relief. "I thought you were in trouble in here."

"I know, I'm sorry," Sophie said, "I should have told you. I was just afraid that she'd get in trouble because of me." The girl took a hiccupping breath and put a hand to her head, "I don't know how much longer I can stand to live like this. I don't like being a fugitive."

Her mother crossed to her, setting the cup on the side table as she came. She put an arm around her daughter. "It's okay, we're going to get through this. Are you sure you don't want to just turn yourself in? Just go and tell them you're innocent?"

Saffron saw a strange uneasiness in Sophie's eyes then. It was fleeting, but definitely present. She pushed away the fear that she was wrong about Sophie.

"I can't. They'll never believe me. And the baby might come before they get it all sorted out."

"All right," her mother soothed, "It's going to be okay. I'm here now," She stroked a stray strand of golden hair from Sophie's face.

Sophie leaned her head against her mother. From out of nowhere, Saffron felt a pang of jealousy. In the busy day-to-day running the farm, she sometimes forgot how much she missed her own mother.

"'Ohana,'" she said softly, involuntarily.

"What was that?"

"'Ohana,'" Saffron said more clearly, "It means family—

people you're connected to, who strengthen you and help you through."

"Sound's like you've been 'ohana to my Sophie," Pauline smiled, "Strengthening her and helping her. And she says you're trying to figure out who really killed Hugo so they'll stop chasing her."

"I'm doing my best," Saffron said.

* * *

THE FAVEROLLES WERE joyous the next afternoon as they purred and clucked at Jasper's feet. He was trotting around enjoying Christmas Eve with Claudette on his back.

Saffron had put the final touches on everything: the poinsettia garlands were out and the leis were ready to distribute to tonight's guests, the Christmas lights were on, and she'd called to confirm that Juno would be there at six o'clock with the malasada truck.

He'd assured her that he would be there and that he'd have all 12 flavors of special-edition Christmas malasadas on hand.

She thought she was ready for any surprises, but when a big black car pulled up in the driveway, she realized she'd been wrong.

From them emerged the judges. Margaux stepped out first, dressed in a dark blue tailored pantsuit and her usual black beret. She hung back as Vladimir Korsov and Perlita Moreno approached Saffron. Only Margaux still carried a clipboard.

After the way she had talked to them, Saffron expected a frosty greeting, but the man with the pencil-thin mustache had just the opposite for her. He smiled and took her hand, squeezing it warmly.

Perlita, too, was affectionate. She kissed both Saffron's cheeks, "Thanks to you," she said, "We've truly enjoyed our time in Hawaii."

"Excuse me?" Saffron said. She often heard things like this from her renters, but that was because she was so directly involved in their lodging and, sometimes, their entertainment. She'd only seen the judges briefly.

"Yes," Vladimir said, his slick black hair catching the sunshine, "Because of what you said, Perlita and I decided to stop looking for the bad in everything, and instead see the good and beautiful."

"It was a monumental switch," Perlita said, "Before, we couldn't wait to leave. Now, we'll be sorry to leave Hawaii, because we took the time to notice the best of the food and the most beautiful flowers."

Saffron was smiling.

"Thank you," Vladimir said, "I feel happier than I have in years."

"I'm glad," Saffron said. Her gaze slipped involuntarily to Margaux Boucher, who, to both their horror, had noticed Claudette careening around the field on Jasper's back.

"Don't expect any thanks from her," Perlita said, "she didn't take your advice to heart. She's the same cantankerous crank she's always been."

"Miss Skye," Margaux called, as if on cue, "Would you like to tell me where, exactly, on the care sheet I left you found instructions to allow these fine showbirds to careen around on a donkey?"

Saffron was chagrined. She would have to admit that she hadn't followed the instructions at all. The birds had been fed the same as the rest of her flock, had undergone no showmanship training, and hadn't once had their feathers combed since they'd arrived. Still, as Saffron watched Claudette with the wind ruffling her fluffy cheek muffs, she didn't think the hens were any worse for the wear.

"I'm sorry, but I haven't followed your instructions very well at all."

"It figures. You simply can't trust an egg farmer to do the job of a showman."

Saffron ignored the slight, "Was there something that brought you out here today?"

"We've come to inform you of our decision on the Grand Champion, and to leave the necessary paperwork here to accompany the birds when the legal decision as to their final custody is made. We've also contacted Mr. Godfrey, who will be meeting us here shortly."

"I hope he gets here soon," she said, "the party begins in less than two hours."

Margaux released an audible grunt of disgust, "I know," she said.

When Perlita spoke up, Saffron knew why Margaux knew about the party.

"We were hoping, since we're here anyway, that we could stay for your Christmas Eve celebration. We're trying to fully appreciate the island before we go back home tomorrow."

Saffron was both flattered and annoyed that they wanted to come to the party. She waved a hand, "It's an open invitation," she said, "Of course you're welcome to stay."

Margaux looked chagrined, as if she were hoping Saffron would turn them down so she could get out of here.

"May we look around?" Vladimir asked.

"Sure," Saffron said, "You're welcome to explore. The beach is particularly pretty this time of afternoon."

Together Vladimir and Perlita made their way down the garland-lined path to the beach. Margaux did not join them.

"I came here to judge, not to vacation," she said pertly.

"You could do both," Saffron said.

"Hawaii is just not my kind of place," Margaux sniffed. Her tailored pantsuit and high heels were enough for Saffron to guess that herself. "I prefer places that are groomed and deliberate and perfect."

Saffron looked around at the trees, their blossoms cascading from their canopies. She looked at the grasses tickling her knees and the bushes exploding with flocks of squawking, brilliant birds. "This place isn't groomed or deliberate," she admitted, "But it is rich and vibrant and alive. And surely you can appreciate that there are lots of different kinds of perfection?"

One look at Margaux's face told Saffron that there were no other kinds of perfection in her mind. Saffron wondered what lengths she would go to for perfection.

She thought of Sophie, huddling in the cottage, too afraid to leave. She had to do something. It was time to find out what Margaux knew.

Chapter Seventeen

Saffron took a deep breath and looked Margaux in the eye, "I'm glad you came out today. I've been meaning to ask you some questions about Hugo Leblanc's death."

Margaux bristled. "What do you mean?"

"I think by this point you know what I mean," Saffron said. "I'm sure you've been asked similar questions by the police."

"And they found no reason to suspect me," Margaux said. She'd crossed her arms across her chest and taken a solid stance. She was defensive.

A breeze had come up, and it tugged at Margaux's beret, which she pulled down more snugly on her tightly drawn-back hair.

"That's because they don't know everything, isn't it?" Saffron looked her in the eye.

"I have no idea what you mean."

"I was outside the tent that day," Saffron clenched her fists to keep her hands from shaking. She admitted to herself that she was afraid of Margaux, but she pushed on anyway, "I heard you arguing with your nephew."

She let the last two words fall deliberately, like bombs, and she watched as they hit Margaux, who tried, immediately, to deny them.

"That's ridiculous," she said, but there was a shadow of resignation in her voice.

"Maybe, but it's true. You're Hugo's aunt, and you'd do anything to keep that information quiet, wouldn't you?"

"I know what you're implying."

Saffron rushed on, "But there's more that the police don't know. You wanted to buy the Faverolles."

"*Everyone* knows that," Margaux's eyes were burning, "Those birds *used* to be the picture of perfection."

"You wrote up a contract on your clipboard there," Saffron said, "but Hugo wouldn't sell."

"You're absurd," Margaux looked at her with suspicion and a hint of fear.

"That may be true," Saffron said, "but I've seen the paper that came from your clipboard."

Margaux looked truly startled. She opened her mouth, but no words escaped.

"So why don't you just tell me," Saffron said, "you argued with him in the judging tent, and he tore up the contract, then you sent him to the photography tent, where you ambushed him and hit him with the cup."

Saffron had sprung too early. She could tell by the way Margaux pressed her lips together, by the steely set to her jaw and the cloud of resolve that settled in her eyes. She wasn't going to say another word. Silence stretched between the two women, neither of them speaking, neither of them breaking eye contact.

Gavin Godfrey's car blazing up the driveway broke both the silence and their staring contest.

Lyle and Gavin bounced their way over. Gavin didn't let Lyle down this time. He kept the rooster cradled gently but firmly under his arm. Lyle looked longingly at the two Faverolles scratching in the dirt. He took note of Claudette, tipping his head to watch her and Jasper with a puzzled expression.

Lyle was perfectly groomed—his poof of head feathers exquisite, every feather gleaming and in place. His toenails were filed and his unique comb oiled to bring out its rich scarlet color.

"Well, I guess we're ready to find out," Gavin said. He was also in peak form, wearing his full show outfit, his hair spiked in a perfect echo of Lyle's.

"I'll have you know that I was of the opinion we should just call you," Margaux said, "But when my colleagues found out you were still on the island, they insisted on meeting in person."

Gavin nodded. Saffron could see that he was happy they'd planned it that way.

Margaux's eyes narrowed, "Why *are* you still on the island, Mr. Godfrey?" She asked, "Are you hoping no one will appear to claim these hens? Are you still after the Faverolles?"

Gavin looked at the peachy chickens, "Of course I'd still like them," he said, "but I'm mostly just here because the show stressed Lyle out. He needed a vacation. Shipping birds by air is stressful, as you know, Judge Boucher, and I wanted to give him some time to recuperate before he had to travel again.

"Are you sure that's the reason?" Margaux asked pointedly, "maybe the local law enforcement requested you stay on the island while they investigate the death of Hugo Leblanc and the disappearance of his wife? Because maybe they think you had something to do with it?"

Gavin tensed, drawing back and holding Lyle protectively. Margaux was trying to deflect Saffron's suspicions, but it only made Saffron more wary of the woman.

The other two judges were walking up the pathway toward them, and Margaux's words came quieter and faster.

"Miss Skye was just insinuating that I may be involved. But I'm not the only one who wanted those birds, am I, Mr. Godfrey? Perhaps she should look at your motives and opportunity. After all, you were in the judging tent just moments before Hugo was killed, weren't you?"

Gavin looked like he might run. "Well, yes," he admitted, "I came back for my pen. But I . . . I only saw Hugo for a minute, and I didn't kill him."

"But you would, wouldn't you? Kill for the perfect birds?"

Gavin didn't get to answer. The other two judges arrived, smiling, and began to talk immediately about the award.

Saffron felt uneasy, as if on either side of her could be a killer.

"It was difficult deliberation, you understand," Perlita explained, "All seven judges had excellent perspective on their favorite bird. Each class had its strengths. And every bird in the show ring—er, in the competition—was an excellent specimen. But in the end, there was really only one bird that truly fit the standard of perfection."

The Faverolles weren't Saffron's birds. They belonged to Sophie, but in that moment Saffron felt a pride and anticipation that equaled any owner's. She felt herself bouncing slightly, trying to contain her nerves. If Sophie won, the prize money and opportunities would go a long way toward helping her become financially independent.

Gavin, the professional showman, showed no outward signs of nervousness. He wasn't arrogant, though, and there was a hint of anxiety in the way his eyebrows drew together over the bridge of his nose.

When all the judges had spoken, Vladimir finally cleared his throat pointedly. Though there were only five people there in the crowd, he spoke as he would have spoken at the show in front of thousands of onlookers.

"We're proud to announce that the winner of this year's Companion and Utility Birds Association Premier Poultry Classic Show Champion Award is the Crested Houdan—Lyle, owned and shown by Gavin Godfrey."

Though she was disappointed, Saffron clapped as Gavin calmly accepted the award. It was a new cup, as big and beautiful as the other. Now, though, it made Saffron shiver a little to see it.

The wind whipped around them, tearing the sound of Saffron's applause away from her hands and sending it tumbling back down the path toward the sea. Gavin should have had the applause and adoration of thousands. Instead, it was just her, sending a lonely ovation through the waning afternoon sunshine.

Margaux held out her clipboard. "We'll need some signatures here," she said, then, patting her pocket, made a frustrated grunt, "I seem to have left the pen in the car. I'll go get it."

"No need," Gavin said, "I've got mine here." He reached into the inside breast pocket of his suit and extracted the pen Saffron had seen before, at the show—black and white enamel, with the etched Houdan rooster on its side.

Saffron paid little attention as the judges and Gavin signed the paperwork. People would be arriving soon, and there were still a few details to attend to.

As Margaux swung the clipboard back toward herself, though, Saffron caught a flash of color. A unique color, one she'd seen before.

It was the fine indigo ink, the one she'd seen on the scrap of paper from her Christmas slippah.

"Wait," she said, her eyes glued to the ink, "may I see that?"

Margaux glanced around nervously, but handed over the clipboard.

The scrap of paper, the contract Sophie had read for Saffron, was written with this pen. Saffron took a step back from Gavin as she handed back the clipboard.

Mano's ukulele Christmas carols were just what Saffron needed to calm her frazzled nerves as the party began. She had hundreds of people arriving for the party—she couldn't focus on Gavin just now. The music was light and playful, a perfect greeting as the townspeople of Maika'i parked their cars and wandered up to the barn where Saffron and Slate, assisted by all the children in their nativity costumes, slipped the beautiful poinsettia leis around guest's necks and greeted them warmly.

The evening was lovely. The surf kept time for Mano's carols. The twinkling strings of Christmas lights lit up the beach and barn, the path and the empty choir risers. Jasper was wandering free for now, Claudette on his back and an enormous poinsettia lei around his neck, reveling in the exclamations and affection the guests were heaping on him. They scratched his ears, petted his wooly belly, and stroked his nose. Claudette rode contentedly through it all, seeming to enjoy the attention just as much. Slate would put Jasper back in the barn just as the nativity program started so he could make his big entrance when he carried Piper Tucker out holding her doll.

The growing wind pushed Saffron's red hair into her eyes and pulled at the flowing poinsettia sundress Mano had given her for an early Christmas present. On the breeze floated the exquisite scents from Juno's malasada truck.

Egg nog, peppermint, gingerbread and sugar cookie. Hot cocoa, fudge, fruitcake, orange, cinnamon, and hazelnut. Chocolate-covered cherry and marshmallow. The sweet familiar flavors mingled in the evening air and drew the crowds to the truck.

Saffron wished Sophie could come out and enjoy the evening. She wished that she could weave the little strands of evidence she had gathered into an actionable accusation against Margaux or Gavin. If she could, she would take it to Officer Bradley and Lieutenant Havili, who were reaching for their malasada order right now. They could make an arrest and Sophie could come to the party, a free person.

Saffron kept an eye on Judge Margaux as she stood stiffly in the middle of the teeming crowd. The more Saffron watched her, the more familiar the woman seemed. Saffron was watching when a particularly fierce gust of wind pulled Margaux's beret completely off her head and under the feet of the townspeople.

Margaux went after it, and Saffron was surprised to see dark hair—streaked with gray, come tumbling down around the woman's shoulders as she chased it. The hair, onyx and gleaming, also reminded her of something. It was a color she'd seen many times: in the iridescent sheen of her rooster, Curry's, hackle feathers, on the wing of the 'i'iwi bird, on the back of a fat spider that spun her web under the eaves of the egg house every June. It was strange to see Margaux with any element of disarray.

Gavin, however, was never hard to spot with his shock of exciting hair and the brand-new silver cup he insisted on carting around. Half the time, when Saffron spotted him in the crowd, Lyle was riding in the cup, poking his head out to greet curious Maika'i townspeople.

The more Saffron thought about it, the more she felt the need to figure out who had killed Hugo. Tonight. Now. While Sophie still had a chance at having her baby without being under suspicion, while the two principal suspects were in the same place as the officers, while Saffron still had the pieces of evidence to hand over.

She looked up to see Dylan and Betsy Sawyer walking up the path. Rather, Betsy was walking up the path and Dylan was following, his head drooping, his shoulders slumped. He did not look ready for a party.

Betsy bowed her head to receive her lei from Saffron. Her spider-black braid glinted in the glow of the Christmas lights.

"Mele Kalikimaka," Saffron said brightly, as she had hundreds of times that night already.

"Joyeux Noël," Betsy replied, but there was no joy in her tone, "I understand you've got our cows here."

Sweat beaded on Saffron's forehead. She hoped she wouldn't come to regret turning down Wyatt's offer to borrow a shotgun, "Yes, they're down by the barn now, getting lots of attention."

The sheep would be herded out of the barn and into their little corral by the kids who were playing the shepherds, the doves would ride in on the wise men's shoulders, but the cows would start and end the evening in their place. Mano and Slate had decided it was just too dangerous for kids to try to move a mama cow and her calf through a crowd of people.

"They should," Betsy said, "They're lovely."

"If they're so lovely, why are you sellin' them?" Wyatt's voice came from the shadows off the path, and he stepped into the light of the Christmas bulbs defiantly.

Dylan didn't say anything. He didn't move from behind Betsy. He didn't even look up at his brother.

Betsy spoke up, though, "Because they belong in the herd in France. They belong somewhere they can be part of a championship strain. And besides, they're ours and we can do what we want with them."

Saffron wasn't about to relive the egg fight of two weeks ago. She cleared her throat and stepped between Betsy and

Wyatt, reaching up to slip a lei over his cowboy hat and down onto his neck.

"This isn't the place for business," she said, glancing behind her to be sure her father had her back. When she saw that he did, she went on, "You can talk about cows and sales and rights tomorrow. Tonight is about carols and malasadas and Christmas."

Betsy's eyes snapped. If there was one thing she hated, it was being told what to do. But quite a crowd had gathered behind them now, and she must have judged it unwise to pursue the topic further. She looked away, and Saffron saw her eyes light on Jasper, standing in the path a few paces ahead. It was as if, suddenly, Betsy had eyes for nothing else. Her boots thudded against the path as she strode forward and caught Jasper's bridle with one hand. With the other, she scooped Claudette off his back.

Both animals protested. Jasper stamped and brayed. Claudette squawked in outrage.

"Hey!" Saffron left Slate and the children to give out the leis and stalked over to Betsy.

Betsy was inspecting Claudette: tipping her head side to side, peering at her toes, and, finally, stretching one lovely, honey-colored wing out and eyeing the flight feathers.

"What are you doing?" Saffron's voice was shrill with annoyance.

Betsy fixed her with dark eyes. She didn't answer Saffron's question. Instead, she demanded, "Where did you get this bird?"

"That's none of your business," Saffron said, "You can put her down now."

"This is not your bird," Betsy's accent was thicker when she was angry. "This is a very fine hen," the woman's voice was sharp with disdain, "It has no place here, riding on a donkey. It's from France, near my parents' farm. It belongs back there." Saffron was trying to think of something to say when Betsy went too far. "I saw this bird at the poultry show in Honolulu two weeks ago," she paused and said loudly, more to the gathered crowd than to Saffron, "from where she was *stolen*!"

The words hit Saffron like slaps. Was this woman really accusing her? Here at her own farm? She'd known Betsy had nerve, but not that much nerve.

Saffron wanted to blurt out that the owner of the hens had brought them here, that the police had decreed they stay here, but of course she couldn't say any of those things without breaking Sophie's confidence. Anyway, she wouldn't give Betsy the satisfaction of knowing she'd made her feel defensive.

"If you have a concern," Saffron said, stepping up and firmly grasping Claudette, "Officer Bradley is right over there." She pulled the fluffy hen close to her, turned, and placed her back on Jasper.

"Go on, boy," she said, "go wish the people a Merry Christmas." As always, Jasper seemed to understand. He trotted off with a derisive snort in Betsy's direction.

"Maybe I will go talk to the officer," Betsy sniffed, "I know that bird." She stalked away, Dylan following her like a puppy.

The people of Maika'i were, for the most part, polite, and they moved on with minimal questions.

The encounter made Saffron doubly resolved to tie Margaux or Gavin to the murder. It needed to be solved, to quell all these wild suspicions. "Dad," she said, "Keep things going here. I'll be right back." Slate nodded. She could see from his tight jaw that he wasn't very impressed with Betsy's little display, either.

Mano's ukulele version of "We Wish You a Merry Christmas," followed her up onto the lanai and stayed in her mind as she went into the house to retrieve the contract and the scrap of paper.

The ink on the contract was from Gavin's pen. But she'd been sure Margaux had written it.

She sifted through the papers on the kitchen table, laying Wyatt's cow care instructions on the table next to the instructions Margaux had left. She also extracted the shaded contract from the pile and took the scrap of paper out of the empty sugar bowl where she had hidden it.

Seeing them all laying on the table together, she was sure of it: the ink on the scrap matched the ink she'd seen from Gavin's pen earlier.

But there was something else strange. For the first time, Saffron saw Margaux's instruction sheet next to the shaded contract. She bit her lip. The handwriting could not have been more different. Margaux's penmanship was, like everything about the woman, tight and neat and controlled. The handwriting on the contract was wide and flowing, scribbled and hurried.

Saffron wished she'd paid more attention to Gavin's signature on the paperwork earlier. One thing was sure—Margaux hadn't written that contract.

"Mo 'opuna," the voice came from behind her and made her jump. She realized as she turned that the delicate ukulele music had stopped outside. Mano stood in the doorway, holding the instrument and looking anxious.

"Sorry, Tutu," she said, "I was just getting something." She folded the contract with the scrap of paper inside and stuck it in the pocket of her sundress.

"You need to get down to the beach," Mano said, his voice urgent, "Kanakaloka will be coming any minute."

Saffron knew Santa Claus was coming in on his outrigger canoe soon, but she didn't think it imperative that she was there. Mostly the children wanted to be there to meet him and tell him what they wanted for Christmas.

"What about the keiki?" she asked, "did they go down?"

"They're already on the beach, but you need to go down, too."

Saffron couldn't fathom why it was so important to Mano that she go down to meet Santa Claus, but Mano was so good to her, she didn't want to cause him any distress. Maybe he wanted to go down, too, but didn't want to leave her. Either way, anything that Mano asked, she'd try to do.

"Let's go, Tutu," she said, "You can tell Santa what you want for Christmas."

Mano laughed, "I might just do that."

Chapter Eighteen

The beach was beautiful. Strings of lights swayed in the wind, casting rolling light over the sand. The kids were lined up, their ankles in the water, their eyes on the horizon.

They were in their costumes: angels and shepherds and

wise men in grass skirts and bathrobes and sheets that floated around their feet as the waves sighed in and out. They all wore lei, and they all had their eyes fixed on a bobbing dot of light making its way around the big lava point off to the left of the beach.

It was magical, seeing the canoe riding the waves toward them. Torches onboard made a globe of light around the figures inside. Two elves dressed in aloha shirts and pointy hats paddled, and Mrs. Claus rode primly in the prow, decked out in a golden muumuu and waving a gloved hand. Behind her, Santa stood with one foot on the seat, perfectly balanced as the canoe made its way in. He was wearing red velvet board shorts trimmed with white fur along with a traditional pom-pommed Santa hat and a flowing white beard. His red and green aloha shirt was made from material that matched Saffron's sundress.

Saffron couldn't tell who it was, but it didn't matter. Whoever it was had all the style and jolliness of Santa, waving to the keiki on the beach and cruising in on the canoe.

She stayed at the edge of the crowd of kids as the elves jumped out of the canoe and hauled it ashore, then helped Mrs. Claus out carefully.

Santa leaped out to the sand and snatched up two of the keiki, laughing heartily, before making his way through the crowd up to a wicker throne, decorated with poinsettias and twinkle lights, that awaited him.

Parents snapped pictures as Mrs. Claus and the elves helped the children line up and approach Santa, who focused on each one as they came and didn't rush any of them through their lists.

The crowd grew smaller and the knot of people around Santa's throne grew tighter until there were only two children in line between Saffron and Santa. She realized that Mano had been edging her closer and closer to the line the whole time.

"And I want a new boogie board because my sister broke mine," said the last little boy, a wise man whose dark green Maile leaf headband set off the red in Santa's unconventional suit.

Mano was urging Saffron forward subtly, and in turning to give him a puzzled look, Saffron missed Santa's reply. When she turned back, the line was gone and Santa was standing up.

"And how about you?" he said, his voice causing Saffron's elbows to draw against her sides in surprise and excitement, "What do you want for Christmas?"

When Saffron threw her arms around him and looked up into Keahi's topaz eyes, she realized he was the answer to his own question.

* * *

KEAHI HELD ONTO HER, too, his scratchy false beard the only thing between his strong jaw and her cheek. The shock of realizing who he was had taken her words from her, and she just stood hugging him.

When she finally remembered that they'd broken up, that they lived a continent apart, that they hadn't had a real, deep conversation in months, she stepped back, a little embarrassed. Her cheeks flushed even redder when she realized that the crowd had gone back up to the barn, leaving them alone on the beach. Even Mrs. Claus was making her way up the path, accompanied by Mano, who shot a few looks back over his shoulder.

"I'm sorry," she said.

"For what?" he always liked to make her say exactly what she meant.

"I was just so happy to see you, I didn't remember for a minute, I didn't realize what I was doing."

"Listen, you don't have to apologize. I felt the same way the other day in town, and I'm sure I looked like an idiot just leaving like that."

Saffron tipped her head, "The other day?"

"At Juno's. The day they had fudge malasadas? Didn't you see me standing there like I was frozen? I had just come in from Boston, and I saw you, but I didn't know what to say, so I just left."

"No, I didn't see you. I had no idea you were back."

"But you called me," he said, "about the pills. I thought that was because you saw me in the bakery."

Saffron laughed, and though the wind whipped the sound away and tossed it to the sea foam, it felt wonderful, "I thought you were in Boston. I was feeling so sorry for you in the cold and gray while I was here in paradise for Christmas. And you were just down the road."

"I'm sorry. I probably should have come by. I just didn't know if Nik would be here, and, you know, if that would be awkward."

Saffron shook her head, "Nik's in Barbados. But it was bound to be a little awkward either way."

Keahi laughed, "I've missed you, Saffron."

The sounds of Mano's ukulele, along with a couple hundred people singing *Deck the Halls*, floated down the path to them.

"I've missed you, too, Keahi."

"So Tutu didn't tell you he'd asked me to be Santa?"

"No," Saffron smiled, "He just said he had it taken care of, and since I've been so busy, I didn't think to ask." She looked down at their matching outfits, "Incidentally, he also didn't tell me that my Santa would be wearing the same aloha print as the dress he gave me for Christmas."

"Tutu's subtle," Keahi laughed.

* * *

SAFFRON WANTED to spend more time with Keahi down on the beach. She wanted to hear all about his adventures in surgery back in Boston and tell him about the egg farm, about Hugo, about her father's unexpected return. She even wanted to tell him about some of the places Nik had shown her, to see if he'd been there or if he'd like to go. But the community carols had started, and that meant the evening was getting closer to its climax: the live nativity. She had to be on hand for that, to be sure everything went smoothly. So she and Keahi walked back up the path and joined the crowd.

Mrs. Claus was quick to re-appropriate her Santa and dragged Keahi off to get a malasada. Saffron worked her way to the front of the crowd, where Mano had situated himself on the risers, the angel choir in place behind him, helping him lead the group in song. The three Faverolles were at his feet, scratching and pecking. Slate must have already put Jasper in the barn so he could play his part later. Claudette seemed at ease with being separated from him, particularly when she found a nice bug to snatch from one of her sisters.

Saffron mingled with the crowd, thinking through every minute of the afternoon at the show. She snapped back to the present when she heard the crowd singing *The Twelve Days of Christmas.*

"Five gold rings!" the Walking Wonders trumpeted. Saffron gave them a smile and kept walking. "Four calling birds," came other voices. It was the next line that stopped Saffron in her tracks.

"Trois poules françaises," Saffron heard.

If she hadn't just read it, she wouldn't have recognized it. But in the midst of the whole crowd singing, "Three French hens," the words rang out like a bell.

She turned in time to see Blue standing in the crowd, snapping photos occasionally, while he sang, "deux tourterelles, perdrix dans un arbre de paire."

French. Blue was singing the song in French. She hurried to him, laying a hand on his arm as the next verse began. She leaned in so he could hear her over the other carolers.

"Do you speak French?"

He raised his eyebrows, "Of course I do," he said, "Why is that so surprising?"

"I just, I didn't know you had French ties."

Blue cocked his head, his expression puzzled, "What language did you think my name came from?"

Now it was Saffron's turn to be puzzled, "Um . . . English? Blue? It's a color?"

Blue closed his eyes, shaking his head impatiently and putting his mouth next to her ear, "Not B-L-U-E, Blue, B-L-E-U. Bleu." This time when he said it, Saffron heard the difference. A slight truncation of the final 'u' sound.

"Are you kidding me? I've thought it was Blue this whole time."

"That's not my fault," he said. "My name's always been Bleu."

It was a fair point. She was going to have to start calling him by the right name.

"So you can write French, too?"

"Of course I can."

Her list of suspects was getting longer. Saffron decided to try the element of surprise. She took the folded paper out of her pocket and held it out to him. Her heart was pounding.

"Did you write this?" she demanded. He had been in the tent. He had fought with Hugo. He had lied to Saffron. But she saw no recognition in his eyes as he ran them over the paper.

He raised his eyebrows, "Intrigue?" he asked, taking it from her.

"More than you can imagine."

Bleu unfolded the paper, squinting at the smudges.

"It's some kind of contract," Saffron said, "for the Faverolles hens. Were you interested in buying them, too?"

"No," Bleu's tone was vacant, his mind distracted.

"Yes. Margaux Boucher wanted to buy them, and so did Gavin Godfrey. Someone read the contract for me, and she said Margaux probably wrote it up, or maybe Gavin did, because I noticed it's written with ink from his pen. But the pen was left in the tent. So maybe you wrote it with his pen while you were in there. But either way, the person who read the contract for me thinks that Hugo wouldn't sell and he tore up the contract. I have a little piece of the original."

"That's an interesting theory," Bleu mumbled, still peering at the paper.

"What do you mean, *theory*?"

"It's not a contract," Bleu said, his mouth tight.

"But she said—"

"Whoever read this for you lied to you. It's not a contract. It's a letter."

"Lied? A letter?" none of his words were making sense.

"More of a note, really, a message, I guess," he held it out and Saffron looked at it, expecting to see something new. But she still had no idea what it said.

Bleu sighed, his head bobbing impatiently, and read, "'Someone is trying to kill me. I may not make it to the end of the competition. Should anything happen to me, please investigate the Three French Hens.' It's signed Hugo Leblanc."

Saffron could see that now, when she looked. The looping handwriting made a prominent H and a clear L.

Her mind was reeling. Hugo Leblanc had written this? Sophie had lied? Everything she thought she'd unraveled seemed snarled in her head again. She looked at Blue pleadingly, "Why would he want them to investigate the hens? They didn't kill him."

Bleu shrugged, "Maybe they hold a clue."

Again, Saffron wished the birds could talk. She also wished they weren't scratching in the dirt at Mano's feet. She couldn't go snatch them and inspect them for clues just now, not with the eyes of the entire town trained on them.

She couldn't ask the birds what had happened, but she certainly could ask Sophie why she had lied about the contract.

"Saffron," Bleu said, looking at his feet, "I need to tell you something."

Saffron froze. She could tell by his tone—somber and ashamed—that he'd been keeping something from her, too.

"What?"

"I was there. Just before Hugo was killed. I—I saw him write this note in the photography tent that day," he caught her hand, "I didn't know what it meant—I swear, I didn't read it, I just saw Hugo scribbling it on the clipboard on the table. I was there because Sophie wanted me to photograph the birds. When Hugo came in and saw us, he was furious. He pushed me down and my leg got hurt. I hid behind the table. Sophie struggled with him, and shoved him, then she grabbed the birds and ran out of the tent. He stopped and scribbled this note, then he came after me again, and I was terrified, so I scrambled out of the tent."

"Why didn't you tell me this?"

"It sounds bad. I was there. I fought with him. But I swear he was perfectly fine when I left the tent. I don't know if Sophie came back, or if Gavin met him in there, or if Margaux followed him, but I do know that I didn't kill him."

Saffron believed him. She could see what a relief was for him to tell her.

"I need to talk to Sophie," she said, "thanks for telling me the truth about this," she stuffed the paper back in her pocket.

Saffron skirted the edge of the crowd, throwing one last glance toward the singing angels. *The Twelve Days of Christmas* was just ending, and that meant that the nativity was beginning. She saw Pastor Vaughn stepping up as the crowd erupted in applause and Mano took a little bow.

Once her eyes adjusted to the full moonlight, the night was bright beyond the circle of twinkling Christmas lights. It was easy to work her way to the coral cottage.

She had to be quick. The nativity was beginning. She ran up the driveway, past the house, and across the yard to the cottages. Her breath was coming hard and she had a pain in her side as she knocked.

Sophie's mother answered the door.

"Is Sophie here?" Saffron gasped, making no attempt to hide the urgency in her voice.

"I'm sorry," Pauline smiled, "I finally talked her into getting out for a moment. She insisted on covering her head, but she did finally agree to go over to the nativity with her friend."

Saffron's throat closed with fear. Sophie didn't know anyone here except Margaux and Gavin. She should have been wise enough to be wary of either of them. Saffron could barely choke out the words, "Her friend?"

"Yes, it's such a comfort that she is here with all that has been going on. And such a strange coincidence that they would both end up here. I don't think they've even seen each other since my daughter moved to France and they were in that little singing group together. And now they're both here in Hawaii."

Saffron swallowed hard, "Who, Pauline? Who's her friend?"

Saffron was prepared to hear something that surprised her, but the words that came out of Pauline's mouth did more. They shocked her.

"Betsy Sawyer. Of course, her name was Betsy Boucher when she lived in France, before she got married."

The words echoed in Saffron's ears. The world began to float around her. Betsy. Betsy Boucher. Margaux Boucher. Hair black as a spider's back. Betsy was Judge Margaux's daughter. She was Hugo's cousin. Her family had wanted that strain of Faverolles for a long time. Was she the one who had left the note telling Hugo that he was related to Margaux?

She tried to keep her voice even. The words in Hugo's note streaked through her mind, "Pauline. What was the name of their singing group?"

"It was so cute. They called themselves the Three French Hens."

Saffron had known it before she said it, but the sound of it hit her like a cold wave anyway.

Three French Hens. Margaux, Betsy, Sophie. Hugo wasn't pointing to the Faverolles. He was pointing to the women. And Sophie had known the evidence pointed to her, so she had lied and tried to redirect the evidence toward Margaux.

Saffron had seen it in Betsy's eyes when she saw Claudette on Jasper's back. Betsy wanted Hugo's prizewinning line of chickens like she had wanted the Sawyer's prizewinning line of cattle. If she was willing to marry in order to get one, Saffron had no doubt that she was willing to kill in order to get the other. She had tracked down the lines of animals that had come from her family farm back in France, and she was reclaiming them, at any cost.

Hugo had known the threat came from one of the women. He had seen something coming. But he hadn't known which one until too late.

"Pauline, how did Betsy know Sophie was here?"

"She said she saw Sophie's birds and just knew Sophie would be somewhere nearby," Saffron closed her eyes. It was her fault. She should have kept the Faverolles hidden. Now

Sophie was somewhere with a killer. She was still the legal owner of the hens. Saffron didn't know how Betsy planned to get them, but she did know that her first step would be to get rid of Sophie. She was the only thing standing in Betsy's way. Saffron had to find them.

Chapter Nineteen

She sent Pauline to search, too, and ran straight down the driveway to where the red truck sat lined up with all the other cars.

Inside sat Dylan, his forehead on the steering wheel, his cowboy hat drawn down low. Saffron yanked the door open, but he didn't look up.

"Dylan, where's Betsy?"

"Dunno."

"What do you mean you don't know?"

"She left a little while ago. I went to get us some donuts from the truck, and she slipped off. I saw Wyatt follow her. They're probably together somewhere."

There was despair in his voice, and resignation, "I don't know why I been fightin' it all these years. I oughta just let them go be together."

"You really think that's what she wants?"

"Well, she don't want me, that I can tell ya. Not an old broken-down paniolo. She wanted to be on the deed to the ranch and to have half ownership in the stock, so I gave it to her. Now she's talking about goin' back to

France. Guess she'll take Wyatt and half my herd with her."

Saffron felt sorry for him, but she didn't have time to nurse his broken heart. She slammed the pickup door. She felt sick that Wyatt could be in on this, too. Hatred and bitterness corroded a soul, though, and there had been enough of those things to ruin even people as straightforward as the Sawyer brothers. She ran toward the crowd, looking for Margaux, for Wyatt, for anyone who could help her find Sophie and Betsy.

She scrambled back past Juno's malasada truck, through the crowd, peering over their heads and past their shoulders at the dark farm beyond.

Pushing through the crowd, she ran solidly into a red-and-green aloha shirt.

Keahi put a hand on her shoulder to steady her, "Woah. You okay?"

The choir was singing *Hark the Herald Angels Sing*. Saffron vaguely registered the kids singing a line that had made her smile at practice a few days ago: "Joyful, all ye nations' spies, join the triumph of the skies."

That meant they were nearing the middle of the program. When the nativity ended, this knot of people would spread out and cover the farm and the driveway, making it more difficult to look for Sophie.

She searched for Bradley and Havili, but they were nowhere to be seen. She couldn't waste time finding them. She had to go after Betsy and Wyatt herself. She peered toward the driveway again, running her gaze along the line of cars.

Wyatt's blue pickup truck was still here. If Betsy and Sophie were with Wyatt, they hadn't left the farm. And of course they wouldn't. Betsy would know better than to let anyone see her with Sophie, or to find any evidence of Sophie in a truck she was escaping in. If she was going to kill the girl, she'd do it here and walk away without anyone knowing she'd been involved, just as she had Hugo, probably framing Saffron for it in the process. And what of Wyatt? Could he be so smitten by Betsy that he'd be a party to something so terrible? That was hard for Saffron to imagine, but if he would betray his brother for her, who knew what else he might do?

All those things were streaking through Saffron's mind as she looked up at the kind, concerned eyes of her ex-boyfriend.

Only right now Keahi didn't feel like her ex-boyfriend. He felt like a harbor in the storm, one person she could truly trust and depend on.

"I need your help," she blurted.

His answer came without hesitation, "Of course."

She pulled him away from Mrs. Claus, by the hand through the crowd, glancing back to see his fake beard flying and his Santa hat bobbing, and went toward the house. Searching through it quickly, she told him what was going on. There was no sign that anyone had been there. She grabbed a couple of flashlights and from there, they searched the beach, the egg house again, each of the little cottages. But there was no sign of Sophie.

The only place left was the barn.

The two cut around the back, through the pasture, so the crowd by the barn's front doors wouldn't see them.

"If the Nativity story stops early, it might make Betsy panic," Saffron said, "We need to give Sophie all the time we can."

Keahi nodded.

"Give her time for what?" came a voice from behind them.

Saffron turned to see Slate and Mano wading through the tall grass, munching on a malasada in each hand. Suddenly, she became very afraid for them.

"Go back," she said, "Keahi and I just need to do something. You go enjoy the party."

Mano looked at her skeptically, "You know, I've been

hoping all night to see you two sneak off behind the barn, but I'm not getting the vibe I would like from you both."

Saffron felt her face get hot. She pushed through the half-door into Jasper's stall, shining her flashlight ahead of her.

Jasper stood inside, impatiently looking in the opposite direction, toward the barn doors. Saffron figured he wanted to be out with the rest of the animals. The two oldest Tucker kids were supposed to slip into the barn just before their sister Harley sang the final song—*Silent Night*—and get him. Saffron patted the little donkey as everyone filtered into his stall.

"It's not like that," She told Mano, "Sophie's in trouble. We've got to find her."

"Sophie?" Slate asked, "The girl from the papers? The one who killed her husband at the poultry show?"

"She didn't kill him," Saffron said, "I don't think. I think Betsy Sawyer did."

"Betsy Sawyer?" Mano's voice was puzzled, "Was she even there?"

"Yes. I saw her there. And she wanted to buy Hugo's hens —that's the husband—but he wouldn't sell them."

"So she killed him?"

"She was going to get them one way or another," Saffron said.

A sound from inside the dark barn made her freeze. It was a harsh sound, a gasping, choking sound. She shone her flashlight and saw, in its sweeping beam, the crumpled form of Sophie Leblanc on the straw.

Running to her, Saffron dropped the flashlight and put a hand on the girl's shoulder. Sophie flinched and rolled into a ball, still gasping for air, but covering her head as if she were afraid.

Saffron was aware of another sound. It was the scraping of boots on the rungs of a ladder.

"Lights!" she shouted, raising her voice to compete with the crescendoing music of the choir outside, "somebody turn on the lights—by the door!"

When the barn was flooded with the yellow glow of the overhead lights, Saffron felt a jolt. Where she had expected to see Betsy on the ladder she saw Wyatt Sawyer.

He was reaching up, struggling.

"Get him!" Slate shouted, and Mano headed for him. But Saffron suddenly saw what he was holding onto. Above his head, sticking out of the loft, he held fast to one of the studded blue boots of Betsy Sawyer.

"She-" Wyatt said, his voice coming in grunts as he wrenching at the boot, trying to pull Betsy back, "tried to strangle that girl."

Wyatt was trying to help Sophie, too. At that moment, the other boot lashed out from the loft and hit Wyatt in the face. He fell backwards, ladder and all, blood streaming from his nose, and hit the ground hard. He didn't move.

Slate, Keahi, and Mano rushed toward him.

"Not him!" Saffron cried, "the woman! In the loft!"

A gurgling sound made Saffron turn her attention back to Sophie. In the full light, Saffron could now see what was wrong. A twist of baling twine was wrapped tight around Sophie's neck. Saffron pulled the knife from her pocket and willed her hands to be steady as she slipped the blade beneath it and cut the twine.

It popped off just as it had from Jasper's foot. Sophie coughed as she drew in a gasping breath.

"Keahi!" Saffron cried, "Come quick!"

He was at her side in a moment, running practiced fingers across the reddening mark on Sophie's throat, speaking calmly and reassuringly to the girl.

Sophie responded, uncurling, laying prone on the straw, gasping and crying. She was alive.

"It's okay," Keahi said, "you're going to be fine. Just breathe. Good. Big, deep breaths."

Saffron glanced over her shoulder to see Mano and Slate standing beneath the loft, their eyes on Betsy, who was trapped thirty feet above the ground, crouched and snarling like an animal.

"Those are my family's bloodlines," she said, "I got our cattle back, and I'm taking those hens, too."

"You——" Sophie gasped, "you killed Hugo."

"I didn't mean to do that," Betsy spat, "I expected to find him alone in that tent and make him a hefty offer for those birds, but it was a three-ring-circus in there. Sophie came flying out, and Hugo and the photographer were fighting when I slipped in. As the photographer crawled out, I saw a pathetic note——a cry for help that pointed directly to my mother and me. I tore it up and took the pieces, but Hugo saw me."

Sophie made a little sound. Saffron hated that she had to hear this, but there was no stopping Betsy. She was far too high in the loft.

"I made him a fair offer. I did. He was a fool to refuse it," Betsy was furious. Saffron saw a woman used to getting everything she wants, "I just wanted to get his attention. He was going to walk away without even negotiating. I did hit him with the cup, but I didn't know it would *kill* him. I was just trying to make him listen to me. You can't blame me for that."

Saffron felt a sharp pain in her hand as Sophie snatched at it and squeezed.

"Saffron," the girl gasped, "it hurts!"

Saffron forgot about Betsy as she looked back at Sophie.

Keahi wasn't checking the girl's throat now. He had a hand on her protruding belly and was looking at his watch.

"Oh, no," Saffron said, a slow realization dawning on her.

Keahi smiled reassuringly at Sophie and then looked up, catching Saffron's eye as Sophie let out a deep, guttural groan.

"Looks like the excitement is just beginning," Keahi said, "Sophie, your baby is coming."

Saffron looked around. Here? In the dingy straw of an old barn?

"Should we move her?"

"No time," Keahi said. He called to his Grandpa Mano under the loft, "Tutu," he said, "bring me those blankets on the tack shelf."

Saffron was glad she had washed them.

Sophie's other hand clawed at Saffron's arm, and she turned her attention back to the young woman. Her pale blue eyes were wide with pain and fear. "Stay with me, please? Stay with me?"

"Of course I will."

Keahi was totally calm and in control. He took the blankets from his grandfather and said softly, "You'll want to call 911."

Mano nodded.

"No!" Sophie said, "They'll take me to jail!"

"It's okay," Saffron soothed her, "We can prove that it wasn't you who killed Hugo. I have evidence, and Betsy's admitted it now. It will be all right. We have Betsy, and Wyatt saw her try to kill you. She's going to jail, not you."

Saffron pulled her attention from Sophie for a moment. Wyatt had sat up and was keeping a wary eye on Betsy in the loft. They could spare Slate for a moment.

"Dad?" she asked. He was at her side in a breath. "Go find Sophie's mother."

"Sophie's mother?" Slate looked at her as if she were a total stranger. "I thought you weren't renting the cottages."

"They ended up being more full than I had anticipated," Saffron said, drawing her eyebrows together in an effort to convey that she'd tell him all about it later.

"Okay," he said.

"Your mom will be here soon, Sophie," Saffron said. "Don't worry."

The choir sang on outside, oblivious to the drama unfolding in the barn. The music was sweet, and Saffron saw how it helped Sophie relax between the frequent contractions. Everything went so fast. It wasn't like the goslings' entry into the world. They had come in long stages, easing from one state to the next, breaking through their shells one tiny shard at a time. This baby was in a hurry.

Pauline made it just as her new grandson came into the world.

His arrival was accompanied by the enthusiastically joyful strains of the children's choir singing their *glorias*. This time, they were perfect.

The strains of the song wove through the cracks of the barn and fell around the new mother as she stroked the cheek of her baby, holding him close to her.

The song was about a different baby, a long time ago, but the peace and the magic of this moment was the same. Saffron was caught up in it: the rose blush of the baby's cheeks, the light glinting off the tears on Sophie's face, the glittering specks of dust rising and falling around them, the sweet voices of the children filling the air.

"Now that he's here," Keahi said quietly, "we need to get you two moved out to someplace more comfortable."

He had realized, of course, that the ambulance that they hoped was coming could never make it through the trenches and weeds down to the barn. They'd need to meet it at the driveway. But how would they get sweet exhausted Sophie out of the barn, much less all the way to the road?

As if he'd heard Saffron's unspoken question, Jasper brayed loudly from his stall. The squeaky, earnest sound filled the barn.

Saffron looked at Keahi, who smiled in a wistful way and

caught his Tutu's eye. Saffron saw him give Mano a little nod. "Switch off the big lights until we get them situated," Keahi said softly.

Mano crossed to the doors and turned off the light, then let Jasper out of his stall.

Jasper seemed to know what was needed, just as he had when Saffron was in the water. Mano led him to Sophie. The donkey stood still as Keahi and Slate helped the new mother stand. Pauline offered to take the baby, but Sophie wouldn't give him up. She cradled him close to her, fire in her eyes.

"This is the best gift Santa ever brought me," Sophie said with a smile. Saffron looked again at Keahi. Though he'd abandoned his beard, he was still wearing his Santa suit and hat.

Jasper's small stature turned out to be a benefit as he bowed slightly and Sophie sat securely on his back.

The strong little donkey straightened and, with more care and delicacy than Saffron would have thought possible, walked toward the barn door.

It was at that moment that Saffron saw the two oldest Tuckers slip into the barn, through a side door chattering softly to each other, ready for their big entrance.

He was dressed in a bathrobe, she was clutching a baby doll.

Slate stepped to the side and caught them. He threw an arm around each of them, bending down to explain. They stood smiling as Jasper and his entourage passed them. The Tucker kids understood mothers and new babies, and Saffron saw in their eyes the reflection of the peace and magic she was feeling.

The Christmas lights twinkled and Harley Tucker's voice rang through the clear, warm air like a bell. It grew louder as Mano swung the big barn doors open.

"Silent night, holy night,

All is calm, all is bright."

An audible gasp went up from the crowd as Jasper emerged from the barn, Sophie and her baby on his back.

Pastor Vaughn, obviously surprised at the switch, caught Harley's eye and nodded encouragingly.

Keep singing, he mouthed. She looked over her shoulder, smiled widely, and carried on.

Saffron would remember a lot of moments from that night, but the most beautiful was that one, when the scent of jasmine washed over them and her friends and neighbors, the good people of Maika'i, parted to make room for the mother and child.

Saffron smiled at them as she walked beside Sophie and Jasper. She saw Jan Lin, her cheeks streaked with tears, and the Empress with her little chicken on her lap. The Empress reached out and squeezed Saffron's hand as she went by. They would have so much to talk about at their next tea party.

Saffron saw Mrs. Claus and Fumi and Juno, just some of the many faces lining the way, blocking the wind, watching over the procession.

At that moment, she was surrounded by 'ohana and filled with aloha.

Chapter Twenty

It was Christmas. Three hours new, the holiday felt especially calm and sweet after the turmoil of the previous evening.

Sophie and her newborn were safe in the hospital. Keahi had ridden there with them, and Saffron had given him a little wave of gratitude as he glanced up through the back window of the ambulance. She had no words for how grateful she was that he'd been there.

Sophie also had her mother beside her, and as soon as they could travel, they'd be going back to her home in the Midwest. Antoinette, Babette, and Claudette would not be going with them. Sophie wanted them to live here, where they'd be part of the flock and lend their lovely rose-pink eggs to Saffron's cartons.

Although Margaux hadn't known about Betsy's actions, she hadn't been totally forthcoming, either. Saffron had revealed Margaux and Hugo's familial connection to the other judges before they left for the night. They assured her that Margaux, while not charged with any law-breaking, would be stripped of her credentials. She'd never judge a poultry show again.

Not that she seemed to mind. She'd struck quickly and offered Sophie a small fortune for the Faverolles farm back in France. Sophie didn't ever want to return, and the money would set her up well in her new life. Margaux could leave judging and continue to work on the breed she admired so much.

Betsy, however, wouldn't see her mother for a very long time. She was behind bars, where she belonged. She now faced a host of charges, and both Officer Bradley and Lieutenant Havili had been on hand to apprehend her in the loft.

The live nativity had been a success, Jasper had gotten two scoops of oats for saving the day, and calm seemed to have once again descended on Hau'oli ka Moa Egg Farm.

Saffron was in the living room, feeling giddy and sleepless now that the weight of the past two weeks had been lifted. The night was sweet and calm, and she fought the urge to wake up her father and start Christmas Day.

But three A.M. was a little early, even for Christmas morning. Slate and Mano were asleep in the guest rooms, and Saffron would let them stay that way for a little longer.

Saffron laid their gifts under the tree and plugged it in, setting the dark living room ablaze with sweet light.

The front window reflected the twinkling tree back to her, and beyond it she could see the swaying palms, the wide stretch of beach, and a figure.

Who was that? Saffron's heart skipped.

She knew.

Before she could think, before she could talk herself out of it, she headed for the beach.

Keahi turned as she approached, "Hey," he said, as if it weren't three in the morning, as if she wasn't seeing someone else, as if they weren't over.

"Hey Santa," she responded, "I guess you got all the presents delivered?"

He laughed, and it was music on the breeze.

"What are you doing out here?" she asked.

"Just came to get the canoe," he gestured, and she remembered that with all the excitement, they hadn't sent Santa off across the waves as planned. Instead, he'd ended up riding away with lights and sirens.

"Pretty wild night, huh?" Saffron asked.

"I'll say."

"The nativity turned out more authentic than I expected."

"Every party you throw is a surprise party," he laughed.

The sea shushed in and out, and down the beach a monk seal barked, scolding them for disturbing her.

Everything they hadn't said since Keahi left lay between them. But somehow, as the surf surged over Saffron's feet and the bubbles tickled her ankles, it carried away the awkwardness between them.

"You're an exciting girl, Saffron," Keahi said. There was admiration and affection in his voice.

Saffron wasn't an adrenaline junkie, but when Keahi took her hand, she felt a rush like a roller coaster.

It was so easy, so natural, to slide into his arms, to turn her face up, to kiss him in the moonlight.

Saffron and Keahi had shared many kisses, but none like this one. They'd shared tentative kisses when their relationship was new, and tearful kisses when Keahi left for Boston.

This kiss, though, was a kiss of longing, and of belonging. Through it ran the current of their connection woven with strands of sadness. They still loved each other. Saffron could feel it.

But Keahi wasn't home for good. He was going back to Boston, and they both knew that. In this kiss, mingled with the excitement of reconnecting, was the somber, heartbreaking understanding that it couldn't last.

Saffron didn't want to let him go. She reached out as he stepped back and sat on the prow of the grounded canoe.

"I've missed you," he said again, but this time there was a depth of feeling behind it that made Saffron catch her breath, "a lot."

She was quiet. She looked out over the sparkling water. She wanted to say how much she'd missed him, too, but there were no words for that. A long quiet settled on the beach. She could feel his gaze on her, but she didn't trust herself to look at him. How could she see him and not throw her arms around him again?

"Would you ever consider . . ." Keahi trailed off, then gathered his courage and charged on, ". . . do you think, ever, in the future sometime, you could live in Boston?"

Saffron sucked in her breath, "Don't ask me that," she said.

"Why not?"

"Because," her eyes felt sandy, and she wiped a tear away impatiently, "because I've already thought of that—a thousand times. Of course I want to be with you. Of course I miss you. But this is my home now, Keahi." She waved a hand at the star-studded sky, the moonlit palms, the shimmering midnight beach, "I have my hens, my dad is back, Tutu is here. Everyone in town is my 'ohana. I've never had so much family. I don't want to leave them. I don't want to leave the quirky chickens, with their little squabbles and their enthusiastic greetings whenever I come into the egg house."

"And the colors, Keahi. I don't want to leave the colors I've found here—brand new blues in the ocean, a thousand golden shades in the sand . . ." she breathed in the soft scents of the sea, using them to calm her and slow the rush of her words, "I finally feel like I have a place—a real place in the world."

She was looking at him now, willing him to understand. She saw his smile in the dark, the sad crinkling of his kind eyes highlighted by the moonlight falling around him, "I knew the answer," he said, "but I had to ask." She heard him sigh, "And for what it's worth, I know exactly what you mean."

"I'm sorry," she said.

"Don't be. If you want to know the truth, I'm glad Tutu has you nearby, and I'm glad you have your dad back. I'm happy to see you happy."

Happy wasn't the word Saffron would have used to describe herself right now.

"How long will you be here?"

"Just until tomorrow. I have a little girl coming in for surgery on the 28th, and I have to get back and get rested and prepped before then."

Saffron felt a swell of pride, "You're doing what you need to be doing," she said, unsure whether she was trying to make him feel better or herself, "those kids need you."

He didn't respond, and she didn't say how much she needed him, too. It would only make the next few minutes harder.

He stood and started shouldering the boat toward the water, "I'm going to go. You need to get inside and get some sleep."

"Doctor's orders?"

He chuckled.

"I'm sorry I came out," she said, "and made this even harder."

He left the boat abruptly and came to her in three broad strides across the sand. She saw the effort with which he stopped himself from taking her in his arms again. Instead, he took both of her hands in his, "I'm not sorry, Saffron. I know it's been months since we talked, and I know we live oceans apart, and I know you can't come to Boston, and that it's completely impractical for me to keep loving you, but I do. You're the best friend I ever had, and I love every minute I spend with you, even the hard ones."

* * *

Saffron slept for a few fitful hours after Keahi rowed away on the glittering waves. In her dreams, she was in the canoe with him, rowing toward the horizon, the two of them facing adventure together. There was a touch of melancholy in her mind when she awoke and realized it was Christmas morning and what she really wanted wouldn't be under the tree.

But any despondency evaporated with the sounds and smells from the kitchen. Mano and Slate were already up, making banana pancakes with coconut syrup and harmonizing on a cappella Christmas carols.

Later, with the marigold sunshine streaming in on them and a little emerald gecko making his way across the front window, they tore open their presents like children, laughing and exclaiming, modeling their new aloha shirts. Slate wheezed out a rendition of *Joy to the World* on his new harmonica.

Saffron made out like a bandit herself—Slate and Mano hadn't held anything back. She got egg gadgets and a hand-carved ukulele, new slippahs and a board game called "Name That Manu" that challenged players to identify Hawaiian birds.

In the middle of it all, Saffron heard the deep barking of an old hound dog outside. Panic washed over her as the sheep and the calf in the barn flashed through her mind, along with her hens and Jasper.

Pushing the pile of wrapping paper off her lap, she ran to the door and threw it open.

She barely registered Slate and Mano's calls as she ran barefoot out onto the lanai, heading for the barn.

But what saw as she came out sent her skidding to a halt.

The cow and calf were coming up the path from the barn, toward a blue pickup and stock trailer parked along the driveway.

Behind the cows, walking up the path, was Dylan Sawyer, baying like an old hound to keep the cows moving in the right direction. Beside him, a smile flashing across his bruised face, was his brother.

They tossed Saffron a wave, and a sense of satisfaction washed over her. It was Christmas morning, and she was seeing its magic: peace and brotherhood, joy and understanding. Finally, it felt like Christmas.

Sneak Peek Book 8: Empty Nest

CHAPTER ONE

Saffron pressed her back to the bathroom door and her fingertips to her temples.

"You can do this," she said, summoning every bit of patience and understanding she had.

"Saffron?" a voice called from the other side of the door, "your breakfast is ready!" It was Jan Lin, the woman who ran Maika'i's cell phone store, Sea Cells Mobile.

Jan was nice. Too nice, really. She'd taken a shine to the three goslings that had hatched down in the egg house, and she'd started coming out every day to check on them. She spent hours in the egg house. More than once, Saffron had been startled out of her wits by Jan's voice coming from the pen where the goslings lived with their foster mom, Saffron's chicken, Cupcake.

The underlying problem was that Jan was lonely. Her only son had left for college a few months ago, and she had struggled to find purpose. The goslings seemed to have given her that purpose.

And now, she'd shifted some of her attention to Saffron, too. She cooked for her, tidied the bungalow, sat at the kitchen table and asked probing questions about Saffron's life, which she always followed up with a heaping helping of advice.

Jan was coming by every day now, and Saffron was beginning to miss her autonomy. She'd lived alone a long time, and it was proving difficult to adjust to having Jan at her elbow every time she turned around.

This morning, Jan had arrived before Saffron even awoke. The woman had spent the last half hour making breakfast fried rice—a traditional fried rice with spam and scrambled eggs—to start Saffron's day.

It was a kind gesture, Saffron reminded herself. The least she could do was eat it graciously. She opened the door a crack.

"Saffron!" came Jan's voice, now down the hall, "your closet is disgraceful! Why are there clothes on the floor in here? Are these dirty or clean?"

Saffron rushed to her room. Her closet wasn't perfect, but disgraceful seemed a little harsh. And what was Jan doing poking around in there anyway? She gritted her teeth and stepped in front of the woman, closing the doors to the closet behind her.

"I'll work on that, Jan," she said.

Jan peered at her and held up a finger, "The closet is a reflection of the brain," she said firmly, "Cluttered closet, cluttered brain."

Saffron peered hard at Jan for a moment, trying to think of something nice to say, "I'll keep that in mind."

Over breakfast, Jan regaled Saffron with stories of the goslings. She'd been reading to them, and they liked it.

"I'll bet they do," Saffron said, absentmindedly chewing a scoop of fried rice.

"Do you know their favorite book?" Jan picked up her shoulder bag and looked at Saffron expectantly.

Saffron racked her brain, trying to think of what goslings would like. Before she could come up with anything, though, Jan pulled a large book triumphantly from her bag.

"Mother Goose!" she cried.

Saffron couldn't help but smile. Of course.

"And," Jan said, "if it's alright, I've given them names."

"Sure," Saffron said. She was a big believer in the idea that each bird was an individual and should have its own name.

"I called Vance Carlyle from the wildlife department to confirm," Jan said, and Saffron smothered a smile. Vance had heard a lot from Jan lately, too, "And we have two girls and a boy. Because they love Mother Goose nursery rhymes so much, I've called them Muffet, Bo Peep, and Peter Peter," she was bursting with pride.

Saffron pictured the fuzzy little goslings. "Perfect," she declared.

"And don't forget," Jan said, "Vance Carlyle is coming to check on them today. I think he's going to be quite pleased with how they're growing. Peter Peter has seven feathers starting on his wings!"

"They're growing fast," Saffron affirmed.

"And I want him to take another look at Muffet's foot. She

has a crooked toe, you know, and Vance says it's all right and won't bother her, but it looks a little funny, and I wonder if the other geese will notice it when she's older and exclude her for it. I wonder if there's some kind of goose plastic surgery we could get for her? Just to make it look normal?"

Saffron nodded, "Maybe. But you know, I've got several chickens whose toes are a little off, and they seem to do just fine."

Jan seemed dissatisfied with that answer, "Well, I'm going to ask Vance Carlyle about it, anyway."

"Absolutely," Saffron said, glad he'd be here to entertain Jan for a while, "I might not be here when he visits, though."

"What?" Jan's eyes grew wide and her mouth pressed into a disapproving line, "You're not going to be here for the checkup?"

"Well," Saffron said, feeling suddenly defensive, "I was going to go check out that exotic animal show that's stopping a couple towns North."

"In Pali?" Jan shook her head, "Oh, no, that's not worth your time. You should be here for the checkup."

Saffron let her eyes close briefly. She counted to ten in her mind, "I think Vance can handle the checkup without me, and I think that show looks very interesting."

"Waste of time," Jan stood and cleared their plates, not bothering to ask if Saffron was done or not. Saffron fled the kitchen to keep from saying anything snippy.

"I'm going to get dressed!" she said. She locked her bedroom door behind her and sunk onto the bed.

On her nightstand was a flier. Saffron reached for it.

"An Exciting. Exotic. Exhibit." The flier read, "Limited time only! Traveling show! Amazing Armadillos! Beautiful Bobcats! Cuddly Koalas! Come and see them all!" Saffron kept reading and counted eleven exclamation points on the flier.

It was done in an old circus-style, brightly colored and illustrated. It had caught her eye when she'd dropped off an egg order at the Paradise Market yesterday, and she'd decided to drive up to Pali and see the show.

Saffron looked through her cluttered closet and pulled out a pair of sage capris and a flowy shirt with a soft floral print on it.

She needed something to distract her. Christmas had just passed, and it had brought a lot of excitement. Over the holiday she had harbored a fugitive, acquired a donkey, witnessed a murder, and shared a sweet moonlight kiss that had left her feeling conflicted and confused.

She needed something fun and different to do. She'd even thought of a vacation, but when you live in paradise, there's really no place you'd rather go. So Exciting Exotics seemed like a great distraction.

A tapping on her window caught her attention. Curry, the rooster who lived on her porch, was ready for a morning treat. She opened the window and he hopped in onto her nightstand.

"You're so needy," it felt good to say the words out loud, and she gave Curry the rest of the speech that she would have liked to tell Jan. "There are lots of more interesting places you could be if you're feeling bored, and lots of people you could spend time with if you're feeling lonely." It was a relief to say it, even though Curry completely ignored her, instead pecking and snatching at the handful of seeds she had poured onto the stand for him.

His low, contented chuckling brought a sense of calm to the room, and Saffron chided herself for getting so worked up. The morning was pristine—the warm air that moved in through the window was candied with the scent of gardenia and melodious with the songs of island birds. It was a cloudless day, and the mountains stretched to the sky behind the farm like enormous gems—emeralds that glistened with the morning dew.

Curry suddenly raised his head, his treats forgotten. He spun toward the window and began to make a tuk-tuk-tuk sound, low and popping. That was his warning—someone was coming.

Could Vance be here already? It seemed a bit early for him to be working. But Curry leaped out the window, flapping down onto the lanai and heading for the front door. Saffron definitely had company. Well, *more* company.

When she opened the front door, she was delighted to find her adopted grandpa, Mano, and her father, Slate. They were grinning widely.

"Hello," called Jan from the kitchen. Mano winked at Saffron as he returned the greeting.

She greeted them and invited them in, but the shook their heads in unison, "No, you got to come out," Mano said, "We have something for you."

"What?" Saffron said, "We just had Christmas. You guys spoiled me rotten then. What else could you possibly give me?"

They exchanged a glance, "We tried to get this done for Christmas, but it was a little bigger job than we expected," Mano explained, "Come see!" He leaned around Saffron and called toward the kitchen, "You want to see, Jan?"

"No, thanks," she said, "I'm finishing up the dishes in here, then I need to get down to the egg house and check on the babies."

Saffron walked with Slate and Mano out on the lanai, then down the steps and around the corner of the house.

There, on the path to the egg house, stood Jasper, Saffron's new donkey. His best friend, Claudette the hen, was settled happily on his back, and behind him was the most beautiful little donkey cart Saffron had ever seen.

It was made of carved wood, hand-polished and sealed. It had four little wheels and shafts that went up on either side of Jasper and were connected to a harness.

The sides were carved with intricate images of Saffron's chickens. Saffron recognized them. She also recognized Mano's work immediately.

"Come see!" he called.

She approached it.

Inside was a big square area.

"For the eggs," Slate explained, "You can use it to pull the loads of eggs up from the egg house every day instead of hauling them yourself with that old rickety cart you've been using."

It was true. The old one was getting difficult to use. One wheel was bent and the bolts in the bottom were constantly getting loose.

"Wow," was all she could think to say.

"That's not all," Slate said, "It's a convertible! Show her, Mano!"

Mano reached down into the floorboard and pulled up on a little handle near the side of the cart. A section of the floor pulled up and locked in place creating a seat for two—complete with arm rests.

Saffron's eyes widened, "What?" she managed.

"Your dad designed that," Mano said, "so that you can ride in it when you want, but have plenty of room for hauling eggs if you want."

"Dad, that's amazing," Saffron said.

"We had to be space-efficient," Slate shrugged off the praise, "Jasper's not a very big donkey, you know. He can easily pull a full load of eggs, or two people and a smaller load of eggs."

"Like my business deliveries?" Saffron asked, picturing herself riding into town in the little contraption.

"That's exactly what we were thinking of when we designed it," Slate said.

"And there's more!" Mano said, reaching under the seat,

where he pushed a little button that Saffron hadn't noticed before.

Up sprang an umbrella over the seat.

"Gotta protect our redhead from the island sun," Mano said affectionately.

Saffron was speechless.

"How did you do the metal parts?" she asked, "The frame? The wheels?"

"We just found someone on the island who had welding equipment," Slate said, "Well, you want to take it for a spin?"

Saffron was excited, but a little nervous, "I've never driven a horse cart before," she said doubtfully. She now noticed the reins looped around a little handle on the front of the cart.

"Oh, you can do it," Mano exclaimed, sliding into the seat and holding out a hand, "It's easy. I'll show you!"

Saffron looked doubtfully at the little donkey, "Are you sure Jasper can pull us both? I'm not, you know, a tiny person."

"He's been pulling us both all around, testing it," Mano assured her, "He loves it—it's like it gives him purpose. Come on, you'll see."

She took his hand and slid into the seat.

Mano lifted the reins. With a steady hand and a firm voice he spoke to Jasper, "Walk-up!"

The fuzzy creature walked forward, pulling the cart as if there was nothing behind him. They moved up the path and past the house, heading for the driveway.

"Walk-up!" They went a little faster, garnering a squawk and a flap from Claudette, whose feathers ruffled a little in the breeze.

Jasper trotted along, eyes forward, taking seriously his job as they turned out onto the road.

The cart moved a little faster and easier on the blacktop, and Saffron watched as Jasper's enormous ears flicked this way and that, taking in the sound of an 'i'iwi bird, the sighing of the ocean, and a honk from a passing car whose occupants waved cheerfully at the donkey and his passengers. Jasper never flinched, never panicked.

"How did he learn this?"

"He must have been trained when we got him," Mano said, "He knew what to do as soon as we hooked him up. And he seems to really enjoy it."

Mano was right. In fact, when they moved to a wide, sandy spot to turn back, Jasper gave a little huff of annoyance before obeying the "Haw," command and making a sharp u-turn to the left to head home.

"How did you learn the commands?" Saffron asked.

"The internet," Mano said simply. Without warning, he handed her the reins.

"Oh, no, I don't——" Saffron started, but then she felt something. The reins were alive——a direct connection to Jasper. It was as if, suddenly, a whole new world of communication opened up between her and her long-eared friend. She felt his eagerness, his confidence. She felt his hesitance when a car pulled in front of them and his relief when it pulled away and disappeared down the road.

She didn't pull on the reins, or slap them against him. She could sense that such things would scare Jasper. Instead, she tightened the left one slightly and said, "Haw!" when they got to the driveway. Jasper trotted happily back toward the house.

She was so busy communicating with Jasper that she had tuned out Mano. She refocused just as he was saying, "That's great! You never want to smack him with the reins, just tighten a little or loosen. Good," Mano beamed at her, "It looks like Jasper's not the only one who's good at this."

Slate sat on the porch grinning and eating a plate of left-over fried rice. He waved as they approached.

Saffron's attention was drawn by more waving. Running up

the path, her short black hair flying in the wind, was Jan. She wore a look of panic on her face.

Instinctively, Saffron tightened both reins and called, "Woah!"

Jasper stopped and Saffron handed the reins to Mano and jumped out, meeting Jan on the path.

"What is it?"

"The goslings!" Jan was nearly hysterical, her voice cracking and her eyes brimming, "they're gone!"

Saffron glanced back at Slate, but he waved her on, standing to help Mano with Jasper and the cart.

Saffron's stomach was in a knot as they streaked through the doors and down the aisle of the egg house. On the sandy floor, Saffron saw the delicate gem shapes of little webbed feet. She followed them all the way back to their origin: Cupcake's broody pen, where the goslings had hatched and been raised for the last three weeks.

The goslings were usually crowded around the feeder, or swimming, or cuddled up with their mother, chirping and peeping and creating a general ruckus. But this morning an eerie silence had fallen over the pen.

There were no goslings at the feeder. The water in the pool sat still and untouched, and in the corner lay a barren and empty nest.

* * *

Continue reading Empty Nest: Book 8 in the Aloha Chicken Mysteries!

* * *

DEAR READER,

Mele Kalikimaka! Thank you for spending Christmas at

the Hau'oli ka Moa Egg Farm! I hope you enjoyed Three French Hens, and I hope you'll read more of Saffron's adventures in Book 8: Empty Nest. If you did enjoy the book, please consider writing a review on Amazon and Goodreads. I love hearing from my readers and your reviews help other readers find my novels! I truly appreciate every review and every reader who spends time with Saffron, the hens, and me!

-Josi Avari

Made in the USA
Coppell, TX
23 February 2025